I NEVER GOT A GOOD-BYE KISS

"You got it, you just didn't know it was the last one."

"After four years I think we deserve a good-bye kiss," Will said, his voice going low and sexy and making her want to run. She just wasn't sure she wanted to run into his arms or back up the hill toward the crowd.

"What are you afraid of?" he asked in that same low tone.

"I'm not afraid of you, Will. I could sleep with you and remain completely unfazed."

"Liar."

Meghan let out a puff of air, angry at his arrogance and at herself for being momentarily sucked in by him. He never would change. He was all about the hunt. "Will, leave me alone. I can't believe I actually . . ."

His mouth was on hers, gentle, warm, and horribly intoxicating.

Books by Jane Blackwood

YOU HAD ME AT GOODBYE

THE SEXIEST DEAD MAN ALIVE

A HARD MAN IS GOOD TO FIND

Published by Zebra Books

Jane Blackwood

Between You and Me

Zebra Books
Kensington Publishing Corp.
www.kensingtonbooks.com

ZEBRA BOOKS are published by

Kensington Publishing Corp.
850 Third Avenue
New York, NY 10022

All Kensington titles, imprints, and distributed lines are available at special quantity discounts for bulk purchases for sales promotion, premiums, fund-raising, educational, or institutional use.

Special book excerpts or customized printings can also be created to fit specific needs. For details, write or phone the office of the Kensington Special Sales Manager: Attn. Special Sales Department. Kensington Publishing Corp., 850 Third Avenue, New York, NY 10022. Phone: 1-800-221-2647.

ISBN-13: 978-0-8217-7951-4
ISBN-10: 0-8217-7951-6

First Printing: September 2007
10 9 8 7 6 5 4 3 2 1

Printed in the United States of America

Acknowledgments

I'd like to thank Sheila McCurdy,
sailor extraordinaire and multi
Newport-Bermuda veteran,
for her invaluable help writing this book.
Any mistakes made are my own.
I'd also like to thank my brother,
Arthur Blackwood,
another terrific sailor,
for not laughing too hard at one
glaring error I made early on.
Last, I'd like to apologize to my husband, Jim,
for making quahogs a villain in my story.

Prologue

1975

She'd never seen a cuter boy in her life, never got sweaty or flushed just looking, never wanted to touch one this badly. Maybe because he wasn't a boy. Maybe it was because he was a man, working with his hands, all muscle and dirt. Just the thought of getting his dirt on her white shirt got her all excited—and apparently all the other girls, too. Everyone thought Jared Scott was just about the handsomest boy in East Greenwich. He was tanned from working outside on the docks and his hair was thick and long and nearly black. So what if he lived in the Harbor section and she lived on the Hill. So what?

Of course, it made all the difference. She knew it, her friends knew it, and she was definitely sure Jared Scott knew it. He was a high school dropout. He smoked, and some kids hinted that it wasn't just cigarettes but maybe marijuana. He'd had a brother killed in Vietnam, which was about the most tragic thing she could think of. Just looking at him, all sweaty and dirty and sad, made her want to be with him. He was poor, too, and somehow that made him even more appealing. Suffering, poor. God, he was so cool.

She'd gone after him with the single-mindedness that she did everything, including picking out her car or deciding which shade of lipstick would drive her mother insane. It hadn't taken long to get him to ask her out, which was sort of a disappointment 'cause she liked getting boys to like her. Jared Scott liked her right away. He taught her how to smoke, he taught her how to drink, and he taught her how to make love. She stayed out late, lied to her parents, loved the thrill of being with the one boy in town they'd absolutely die to see her with. She'd drive her car to his house and scooch over to let him drive the rest of the night. He was too poor to own a car and she liked the fact that she was the one who let him feel what it was like to be, if not rich, then comfortable. That's what her parents always told her they were—comfortable.

Jared was not comfortable. She'd been in his house, said hello to his father, who wore a stained T-shirt and looked at her with blurry eyes. His mother was huge; really, really big so that she hardly even got up during the day, except to pee, Jared told her. That made her laugh and he laughed too, except not quite as loud.

Jared told her a million times he loved her and it was nice to have a boy like him fall for her so hard. And when she got pregnant, it was wonderful because he said he'd take care of her and they'd live together and raise their little baby and be happy forever. She wasn't worried about anything until she told her parents about the baby and they went nuts and kicked her out of the house. Even that was thrilling because her friends all felt sorry for her and Jared. God, he was just about crazy mad that her parents had done that. She didn't care. She and Jared got married by the Justice of the Peace and rented a tiny little basement apartment in the Harbor section of town and they put up cheap little curtains and her belly grew and she was really happy until her father had some men take her car away. Then she didn't have anything, not a car, not clothes that fit her, they didn't even go to the movies anymore because Jared said they couldn't afford it. Jared worked all the time and he didn't make squat and she couldn't buy any clothes or lipstick or even go to Norman's Restaurant for lunch with the other kids.

Then the baby came and everything was great. All her friends gave her presents and wanted to hold the baby and said how lucky she was and she truly felt like the luckiest girl in the whole world with her baby and her handsome husband. They called the baby William after Jared's father and even though she thought his father was a complete loser, she said it was okay.

William was cute, she supposed, but she never got to do anything anymore and she missed her friends. They all stopped coming around after a while and she knew it was because she always had a baby with her. She even missed her family, who wouldn't come to see little William. She wasn't sure when she started hating Jared, but it was about the time she started hating her life. It hit her like a rock between the eyes that she'd just done about the dumbest thing she could do—marry a poor man. They didn't even have a television. All they had was a radio that Jared took from his old room. At least she got to listen to that and dream about being a rock star's girlfriend and going out to fancy restaurants and buying new clothes. She never got to do anything anymore and it was mostly because of William. Jared loved him and that was nice, but it started driving her crazy, how stupid he was to love their life when it sucked so bad.

She figured she lasted as long as she could, given the fact she hated everything about her life. She wasn't mean to William, didn't hit him or anything. But she didn't really play with him either. He liked to play by himself anyway in the little dirt patch in the back yard. Stupid kid. Just like his father. Looked just like him, too. It drove her nuts. And Jared, the idiot, started talking about having another baby when William was three. Like she wanted to add another weight to her chain. Right.

She left the day she saw a bunch of her friends ride by in a new Camaro convertible, metallic blue and so sweet she almost cried. They didn't see her, or if they did, they wished they didn't. She was pushing a stroller they'd bought at the Salvation Army, one of those cheap things that collapse if you hit a big bump. She was wearing cut-offs from high school and one of Jared's old T-shirts as she watched her friends drive by. She thought, I should be with them. What the hell am I doing pushing a stroller? What the hell am I doing married to a loser?

She pushed the stroller back home, ignoring William's whining because he thought they were walking to the park. Jared would be home from his first job in twenty minutes. William would be fine. So she packed a bag and left a note, told William to be good and walked out.

On Land

Chapter One

In some former life, Will Scott figured he might have been a sea captain, one of those larger-than-life guys who raced around the horn to California before ambitious men decided to build one hell of a long train track. Life would have been a series of long ocean voyages with a few stops along the way for lusty women and spiced rum. Just thinking about it made him smile. All those women cheering from the shore, happy to see him, fighting over who would have the honor to get him first.

And then the image blurred and the women started to all look the same, with short blond hair and soft blue eyes and they were all holding out their hand for a wedding ring looking sad and he was frantically telling his crew to come about, turn away, before those women got their claws into him. Will shook his head with disgust. Two things had gotten into Will Scott's blood and brains and soul and heart, even though he hated the thought of something squirming around him like that: sailing and Meghan Rose.

Sailing was easy to live with. Meghan Rose was not.

Will sat in the sparse cabin of a forty-foot Swan and realized he hadn't thought about Meg in at least three days and was congratulating himself on that fact until he realized that he was, indeed, thinking about her. He couldn't help himself. She'd become as much a part of him as the salt air he breathed in every day, as constant as the breeze blowing off the bay, as irritating as a heavy fog rolling in off the Atlantic.

Will swore under his breath, resisting the strong temptation to reach into the cubbyhole behind him and take out a tattered picture he had of her. It was the only one he had, torn out of a four-year-old *Sailing Magazine* issue that featured the country's top women sailors. The fact that it was the only picture he had of a woman he'd been with for four years said a lot about the kind of boyfriend he'd been. But he gave himself credit for keeping the one he had. The picture wasn't a great one; Will could hardly make out her features, but there was no mistaking Meg. Her back was to the camera, her hair bright and yellow blowing back from her face. He could just make out the curve of her jaw as she looked up at the jib she was adjusting. Some other chick blocked the rest of her, but Will figured he could fill in the blanks just fine after four years of learning every curve, every dip, every smooth line of her body. Why take out the damn picture when he could see the thing in his head just fine? Man, he was as pathetic as his father. He should throw the magazine scrap away. Just like he'd thrown her away.

Just like that.

But the hell of it was he couldn't let go, not completely, even though he was the one who let her go.

So, she broke his heart. He figured he deserved it after breaking hers. Will forced himself to concentrate on the satellite images of the Gulf Stream laid out on the small dining table in front of him. The boat's cabin was barebones, stripped down for racing, containing only the minimum needed for sailing. The forward berths had been removed long ago, leaving the bow jammed with sails—ones for light wind, heavy wind, and everything in between. *Water Baby* was not made for comfort, as his crew often complained when they tried during the longer races to get a few hours' sleep on the hard canvas bunks. She wasn't pretty on the inside, but her outside was built for speed and was so beautiful that just looking at her could bring a tear to a racing man's eye.

Just outside, seagulls screeched as they followed a fishing boat into Newport Harbor, and he could hear the sound of one of his neighbors washing down his deck. *Blue Grass* must have come in while he was working in the cabin, he thought, recognizing the owner's southern accent as he yelled at his wife to "stop messin' wid the dishes, honey, and come hep me brush the deck." Then came the heavy clump of a big man moving down the dock, steps that stopped just outside Will's boat. He looked up through the porthole, but could see only a pair of hairy legs that could have belonged to any of his crew.

"Bad news, me captain." Will rolled his eyes upon hearing his best trimmer's bad imitation of a pirate. Thad Westwood was the best crewmember *Water Baby* had ever had, except, perhaps, for Meg. He could take every ruffle out of a sail and make a boat fly, but Meg could read the wind as if it were coming at her in large print and make an adjustment before most people knew they needed to.

"Go away," Will shouted back. "There is no bad news two weeks before the Newport-Bermuda."

"'Fraid so," Thad said, heaving his beefy body onto the boat, making it dip and causing the lines that tied the boat to the slip to stretch and squeak. Something about the way he sounded climbing aboard made Will tense. Thad might be a big man, but he was as graceful as a dancer on a boat. For a second or two, Thad blocked the light of the sun as he moved down the companionway. And then Will saw it: a cast, brilliant white and new, covering his arm from fingertips to shoulder like a benevolent albino boa constrictor.

"No."

"Yes."

"It's not broken. Tell me that thing," Will said, pointing at the cast, "is coming off in a week or is your idea of a joke."

"I messed up, dude. Drank too much tequila and went out on an egg beater last night with some skirt I met at the Black Pearl. When she was coming into her slip, I crushed my arm into the piling. I twisted the shit out of it and broke it in two places."

Will shook his head and swore viciously beneath his breath. It wasn't as if he was the kind of guy who didn't care if Thad was in pain or not, but hell, he'd just lost his best trimmer and he was sailing the most important race of his life in two weeks. Last race they'd come in third and only because they'd lost a rudder halfway through the race. This year the stakes were much, much higher. "You are screwing me good," Will said, staring at the cast. "How in hell am I going to find a replacement for you two weeks before the race? You know anyone worth having was taken months ago."

"Gary can . . ."

"Gary can't," Will said, closing his eyes and trying to find a bit of humanity lurking beneath the growing rage and disappointment. Gary actually could take over for Thad as his trimmer, but he needed better than Gary this year. He needed the best.

"I screwed up," Thad repeated helplessly.

"Yeah. You did." Will sighed and rubbed his hands over his face. The Newport-Bermuda race was considered one of the most prestigious ocean races in the world and this year he had to win it. He had *Water Baby*, outfitted with a new keel that made the boat scream through the water, and he'd had the best crew around, guys who'd been crewing ocean races for years.

He nodded toward Thad's arm. "Must have hurt like hell."

Thad managed a grin. "Naw. I only screamed like a girl for an hour." They both laughed until they simultaneously remembered what they were laughing about. "I'm sorry, dude. You gonna tell Frank?"

Frank owned *Water Baby*, and until he lost a leg to diabetes ten years ago, had captained the Newport-Bermuda race fifteen times. Thirty years he'd been trying for the elusive Lighthouse Trophy, one year coming so close he claimed losing it made his hair turn gray. Five boats had sat off Bermuda with the island in clear sight, bobbing in no wind, sails hanging down like wet laundry. Frank had watched in despair while lighter, smaller boats drifted past him. Will was only a kid then, but he never forgot the look on Frank's face when a boat that had been two minutes behind drifted by and got the horn blast that ended the race for him. Ever since that day, Will had been driven to win the cup.

"You can tell Frank," Will said, and almost laughed out loud at the look of horror on Thad's face.

"He'll kill me."

"Maybe I can steal someone else's trimmer," Will said, not really meaning it. He'd never sink to that level, no matter how desperate he was.

"Too bad Meg's not around anymore," Thad said, letting out a booming laugh at what he clearly thought was a joke. When he caught the expression on Will's face, he sobered. "No way, dude. Not Meg. You had half your crew quit on you two years ago."

Will grinned. "She's the best trimmer I've ever known." He ignored Thad's mock hurt expression that he hadn't thought Thad the best.

"But she's gone. No one knows where she is."

Will continued to smile.

"You know where she is, don't you," Thad said fatalistically.

"I just might."

Thad leaned over the small table separating them, placing one meat-hook hand on the teak surface. Will figured Thad was trying to persuade him by putting on his tough-guy act, but Will never had been intimidated by Thad's large size, cobra tattoo, or cleanly shaven bald head. He supposed Thad figured he looked like a badass and most people did think that, but Will just couldn't get the Mr. Clean jingle out of his head every time he pulled this crap. "Maybe I'm not your trimmer this year but I care about this boat and this race and you. Dude, if you let her on this boat, I'm telling you it'll be a disaster and I'll never sail with you again."

Will waved him away. "I could never convince her to crew for me. And that's about the idlest threat I've ever heard."

Thad shrugged, good-naturedly giving in on his threat to not crew for Will. Like a drowning man grabbing at a passing plank, he said, "You're right. She'd never get on a boat with you. She told me herself."

"She told everyone," Will said dryly. "But if I did manage to convince her, it'd be different. We're not together any more. We'd be captain and crew, that's all."

"You don't believe that any more than I do," Thad said, shoving a couple of rolled-up charts out of the way so he could sit on the berth across from his friend. "I could help out as rail meat, you know."

Will eyed the cast. "Won't that thing slow you down? I can't afford to lose any time this year, you know that."

"You can't win this race without me," Thad said without a hint of false conceit.

"I can if I get Meg on board."

Thad forced a smile. "But you and I both know that's not going to happen."

"I'll charm her."

That's when Thad let out another of the booming laughs he was known for.

"I can be charming," Will said, slightly bothered by his friend's uncontrollable laughter. "I can be nice. Sort of nice."

"Will, you're a good guy. Hell, we've been friends for years. But I used to wonder what a nice girl like

Meg was doing with you. You never remembered her birthday, you never got her a card or flowers."

"I got her rain gear. Henri Lloyd. That stuff's expensive."

Thad stared at Will until he shrugged, acknowledging that Thad was probably right. "Well, I'm not trying to get her back, I'm just going to try to get her back on the boat."

"Same thing."

Will waved a tanned hand at him. "No, it's not. I'm over her." When Thad gave him a look of skepticism, Will insisted. "I am. I don't know if you've noticed, but I haven't been living like a priest for the past two years."

"Yeah. Different girl every night."

"Damn right."

"You been on a second date in a while?"

Will let out a sound of disgust. "Listen to this guy," Will said to an imaginary friend. "Where were you when you broke your arm? Hoping to get your pole waxed, that's where. Not out picking out rings to throw on some chick's finger."

"Okay, you got me there," Thad said, making Will laugh. "But at least I know I'm going to settle down some day. A long day off. Far, far away." Thad grinned. "Hell, I don't know what the heck I'm talking about. I only know that some day, it's going to happen. I'll be living in a house with a wife and two kids." Thad suppressed a shudder.

Will shrugged and got ready to lie. "The wife thing. The kids. That's not me."

"The Meg thing isn't you either."

"She was a lousy girlfriend, at least for me. But she's a great sailor." A great everything, but Thad didn't need to know that.

"She'll never do it."

Will dug his heels in, warming to the idea of having Meg on the boat again. Heck, more than warming to it. He was beginning to think that the only way he was going to win the Newport-Bermuda was to have her as his trimmer. "I need her on this boat."

"Shit."

"It's the only way I can win this race without you and you know it. Deep down inside."

"You are so wrong. Gary would do fine."

"I have to do more than fine this year."

Thad scrubbed his bald head with his good hand. "I know it. But Meg won't do it. Tell you what, you convince her to crew for you and I'll be on board one hundred percent. I'll be rail meat, I'll cook, I'll do whatever menial task you'd give the newbies. I just want to be on this boat when she crosses that line in Bermuda."

Will grinned. "You really don't think I can convince her, do you?"

"Not a chance in hell that woman will step on this boat with you."

Will leaned back and put his hands behind his head like a man who didn't have a worry in the world. "Welcome to hell."

Meghan Rose was having the worst—strike that—one of the worst days of her life. Two of her hard-fought-for clients had decided to take their houses off the market and one prospective buyer who'd been so enthusiastic about the Benson house twenty-four hours ago was now backpedaling so fast it was dizzying.

She clutched the phone painfully even though she kept her voice even. "Bathroom tile can easily be changed," she said. Perky, perky, even though Meghan did not think of herself as the "perky" type.

"It's not just that," her client said, and from the way she was hesitating, Meghan knew something more substantive was bothering the woman. "It's the neighborhood. It's a bit more ethnically diverse than we were looking for."

Okay, Meghan thought, many aspects of real estate are distasteful. You want to sell houses. You want to make people happy. You want . . . to scream at this woman.

"I'm afraid I don't know what you're talking about."

"It's the Hispanics," she said, lowering her voice as if the offending "Hispanics" might hear her. When the woman didn't get a response from Meg, she said, "Across the street. You know, in the yellow house."

Meghan was dumbfounded. "You mean the DiSilvas? They're fourth generation, not that should make a difference. He's vice president of a bank and she's a high school teacher. I'm afraid I don't see what could be objectionable."

"No, no. I know. I'm certain they are very nice people."

"Nicer than you," Meghan mumbled.

"Pardon?"

"I'm afraid I can't help you, Mrs. Carter. I can find you a good house in a good neighborhood and negotiate a fair price for you. But I can't, in good conscience, take a poll of the neighbors to find out if they are white enough for you."

"Oh, God, I didn't mean to sound like a bigot. But a house is a big investment, you know."

Meghan's grip on the phone tightened. The Carters were looking in the eight hundred thousand dollar range, which meant a very nice commission. She could hear Alan's voice in her head telling her that her main goal was to make everyone happy. That's how she'd build a client list, that's how she'd begin making money. But although she loved it when she found a young couple the perfect house, she hated other parts of the job, the parts that made her be less than honest, the parts that made her wish she was back on a boat feeling the warm, salty wind in her face.

"Why don't we just keep looking," Meghan said, though being nice to this woman was making her slightly ill.

Mrs. Carter let out an audible sound of relief. "Thank you for being so understanding."

Meghan could not bring herself to utter even a syllable of agreement. She hung up feeling ashamed that she hadn't given that woman a piece of her mind before telling her she couldn't help her.

Alan came into the office at that moment, and seeing her expression, immediately came over to her. He was like that, could sense something was bothering her in one look. It was why he was such a good salesman. That and his amazing good looks. He looked like something out of a 1940s movie magazine—sandy hair always perfectly combed, blue eyes, beautiful white teeth, and a winning smile. That package and an innate ability to almost instantly see whether a client loved a house, hated it, or was indifferent had made him one of the most successful real estate agents in the state. He could read people, including her, which was a refreshing change from dating a man who wouldn't have noticed if she'd fallen overboard unless it affected how well his boat was sailing.

"What's wrong, baby?"

She didn't like that Alan called her "baby," especially in the office, but no matter how many times she'd asked him to stop, he didn't. But if that was his biggest flaw, she'd take it, just like she took the engagement ring he gave her that wasn't exactly what she'd wanted. She would have picked out something slightly less—she wouldn't say gaudy, but perhaps less flashy, more subtle. But who cared? It was a ring and it was beautiful and it meant she'd finally found someone who wanted to build a life with her, who wanted the same things she wanted—a home and a family and permanence. Alan was a rock—steady, strong, and wonderfully dull. Alan was just what she needed after years and years of not having a real home or a man with whom she felt safe. Alan was safe and that's what she loved about him most.

"The Carters want only white neighbors so they passed on the Benson house."

Alan furrowed his brow. "Pine Hill is about as white a neighborhood as you can get." And then his face cleared. "The DiSilvas. Of course."

Meghan raised her eyebrow. "Of course?"

"They put out their Portuguese flag."

"Right next to the American flag," Meghan pointed out.

Alan shrugged. "You just have to get used to people like the Carters."

"I don't want to get used to people like that,"

Meghan said forcefully, feeling disappointed in Alan's reaction.

Alan sat on the corner of her desk. "People like them drive me nuts, too. But they still have to buy a house and why not buy a house through us? Listen, if it bothers you that much, I'll deal with the Carters and give you two percent of the commission. Sound fair? That way the firm still gets the sale, you can keep your sensibilities. And some of the commission."

Meghan scowled. "Sometimes I hate this business."

"Me too," Alan said, giving her a quick kiss on her forehead. "But I have a remarkable ability to deal with the scumbags of the world and still come out with my moral outrage in check."

"I don't know if I can do that." Meghan gave Alan a hard look. "And I'm not sure I like that you can."

"Listen. Half the people we deal with are jerks. If I made judgment calls and only sold houses to and for nice people, I wouldn't be one of the top agents in the state. And half the people we think are nice probably beat their wives and molest their kids. Frankly, it's good to know up front about the Carters. Think about the DiSilvas trying to live across the street from people who think less of them just because their ancestors came from Portugal."

"You can put a positive spin on anything, you know that?" Meghan asked, with a small amount of grudging admiration. "I suppose you're right. I can't change the Carters of the world. But I can't deal with them, either. I'll take that two percent, but only because I've spent so much time with them already. I deserve something for that, I guess."

"Fair enough." Alan gave her a fond look. "And

it doesn't really matter anyway, it'll all be in the same pot soon enough."

Meghan forced a smile, not really liking the idea of a single pot. She'd been self-sufficient for a long time and the thought of sharing her money wasn't easy. After a decade of living week to week, she finally she had money in her savings account. It was a wonderful feeling to see that amount grow and know she'd done it herself. But she supposed she'd get used to joint accounts, just like she'd gotten used to living a normal life, having a normal job and a normal boyfriend.

Normalcy. It was a beautiful thing. She had a car, an apartment, she went grocery shopping and bought doo-dads for her kitchen. She actually had enough food in her fridge to make a meal if someone happened to stop by. Her nomad life was over and thank God for it. She loved feeling as if she were part of a community. She loved waking up in a house instead of someone else's boat or a hotel. Every day that went by, she realized she'd made the right decision about leaving the sail racing circuit. She'd walked away from everything with hardly a look back. Heck, she hadn't even gone to the beach last summer. Newport seemed like a lifetime away, even though it was only a forty-minute drive. She hadn't heard the clang of a halyard on a mast in two years.

She'd found Alan when she wasn't even really looking, wonderful Alan with a real job and a real house with furniture that came from a high-end furniture store. She'd be living there within a year, having a baby within two, growing old and happy and content and she didn't miss her former life at all. Not one single bit. And especially she didn't miss *him.*

"Meghan," Jennifer, the receptionist, rushed to her desk, her cheeks flushed. "There's the most gorgeous man up front asking for you."

Meghan didn't care how gorgeous a guy was, she only cared whether he could afford to buy one of her listings. "Is he looking for a house?"

Jennifer blushed. "I didn't ask."

"You do work in a real estate office," Meghan said blandly. She gave Jennifer a fond look before standing up and following her to the reception area of their large agency. Leonard Della Real Estate was the largest independent agency in New England and had more than five hundred agents and a massive amount of listings. Some people still blamed Leonard Della, who'd been dead for ten years, for the state's skyrocketing housing prices.

Meghan walked past other agents, most talking on the phone or checking out the latest new listings in hope of finding the perfect house for their clients. It had taken Meghan a while to feel as if she belonged in this office. Two weeks after she'd gotten her real estate license she'd made her first sale and immediately went out and spent what felt like a fortune on new clothes. Her closet had been filled with shorts and T-shirts, all emblazoned with the title and logo of ocean races, along with the year. She had a T-shirt from 1994 to 2004 for the Newport-Bermuda alone, as well as a fine collection of boat shoes. She'd started racing when she was eighteen because she didn't want to go to college right away and thought competitive racing would be fun. And God, it had been for a long time. She hadn't cared that she didn't have a real home, was actually proud of it. No ties, no worries, just living free and easy. It had been an idyllic life.

And then one day she woke up and she was twenty-eight and still living a life as if she were eighteen and it scared the hell out of her. How had ten years flown by? Was she going to go to college now? Not likely. She was still poor, and other than a great tan and a toned body, she didn't have much of anything. She'd started having panic attacks before races, and Will would hand her a paper bag, tell her to breathe into it, and get the hell on the deck as fast as you can, kiddo, because we've got to get these sails up and head out to the starting line.

Will. God, she'd loved him. He was the strongest man she'd known in spirit and in body. She was twenty-four when they'd met and the chemistry between them had been instant and insatiable. She'd been attracted to his single-mindedness, his ability to win at all costs. Something about Will made people around him want to be their best and for a long, intoxicating time, that had been enough. Pleasing Will became a full-time effort. And then she noticed he wasn't putting in much effort toward her at all. They still had great sex, worked together amazingly well, but there was no feeling of permanence. Even after four years, Meghan still felt like she had to try to win him over.

And damn, that was so tiring.

He never talked about their future, only the next race, the next innovation to Frank's boat. When Meghan started talking about somedays, he'd close down or laugh or quickly change the subject. And when she'd given him the ultimatum, he hadn't budged. See ya, kiddo.

Meghan walked away from *Water Baby* without a

second glance and then proceeded to wait for two months for Will to come to his senses. Then she'd seen a copy of *Sailing Weekly* and saw *Water Baby* on the cover and seen him at the helm, head raised up to look at the mainsail. She stood there in CVS Pharmacy holding her box of tampons and felt as if someone had just ripped her heart from her chest. He'd gone on without her, he hadn't looked back. Nothing had ever hurt as much as that moment when she finally realized that for four years, the only one who'd been in love was her. Desperately, frighteningly in love.

And he was out sailing.

Six months later, Meghan had her real estate license in hand and had begun dating Alan. For the first time in her life she felt truly loved and at peace. She didn't have to fight for Alan's love; he gave it freely and surprisingly easily. Now, she was over Will. Completely, utterly over him.

When she reached the reception desk, she saw Alan already talking to the man who'd asked for her, and her heart skipped a crazy little beat. *Just because you were just thinking about him doesn't mean you conjured him up out of thin air.*

Then Will, looking mussed and sexy as if he'd just stepped off his boat, which he probably had, turned around and grinned. "Meg. I've come to get you back."

Chapter Two

As soon as the words were out of his mouth, Will knew she'd misunderstood him because her stunning blue eyes immediately darted to her fiancé, then narrowed in suspicion and anger.

"I need a trimmer," Will clarified, and watched with fascination as her arms folded neatly over her gray pinstripe power suit. Amazingly, she looked just as sexy in her suit as she had wearing her low-slung cargo shorts and bikini top.

"So, this is Will," Alan said.

"William," Will said, just to be ornery.

"I'd like to say I've heard a lot about you, but the truth is, Meghan only mentioned you once," Alan said, letting out an awkward laugh.

Meghan raised a neatly trimmed brow but remained silent. He wished he knew what was going on behind her impassive expression. Usually she was easy to read. She was probably contemplating several ways to dismember him, starting with some key areas. She was still beautiful, still fit and trim, though her hair was slightly longer and less blond. And it was neat, perfectly styled, just like the rest of her. He didn't like the way she looked at him, taking in his shorts, his wrinkled white shirt, his bare feet jammed into a pair of old boat shoes, as if there was something wrong with the way he was dressed. Will hadn't been ashamed of who he was in a very long time and he wasn't about to start now.

"Nice suit," he said to her, knowing he sounded as if he meant the opposite, but she didn't give him the satisfaction of getting angry. She smiled and thanked him.

Alan, the fiancé (which the guy had managed to impart within about five seconds of meeting him) looked like a shady lawyer to him—all smiles in an Armani suit.

"As much as I appreciate a good joke, I hope you're here looking for a house," Meghan said, not cracking a smile.

"Sure I am," Will said. "What do you have in the half-million dollar range?"

"He can't afford a house," Meghan said with a snort, looking to Alan.

"Meghan," Alan said in a slightly chastising manner, and Will got the satisfaction of seeing Meg's annoyed look. His girl was still in there. Somewhere.

"I'm loaded," Will said, turning to Alan. "She only wanted me for my money, you know. Watch out for that one."

Meghan laughed and Will felt an odd and scary catch in his chest. "The only money he has is in his pocket," Meghan predicted with razor-sharp accuracy. "He couldn't buy a trailer if he wanted to."

Will felt the old irritation grow. "Actually, Meg, my father died and left me with something," he said.

Yeah, twenty grand in debts from an upholstering business that had never made money because Jared Scott drank every cent of profit and then some. Will had never worked a day in that business and never understood why the old man, who on a good day couldn't stand his only son, had added him to the business. Will figured his father knew what he was doing when he died leaving unfinished work and unpaid bills. Oh, and that wonderful letter from his mother, nicely framed. One final cruel joke.

"I'm sorry, Will. I didn't see the notice," Meg said, with obvious caution. Meg had never met his father, and he'd rarely spoken about him. Frank was his father as far as he was concerned, and had been ever since he was a half-starved kid who was as hungry for food as he was for parental love.

"It was a while back," Will said tonelessly. He didn't want to talk about his father's death and he wished like hell he hadn't brought it up. "Anyway, I'm looking for a house," he lied. "Getting ready to settle down."

Meg gave him a long look. "No, you're not. You really are here looking for a trimmer."

"What's a trimmer?" Alan asked politely and they both turned to him, as if surprised he was still standing there.

"Come out to lunch and I'll tell you all about it," Will said, bringing an arm around the other man's back to push him toward the door.

"It's three o'clock," Meghan pointed out. "Frankly, I don't want to go anywhere with you. Particularly not on a sailboat. You wasted your time."

Oh, she was good and mad, and for some reason that made Will feel better, more secure about where he stood with her. "Then I'll buy you coffee," Will said, undeterred.

Meghan could not, not, not believe Will had the audacity to come into her office and try to get her back on a boat with him. She knew Will was the most self-assured—no, arrogant—SOB to ever walk the earth, but even she was shocked at him showing up out of the blue. When Meghan saw Alan begin to follow Will out, she held his arm. "We're wasting our time," she bit out, trying desperately not to sound as angry as she was.

For a brief moment, Alan was stuck in a tug-o-war between the two before a flash of irritation made Meghan release his arm. "Let's see what he has to say," Alan said, a slight edge to his voice.

"Yes, let's," Will said, grinning in a maddening way that made Meghan want to scream.

What the hell did Will think he was doing? If he thought he could get her back on his boat, he had another thing coming. Meghan watched the two men walk in front of her, noting with some satisfaction that Alan was taller than Will. Ha. And way better dressed. Ha. Ha.

Meghan had told Alan very little about Will, other than the fact they'd been together for four years before breaking up. Alan knew she sailed, but thankfully had expressed little interest in the subject. After Meghan quit that life, she didn't want to talk about sailing or Will or anything that reminded her that she'd been a doormat for four years. Sure, Will had never really told her he loved her; it had always been along the lines of "I love you but you're a pain in my ass." She got the warm fuzzies just thinking about it. The underlying message was: Okay, I'm saying the "l" word but don't take it too seriously. But she had. Or maybe she'd taken her own love too seriously. Two years later, she found herself walking with the two men for coffee as if that was something she did all the time, chat with her ex and her fiancé.

"So, you sail?" Alan said with the fake heartiness of a salesman trying to pretend interest in a potential client. Meghan gave an inward cringe and caught up to the men before Alan got himself into trouble. She loved him, but there were times when he turned on the charm that he was downright annoying. She didn't want him wasting an ounce of charm on Will.

"I race," Will corrected.

"Like NASCAR? Big prizes and all that?"

Meghan let out a small sound that might have been a laugh if she'd allowed it out. "Not quite."

"I have done some professional racing," Will said. "But mostly we race for trophies. Cups. You know, like the America's Cup."

Alan smiled. "Of course I've heard of that. Newport lost that in the eighties, right? Is that the race you do?"

"I've crewed it. But I race my boat in the Newport-Bermuda for the St. Davis Lighthouse Trophy. Among others."

Meghan paused and slapped on an interested expression. "You have your own boat now? Will, that's wonderful." If her jab bothered him, he didn't let her know.

"Nope. Still on Frank's boat. And she's got a new keel that makes her fly and enough high-tech equipment to make her sail by herself. This is the year, kiddo. This is it, but I need you"—he put a finger to the tip of her nose—"to help me."

The two men walked ahead and she struggled to keep up in modest one-inch heels, which even after two years she wasn't quite used to walking long distances in yet. When they crossed the street, they turned to watch her stroll ungracefully toward them. "You try walking fast in these," she said, looking down at her cursed shoes. She usually wore a pants suit with flats.

"Why, Meg, you really have turned into a girl," Will said, staring at wonder at her shoes, and Meg had to fight a smile. In the four years they'd known each other, he'd seen her in only one dress.

"I never wore heels before this job," Meghan explained to Alan.

"She used to dress like this," Will said, indicating his own clothes.

"Now I'm a grown-up," Meghan couldn't help but say.

"A beautiful one," Alan said, taking her hand, and Meghan thought she heard a choking sound coming from Will.

When they reached a small coffee shop, Alan held the door for them, giving her a searching look that she ignored. She'd warned Alan that he was wasting his time with Will and he hadn't believed her. Now he'd have to suffer through twenty minutes with the most maddening man God created.

Alan might not be perfect, but everything about Will was annoying, Meghan decided. His windblown chocolate hair, his ruddy, sun-kissed skin, his bright blue-green eyes, his worn cargo shorts, his blown-out boat shoes, the way he raised a dark eyebrow when Alan ordered a double mocha decaf latte right after Will ordered a large coffee—black.

"Sure you can handle a double?" he asked Alan,

who looked confused. Alan was not used to the mean-spirited man-banter that came off Will's tongue as easily as genuine kindness came off Alan's.

"I'm not really much of a coffee drinker," Alan said, and Meghan was proud to see Alan was not sinking to Will's level.

As they sat down at the small round table, Will wedged his way between her and Alan, so she pointedly scuttled the chair away.

"So, Will, are you really interested in real estate or is this simply a ploy to steal my fiancée?" Alan asked, taking Meghan's well-ringed hand in his.

Will didn't miss the obvious caveman move claiming possession of Meghan or the huge rock on her ring finger and couldn't help but be slightly annoyed by it, but only because he found everything annoying about Alan. As far as he knew, Meghan had never been much of a hand-holder and could almost sense how uncomfortable she felt sitting there captured by Alan.

"I want to steal her," Will said. "But only for a few weeks. Then you can have her back forever."

"And here I was thinking you'd come to win me back," Meghan said.

"In my wildest nightmares that is not my intent," Will said. He turned to Alan, sensing he might be able to influence him into getting Meghan on board his boat. "Alan, did you know Meghan is one of the best women sailors . . ."

"Was," she interjected.

"Is. One of the best women sailors in the world?"

Alan turned to Meghan. "Really, darling?"

"That was a long time ago," she said, glaring at Will who had to suppress a grin. She knew exactly what he was trying to do.

"Two years ago we came within a tack of winning the Newport-Bermuda. We were so close I could almost feel the weight of that trophy in my hands. Meghan can trim a sail and find wind that you can't even feel against your face."

"That was frustrating," Meghan said, begrudgingly joining in his reminiscence. "Everything about being on *Water Baby* was frustrating."

"Water Baby?"

"The name of Frank's boat," Meghan explained. "Frank's this old guy who's been trying to win the Newport-Bermuda for thirty years."

"Is he the guy who steers?" Alan asked.

"Used to," Will said. "He was a terrific helmsman, but he's too sick now."

"How is Frank?" Meghan asked. "I keep meaning to go see him."

He's dying. "He's hanging in there," Will said. Frank did not want anyone to know how sick he was, including Will. But when Will wanted to, he could turn on the charm and he'd turned it on to the hospice nurse who worked most days. Will wanted to throttle the old man for not telling him, but figured he'd let Frank have his secret and his pride. It was only when Frank asked Will to win the cup this year that he let Will know just how frightened he was. The race was held only every two years and Frank knew he wasn't going to see the next one.

"I'd sure like to hold that trophy in my hands," he'd said, and damn if the old man's eyes didn't well up. There was a history there that Will knew all about, a desperate promise made to Frank's dying son, which Will had turned into a promise to a dying friend. Will hadn't been foolish enough to promise aloud to Frank, but that didn't make the vow he'd made to the old man any less real.

"I think Frank would sell his soul to win that cup," Will said. "And all I want from you is less than a month of your life."

"Nice try," Meghan said. "I'm sorry Frank made that promise to his son, but there are plenty of good trimmers out there and you know it."

Will shook his head. "Thad got hurt two days ago. Broke his arm in two places and he's in a cast up to his chin." Meghan winced. "Do you really think I'd be here unless I was desperate?" He turned to Alan. "Help me out here, Alan. She's the only trimmer available on short notice. She could win the race for me."

"Is this true?" Alan said, and Meghan didn't like the light in Alan's eyes as he got caught up in the whole win-at-all-costs thing. Alan wasn't a sports fan, but she'd never met another person more competitive than he was about other things. She'd known him for more than a year and he'd been top salesman in the office nearly every month. It wasn't a desire for money, though that was a nice by-product; it was his burning need to be number one. In that one way, Will and Alan were alike, she realized.

"Trimming a sail is an art form and Meg is a master. With her on board I'll win. Without her, I haven't got a chance." Meghan watched Will perform his magic, impressed, despite herself, how he sucked Alan in with his intensity. He was captivating, Meghan had to give him that. "It's a six-hundred-thirty mile race. With Meg here I can get a half-knot to a knot faster than with anyone else pulling the sheets. Do you know what that means over a race that long?"

"Not really," Alan admitted, shifting in his seat, and it was the first time she'd ever seen Alan even the tiniest unsure of himself. "I don't even know what sheets are."

"Ropes," Meghan said.

"It means that given the right conditions, we win the race. It means that without Meg, we don't win."

Meghan wanted to argue, but she knew that at least in this, Will was telling the truth. Without Thad, she really was the only trimmer available who could keep him competitive. She looked at Alan, who was looking at her with the strangest expression.

"I never knew I had such a talented fiancée," Alan said with a weird little laugh Meghan had never heard come out of his mouth.

"Everyone has one thing they're good at. Or maybe two," Will said, looking at Meghan in a way that wasn't hard to misinterpret because it was so blatantly sexual. Then he smiled and Meghan knew he'd been jerking her chain—and Alan's. Except Alan didn't know his chain had been jerked.

"I told you he was an insensitive idiot," Meghan said lightly, and Will just laughed, obviously confusing Alan even more. Poor Alan, he just wasn't used to people torturing each other. Meghan made a show of squeezing Alan's hand and for the life of her she almost burst out laughing at Will's purposefully unconcealed repulsion. She always had found Will funny, even when he was being idiotic.

"This race isn't dangerous, is it?" Alan asked, giving Meghan one of those soft looks that usually made her feel cherished. For some reason, in front of Will, that puppy-dog look made her decidedly squeamish. Which, of course, made her feel irritated at Will, because up until that moment she'd been perfectly happy being cherished by such a wonderful man.

"Only one death. So far," Will said with relish.

"It's perfectly safe," she said quickly. "Okay, not perfectly safe. There are storms. People have gotten hurt. But at night and during heavy seas, we're all tethered to the boat with a harness."

"Unless someone forgets," Will said pointedly.

"I did not forget," Meghan said. Seeing Alan's unspoken question, she found herself being forced to explain how one night she hadn't yet tethered herself to the boat and had found herself dangling off the side. It was every sailor's nightmare to be washed oversea at night. With a boat traveling ten to fifteen knots in heavy seas, you were as good as dead. No one would see you, no one would hear you over the noise of the wind and waves. It was why sailors were so careful about tethering themselves at night and during high seas.

"She forgot," Will said to Alan, whose look of concern was enough to make Meghan forgive Alan for being overprotective. "But don't worry, I won't let her forget again."

"How did you get back on the boat?"

Will started laughing and Meg couldn't help but join in. At the time she'd been scared out of her mind and mad as hell at herself that she hadn't put the harness on yet.

"She was clinging to the safety line dangling off the side of the boat, screaming her head off," Will said. "Seas were pretty high. High enough to give her a soaking."

"My PFD exploded," Meghan said, still laughing.

"PFD?" Alan said, clearly not finding anything amusing in the story so far.

"Personal flotation device," Meghan and Will said in unison.

"She blew up like the Pillsbury Doughboy," Will said, and Meghan lost it, still picturing herself hanging onto the boat looking like a large balloon bobbing in the sea.

"I almost couldn't hang on," Meghan said, trying to stop laughing. "Believe me, at the time no one was laughing." And then, like a ten-foot wave slamming into her, she remembered what happened after Thad and a couple of other guys had hauled her aboard, how Will had held her and didn't give a damn about the boat or how fast they were going, how she swore she'd seen tears in his eyes that she later convinced herself must have been the sea. It seemed Will remembered, too, because she looked at him and he wasn't laughing anymore either.

"What did Frank say when you told him about Thad?" she asked to change the subject, to get that image out of her head.

Will suddenly found the table's mosaic design interesting.

"You haven't told him?"

"I wanted to try to get you first. He's not going to be happy, that's for sure."

"Frank is going to bust a vein," Meghan said, enjoying the image of Frank's reaction.

"He'll understand," Will lied. Frank wouldn't get angry, not at this point, and Will hadn't gotten the courage up to tell him. Because he knew when he did, that terrifying hope he'd seen in Frank's eyes would disappear. The old guy had thrown more money toward that boat and its crew than most owners, all because he'd promised his dying son nearly thirty years ago that he'd win the cup for him. Will couldn't reason with Frank, couldn't get him to recognize that if his son happened to be looking down at him from heaven, the kid wouldn't care about a sailing trophy. Frank had made that promise and that was that. For years, Will hadn't understood the obsession driving Frank to win, but now he understood because the tables had turned and the promise was now his.

"When is this race?" Alan asked, and Will sensed victory, at least in getting the boyfriend's blessing.

"Less than two weeks."

As Alan let out a low whistle, Meghan said, "I can't do it. June around here is one of the busiest times. People with kids put their houses on the market and people looking for houses try to buy during the summer so their kids don't have to switch schools. The agency can't spare me."

"I just need two weeks," Will said, feeling a sick desperation settle into his gut. "Maybe three. You need to get on this boat, to feel her, at least a few times before the race. Meghan, you can't tell me you wouldn't want to be on *Water Baby* when she crosses that line. You can't tell me you can't already taste it, the way it will feel to hold that trophy."

Will could tell he was getting to her, so he kept going. "The crew has hardly changed since you left. All the same guys. They all think this is the year. You should see the money Frank has put into it. We've got handheld GPSs, a weather fax with a computer interface. Hell, he even bought a few night vision binoculars." Meghan let out a little whistle. "Damn it, Meg, you've got to do this."

"Maybe you should, baby," Alan said, squeezing her hand, and Will watched their exchange with interest.

"What?"

"I've sensed a bit of restlessness in you."

"You have?" Meghan didn't know how he'd sensed any such thing, given that she was pretty certain she'd been content—up until an hour ago when Will had waltzed into her office.

"I can take on any listings you have for that short a time. You'll still get the commission if I make any sales. Not that it matters at this point who gets credit for our sales."

Meghan pressed her lips together, for some reason irritated by yet another reminder that her money would soon be "our" money.

"One last race, Meg. One last try," Will said, and there was something about his eyes, something so uncharacteristically desperate that Meghan almost caved then and there.

"I want to think about it." She watched as Will closed his eyes, almost as if in thankful prayer. "I haven't said yes," she said, wishing she could say no outright like she wanted to. One last time. That was what was getting to her. She'd left the sailing world so abruptly and with so much rancor, it had left her with a bitter taste in her mouth. Her quitting sailing had nothing to do with her love of being on a boat, of racing, of feeling the power of the sea beneath her feet. It had all been about the man sitting across from her, the man who broke her heart and who was now asking for her help. She ought to tell him to go to hell for hurting her so badly. But the lure of the sea, which she'd thought was long gone, was suddenly back so strongly she knew she was in for a fight.

"Two weeks?" she asked, glancing to Alan.

"I think we can spare you," he said, and gave her hand a little squeeze. "Just as long as Will here isn't trying to steal you back," he added with false-sounding good humor.

"Believe me," Will said with what sounded like total honesty. "The only thing I want is a good trimmer and Meg's the best."

Meghan took a deep breath, feeling a thrill in her stomach she hadn't felt in two years, a feeling that scared her to hell. "I'll try to call you tomorrow," she said firmly, trying to get hold of her emotions. She had to think about this rationally, something she'd never done when Will was within ten feet of her, and she wanted to give Alan a chance to pull a he-man and forbid her to go. Meghan knew she was in no danger of falling for Will's questionable charms, but she knew her being on a boat with her ex had to bother Alan a little bit.

As they walked out of the coffee shop, Will filled her in on the crew: who was still on the boat, who wasn't, who got married, who got divorced, as Alan followed behind them thinking about his next appointment.

Chapter Three

Frank Walcott hated this dying business, but he supposed there wasn't much he could do about it. Everyone had to go and it was almost his time. But damn it, he didn't want it to be just yet, not when the race was so close, not when he knew, he *knew* Will was going to do it this time.

He let out a sigh, closing his eyes to picture his boat with him at the helm and Will pulling on the main sheet. The kid loved sailing from the start, almost as if he'd been born to it, though God knew he hadn't been. Little guy had been born to nothing. Frank still remembered Will when he was just a skinny kid wandering around the neighborhood like a stray dog. He'd watched the kid from his deck just to see how long he'd sit there staring out at the bay. Will lived across the street, in the old Jones place. The place was basically a shack, a one-bedroom pit that should have been torn down years ago. He'd looked to be about ten years old, scrawny, with hair too long and clothes that were either too big or too small, depending on the day.

Frank had met the kid's father once. The guy

seemed nice enough, but it struck Frank that he wasn't the single-dad hero kind of man, just a guy dealt a lousy hand and dealing with it in a lackluster way. Frank would watch for the father's battered Buick Century and wondered how old a kid was supposed to be before they were allowed to be left alone at night. He'd see the boy sometimes wandering down to the beach right before sunset. He'd sit on the same rock and stare out for long minutes. The kid didn't have a bike or even a skateboard that Frank could see. Wasn't much room in that shack for kid stuff anyway.

The day they'd met, Frank had watched him for ten minutes before his wife joined him on the deck.

"Back again?" Nancy had asked quietly. "That boy's alone too much."

Frank let out a grunt in answer and watched for a few more minutes before letting out a sigh and going down to the beach to talk to him. Frank hadn't had much to do with kids in years, but this boy wasn't exactly a kid. Kids were noisy and impolite and generally annoying. This one was like a ghost—silently walking, leaving no sound in his wake, not even looking your way should you happen by him. And that bothered Frank. Wasn't right for a kid his age to be so quiet.

Frank stood back a while, waiting to see if the boy would turn toward him, but he didn't. He kept staring out on the bay and when Frank followed his eyes, he saw what the boy was looking at—a cat boat, pretty as can be, its large sail stark white against a bank of clouds gathering in the distance.

"You sail?" Frank asked, thinking he might startle the kid.

Will had shaken his head but didn't turn

Frank's way, as if he knew who he was talking to already. "No."

"Like to try it?"

If the kid could have gotten any stiller, he did just then, his little body turning to stone.

"I have a boat," Frank said, wondering why in hell he was trying to befriend a ten-year-old kid. "I can always use another crewmember."

Will had turned to him, his dark bangs almost hiding the near-painful hope in his eyes. "Okay," he said, so cautiously Frank figured he didn't believe the invitation was real.

"I'm Frank," he said grimly, holding out his hand.

The boy took it and smiled for the first time. "Will."

"Well, Will, tomorrow's Saturday and I always take my boat out on Saturdays. If you don't get in the way too much, you're welcome to come any time."

The smile disappeared. "I have to ask my father."

"I can ask if you want," Frank said, instinctively knowing things would work out better for the kid if he did all the talking. Frank didn't know he had an instinct for dealing with this kid, but maybe he did. Then again, maybe it was that he had an instinct for dealing with men like Will's father.

"Okay. Ask tomorrow. He works late Fridays."

Frank said his good-byes and went back into the house where he'd lived with his wife for twenty-five years.

"Something's not right over there," Nancy had said, peeking through the curtain at the lone figure walking across the street.

Frank stared at Will until he disappeared into the tiny house. "I asked him to go sailing."

Nancy had given Frank a sharp look before smiling. "What did he say?"

"That kid wants to go sailing so badly he's about to bust. His old man better let him."

Frank's reminiscences were interrupted when his day nurse entered the room. Frank liked his day nurse, a woman in her thirties who reminded him a bit of what his wife had been like in younger days. Even Nancy had noted the similarity and had given him a playful warning about her.

"Time for your two o'clock meds," Collette said, handing him two Dixie cups filled with pills and standing by with a large glass of water.

He took them without hesitation, because Frank Walcott wanted to live more than any other man on earth. He wanted to live, live, live and he cursed a thousand times a day the diabetes that ate away at him. And he cursed himself as much, too, knowing that if he'd taken his disease a bit more seriously twenty years ago, he wouldn't be dying, his heart failing, his limbs withering.

The race was in ten days. He had to live at least that long because he'd never seen Will so confident, so excited about the Newport-Bermuda. Will had always been cautious with his predictions, but that was before *Water Baby*'s redesign, before Will had assembled the best damn crew in the racing circuit. He could almost feel that trophy in his hands, see the name of his boat engraved on the plaque. It was the last thing he had of his son, a tiny thread connecting them stretched so thin over the years, Frank had to fight to see it sometimes. If he stopped trying to win that trophy for Jack, he would be gone for good, lost to him in a way he wasn't now. Frank knew he was a little crazy about the whole thing, but Jack had loved sailing as much as he did. It was the one thing they could do together without rancor or competition. And when he lay dying in hospital, slipping into a irreversible coma, Frank had made his promise. *"I'll get you that trophy, Jack. I swear it."*

Four days before Jack's seventeenth birthday, he died, leaving a hole so big in Frank's life he didn't think anything could ever come close to filling it. Because despite that promise, Frank's heart wasn't in sailing anymore. Without his son by his side, it seemed empty and pointless. He'd entered the Newport-Bermuda and placed thirtieth and thought long and hard about why he should go on living. Then Will moved into that shack across the street and saved Frank's life.

And now, thirty years after making that promise to his son, he just might come through for him.

"Hey, Thad," he heard Collette say, and Frank tried to straighten up and look less like a dying man and more like a sick one. What he saw truly made him sick.

"Crap."

"Nice to see you, too, old man," Thad said, pretending he didn't know what Frank was talking about.

"Does Will know?"

"Yeah, Will knows. He's working on it."

Frank sort of melted into his bed, a large bit of hope stolen by the sight of that cast on Thad's arm. He knew instantly that the chances *Water Baby* had of winning the Newport-Bermuda were significantly altered.

"How'd it happen?" Frank asked, just to be polite,

because he wouldn't let Thad know how spitting mad he was.

"Jammed it against a piling," Thad said.

"So, what's Will working on?"

Before Thad could answer, Will did as he walked in. "Only on getting the best damned trimmer *Water Baby*'s ever had."

Thad shook his head and smiled, as if baffled by the insult.

"Meg," Frank whispered.

"Meg did not agree to sail with you," Thad said with an edge, obviously still smarting from the slight.

"Has she agreed?" Frank asked, and he didn't like Will's expression when he did.

"Not yet. But she will." When Thad snorted, Will said, "She said she had to think about it, but I could tell she wanted to. Hell, even her boyfriend thinks it's a good idea."

"I thought they were engaged."

"Fiancé, then. Even the fiancé agreed she should do it."

"Then we still have a shot," Frank said.

"Better than a shot, Frank. Better than that. I've got to get Meg back up to speed. *Water Baby* is a different boat than the one Meg sailed two years ago. But she's a smart kid. She'll get a feel for the boat in one practice session."

"She hasn't said yes," Thad unnecessarily reminded him.

"She will."

"When is she supposed to let you know?" Frank asked.

"Some time today." Will didn't like the way Frank's eyes slid to the clock by his bed. It was already two-thirty. If Meghan was going to call, she would have done it by now. "She'll call. And I'll let you know as soon as she does. Believe me, Frank, she'll do it. I could see the fire in her eyes when we were talking about the crew and the boat. She'll call."

But by ten o'clock that night, panic set in and Will knew he was going to have to take more drastic measures to get Meg onto the boat.

More than forty-eight hours after Will had tried to rock her world, Meg decided she would not—could not—get back on a boat with that man. Her life now was wonderfully calm, smooth, and boring. And that's the way she liked it. She'd had enough drama in the past few years to last a lifetime. She was stronger than the lure of the sea, stronger than a charming, handsome heartbreaker.

Meghan opened her refrigerator to see what she could whip up to eat. Alan was showing two houses and wouldn't be done until late, so she was on her own. It was nice to have a night off—a rarity lately. As her client list grew, so did the phone calls. She'd actually turned off her cell phone a few times just to have some peace and quiet, even though she felt guilty about it.

When Alan wasn't coming over for dinner, she usually threw a Healthy Choice meal into her microwave, tossed a handful of cheese onto whatever it was, and ate in front of the television. Pure gooey bliss. Alan liked to cook and usually prepared something incredible to eat. He had weekly themes—Mexican, Italian, Indian, Tex-Mex—always served with the perfect wine. Meghan watched him cook and drank wine and sometimes even chopped something up for him, but for the most part, she let him reign in the kitchen. Her mother, who'd always lamented about her bohemian daughter, couldn't get over the fact that Alan did nearly all of the cooking. "I hope you appreciate that boy," she said more times than Meghan could count. Marge had not liked Will. At all. Not even a bit. She was almost pathological in her campaign for Meghan to get rid of Will, which Meghan to this day could not figure out. Sure, Will may not have been a mother's dream for her daughter, but he was a nice guy. Now her mother was on an equally pathological plan to get Meghan down the altar with Alan.

Meghan was about to pull out an enchilada meal—after all, it was Mexican week—when someone knocked at her door. She opened the door a crack and winced before unlatching the chain and opening it further. Will was standing on the other side, looking like he'd just blown in from the bay. He wore a clean white T-shirt with *Water Baby* stamped in one corner, and a pair of tan cargo shorts. His brown hair was sun-streaked and wind-tousled and his eyes were a remarkable blue-green against his tanned face. In that moment she forgave her younger self for falling in love with him; he was just that damn appealing.

Before she could open her mouth to tell him she'd decided to not race, he held up two white paper bags—one with telltale grease spots on it.

"Tell me that's not clam cakes," she said, her mouth watering as the smell of fried clam-stuffed fritters drifted to her nose. She couldn't remember the last time she'd had clam cakes.

"And chowda," Will said, putting on the New England accent.

"Clear or milk?"

Will pulled a shocked face. "Clear. Anything else isn't real chowder. And you know it." He grinned. "Care to join me?"

"Come on in," Meghan said with real reluctance. She had a feeling she was the little pig inviting the wolf into her cozy brick house. "But don't think a bribe of clam cakes and chowder is going to affect my decision."

He looked shocked again. "I would never stoop to that level. But it's not a bad idea. Did it work?"

Meghan fought to hide a smile. "No."

Will followed her in, his eyes taking in her small apartment. "Cozy. And bright." He chuckled and shook his head as if unable to believe what he was seeing. Sure, she'd gone a bit crazy with color when she'd first moved in, putting her stamp on the place in an almost frenetic way, but she loved her little home. To her eyes, the bright yellow walls trimmed with purple and lime green couch were perfect. She'd thrown a couple of purple pillows on the couch to tie it all together and had thought her place wonderful. Alan had made the mistake of offering her sympathy and his help painting it when he saw it for the first time, assuming it had been painted these colors when she moved in.

"It's really . . ." Will stood there in the room searching for the right thing to say. Meghan waited for the insult to come and when he did speak, she wasn't sure he'd insulted her or not. ". . . you."

"Is that good or bad?"

"You can't be depressed in this room, that's for sure." He moved into the kitchen with its sparkling white walls and bright blue trim and she thought she heard him say something under his breath before he said, "Very nautical." He walked toward the only other room in the house, her bedroom, and Meghan had the sudden urge to block his way. She'd painted it bright blue with lemon yellow trim but Alan joked he couldn't have sex in a room so blindingly bright, and he had offered to paint at least that for her. She'd still been in the I'll-do-anything-to-make-you-happy stage of their relationship, so she'd agreed. He'd picked a sort of brownish-beige color with off-white trim. It was very pretty and contemporary and . . .

"Depressing. Didn't get to this room yet?"

Meghan was not about to admit to him that Alan had picked that color, so she said, "I like it. It's pleasant."

"If you're half dead, maybe."

"Ha ha." She agreed, but at the time it had seemed like such a small thing to do for Alan. How much time did she spend in her bedroom anyway?

"Tour's over. Let's eat. Do you have a deck or anything?"

"I do, but it's connected to my neighbor and it's not really private. Anyway, it's just overlooking a parking lot."

He gave her a long look and she knew he was thinking of his place—what used to be their place—with a rooftop terrace and a view of the bay. His apartment was part of an old Victorian that had been carved up into six units years ago. Will was by far the youngest tenant and the only one who ever ventured up to the shared terrace. He'd taken over it, planting a few tomatoes and green peppers.

"Still have your garden?"

"I had to expand it because the demand for my tomatoes was so high," he said as he took out the two pint containers and handed Meghan a plastic spoon.

Funny, but eating chowder with a plastic spoon seemed perfectly right, even though she had a drawer full of real spoons two feet away.

He handed her a clam cake, and she took a bite, closing her eyes to savor the taste. "Heaven." She opened her eyes to find Will giving her the strangest look.

"You need to go sailing," he said at last.

Meghan took another bite, feeling herself weakening. What would it hurt, one last time? "Maybe."

"Try some chowder," he said with a diabolical look.

She wanted to hate him, she really, really did. She wanted to kick him out of her kitchen, out of her life forever. Instead she picked up the plastic spoon, dipped it into the chowder and took a taste. Then Meghan dropped the spoon with a sick look on her face.

"Why are you doing this?"

"Because I want to win this year and I need you." She'd never seen him so serious. "Please, Meg."

"Part of me still wants to kill you."

"I know."

"A big part."

"I know."

She stared at the chowder, not saying anything. Something must have changed in her expression, something she wasn't even aware of, because across the table from her, Will grabbed her hand and squeezed. "Thanks, kiddo."

She pulled her hand away, hating the way his hand felt so warm and rough against hers, hating that the single touch made her want to say yes, as if he had some sort of weird power over her. It was as if her body had a clearer memory of him than the rest of her, an instinctive pull that sent her instant and extremely unwanted images of Will naked.

She cleared her throat. "I'll call you tomorrow."

"Jesus," he let out on a hiss of breath.

"It's a big decision."

"It's not that big. Christ, you might think I was asking you to marry me."

"That," she said, pointing a finger at him, "would be an easy decision."

He glared at her a moment, then burst out laughing. "Okay. Call me tomorrow. Eat your chowder."

While they ate, Will filled her in about the boat and the tenants who'd once been her neighbors. She missed that old building and hadn't realized it until he started talking about Mr. Gooden, an old guy who was terminally boring and could talk about nothing endlessly. His wife had died while they were there and he used to look at the two of them with the saddest eyes. He moved away and Will had lost touch with him.

"Mrs. Robowitz is living in a nursing home. Her daughter took over the apartment for a while to be close."

"What happened?"

"Alzheimer's. But she's ninety-three. You got to die of something when you're that old."

Meghan let out a bit of guilty laughter. "True. Are you sure you're not some psychotic lunatic who's killing off all the tenants one by one?" He laughed and Meghan smiled, realizing she hadn't had so much fun talking to anyone in a long time. Alan was a terrific guy, but he really didn't have much of a sense of humor.

After the chowder and clam cakes were devoured, Will strolled around her small living room taking in the pictures she had propped on the mantel of the fake fireplace. A picture of her family was front and center, and beside that, a picture of her and Alan cheek to cheek looking like the perfect couple. Meghan liked the photo because it wrapped up her life quickly and easily—here I am, happy at last.

She saw Will frown as he took in the photographs. "You weren't expecting to see a picture of you there, were you?"

He started, as if he forgot he was staring at the pictures. "It's as if you erased the last ten years of your life."

"You just weren't that important," Meghan said, simply to be mean.

Will gave her a level look. "I don't mean me, I mean your life. Sailing. You'd never know you're one of the best women sailors in the world."

Meghan swallowed and felt her cheeks flush. "That part of my life is over," she said with a firmness she didn't really feel. After all, she was still burping up clam cakes and chowder.

"Almost over," Will said with a grin. He cocked his head to the side, pure manipulation that used to work like a charm. "Come on, Meg. Once more. Once," he said, holding up his index finger. When she didn't immediately cave, he let out a puff of frustration. "I can't win without you. Is that it? You're taking secret pleasure in watching my desperation?"

Meghan crossed her arms. "You know I'm not that petty."

He grabbed her hands, enfolding them in his warm, rough ones and she steeled herself against his power. "One last time. One final race. Jesus, Meg, I'm begging you, here. What do you want me to do?"

Say you made a mistake letting me go. Say you really loved me. Make me feel like less of a fool for loving you. "Nothing, Will," she said, feeling tired suddenly. "I'll think about it and call you tomorrow. Either way."

Will dropped her hands, feeling a surge of anger at himself. He apparently had overestimated Meg's love of sailing—or her dislike of him. If it wasn't so damned important that they win this year, he wouldn't have chewed up and swallowed his pride like this. He smiled, just to let her know it would be all right either way. There was a chance they could win without her. The boat was in terrific shape, his crew the best bunch of amateurs on the East Coast. *Water Baby* might pull it off. But with Meg, he knew the odds were that much greater. God, he wanted to squeeze a yes out of her. He couldn't get Frank's expression when he told him he was getting Meg out of his head, that damned hope.

They both turned when the front door opened and Alan walked in, stopping still when he saw Will standing inches away from his fiancée. Will had to admire the guy for recovering quickly and stretching out a hand for another of his painfully strong handshakes.

"Nice to see you again, Will. Still trying to get Meghan out on that boat of yours?"

"Thought I'd bribe her with clam cakes and chowder. Hasn't worked yet, though," Will said with a look to Meg.

"How'd it go tonight?" Meg asked, changing the subject.

"One couple was very interested in that house on Hornet Drive. I think they'll be making an offer within the next two days. You get any calls tonight?"

"Not tonight," she said, strangely chipper.

"That's strange. I got a call from a man who wanted info on that little cape on the south end and I gave him your number. You turned your cell phone off again, didn't you." Alan ruffled Meg's hair as if she were a child, a gesture that made Will slightly ill.

"I wanted to enjoy my night off."

"No such thing in real estate, baby. I keep telling you that." Alan turned to Will. "She does stuff like this then complains when she doesn't get sales."

"There's more to life than work," Will said, feeling he had to come to Meg's defense, since clearly she was just going to stand there and take it.

"You ought to know, Will," Meg said, and Will felt blindsided. Heck, he'd just been feeling sorry for her and here she was ganging up on him.

"I'll admit it," he said. "I'm a happy guy."

"It's true, money doesn't buy happiness," Alan said generously. *Prick.*

"It just buys you the stuff that makes you happy," Meg said, and Alan and she shared a little moment. Will wanted to puke.

Will hated that he felt like the third wheel, even though that was exactly what he was. Even though Meg and he had been apart for two years, a part of him had continued to think of her as his. As if holding onto that pathetic scrap of magazine somehow meant he was holding onto her.

"Oh, don't get all pouty, Will. You know you'd love to buy your own boat if you had that kind of cash."

"How do you know I don't?" He could. If he took out a loan. A big one.

Meg raised an eyebrow, making Will laugh. The

three of them stood awkwardly in her living room for a few minutes before Will announced it was time for him to leave. "Don't forget to let me know," he said. He walked out the door and down the steps and looked back to see Meg standing in the doorway smiling at him, and Alan standing behind her with an even bigger smile on his face. Somehow that seemed so wrong, insanely out of kilter. What the hell was she doing standing at the door with some other guy smiling over her shoulder?

Will waved and turned away, forcing that image out of his head. He'd had his chance with Meg and he'd blown it. The best—no, the only—thing he could hope for was to get her back on *Water Baby* so they could win that trophy.

Meghan stared at the phone, her stomach feeling the way it did when she was a kid and it was time for her to read out loud. She'd had a terrible lisp until a speech therapist had gotten hold of her in the fourth grade. What had been cute in kindergarten was fodder for cruelty once she reached the first grade.

"Haven't you called yet?" Alan asked, once again perching himself on the corner of her desk. She looked at him, amazed as always that he could read her with a single look.

"How do you do that?"

He flashed her his smile, recently professionally whitened teeth dazzling, and asked, "Do what?"

"How do you know exactly what I'm thinking about? I'm starting to think you're psychic."

Alan laughed. "You are the easiest person on earth to read. I do try to tell what other people are thinking. Helps out a lot in this business. But you are an open book. You want to sail, but you don't want to sail with your ex. You're a little bit worried that I'm worried, which I'm not."

Meghan shook her head in disbelief. "Amazing. Still, I'd be crazy to do this. Will and I are like oil and water. I really don't know if I want to be on a boat with him again."

"Then call and say no," Alan said reasonably. Alan, in addition to being psychically gifted, was always reasonable.

"But part of me wants to race. Badly. One last time."

Alan smiled and Meghan wished she didn't interpret it as a condescending smile. "Then call and say you will. But make a decision, because I've got to make some quick arrangements if you are going to be gone for two weeks."

Meghan gave Alan a sharp look, wondering if she'd just imagined some testiness in his tone. "Are you angry with me?" she asked out of simple curiosity.

"Actually, yes. It's the one thing about you, baby, that drives me a little crazy. Make a decision. For God's sake, just say yes or say no but say something."

Meghan slumped onto her desk, her head resting on her forearms, knowing he was right. "It's a big decision," she said, her words coming out muffled.

"No, baby, it's not. You either race or you don't. I'll be here to cover for you if you're gone. If you stay, then you can take care of your clients yourself."

Meghan kept her head on her desk. He didn't understand. He didn't know her history with Will, he couldn't know how being on a boat with him might, just might, be a dangerous thing for her. Will had this thing, a magnetism, that completely controlled her. Meghan knew she loved Alan, she knew she was over Will. But seeing him again, seeing the passion he had for sailing, seeing how vibrant and healthy and alive he was . . . well, it was just a tiny bit disturbing. No, not disturbing. Something else, something more toxic.

"You're afraid," Alan said, with deadly accuracy.

Meghan instantly lifted her head. "No. What would I have to be afraid of?"

"I don't know, Meghan," he said, as if he really did know. "You tell me."

Meghan rolled her eyes. "If you're hinting that I still have feelings for Will, you're crazy. And you just told me three seconds ago that you were not bothered by my going on the boat with him."

"You certainly didn't seem to dislike the guy."

Meghan threw up her hands. "That's it. I'm not going. If it's going to cause a problem between us, I won't do it. Honestly, Alan, I thought you had more faith in me than that. You don't trust me."

Alan sat on the chair in front of her desk reserved for clients. "I trust you; it's him I don't trust."

Meghan laughed. "I can handle Will, believe me. Anyway, I know him. He's scared to death of me because I want to get married. The last thing he'll do is make a move on me. And besides, Will might be a lot of things, but he's basically a good guy. He knows I'm engaged."

Alan leaned back, propping an ankle casually across one knee. "He did go right to me," he said, clearly mulling over the evidence. He sat upright abruptly. "You do it. Go sailing. I'll meet you in

Bermuda and we'll make a little pre-honeymoon of it. You don't have to sail back with him, do you?"

"No. He just needs a skeleton crew for that." Meghan knew she sounded less than enthusiastic, but for some reason she felt hesitant combining her two worlds. Sailing Meghan was a completely different person than the one Alan knew and she wasn't certain how Alan would react to seeing her so out of her element—or at least the element he knew.

"Then it's settled."

"Great," Meghan said, forcing a smile. She didn't know why she was so lukewarm about spending some time in Bermuda with Alan, but she was. It was *her* thing, *her* memories, and she didn't know that she wanted Alan part of it. If *Water Baby* actually won the race, there would be parties and dinners with the crew and Meghan didn't want Alan there. Sailors knew how to party and she'd certainly held her own over the years. After one particular party and one too many glasses of rum punch, Meghan had joined the rest of the crew skinny-dipping in Hamilton Harbor. She and Will had made love that night within shouting distance of the raucous and quite oblivious crewmembers. In a million years she couldn't picture Alan part of that scene of wild abandon. It would be like inviting a stuffy banker to a surfer's convention.

Then again, maybe she should invite him—and just for that reason.

"Despite your lack of enthusiasm, I am planning to join you," he said dryly.

"I'm sorry, Alan, I just can't picture you hanging out with a bunch of sailors. They're a pretty rowdy bunch."

Alan laughed and shook his head. "If you can handle it, I'm certain I can," he said, full of good-natured oblivion. Alan would not handle it. He'd find them obnoxious and childish, which they were, but Meghan loved them all just the same. Heck, she'd done her share of childish, obnoxious things when she was with them.

"I'll start making plans now," Alan said, with an enthusiasm Meghan couldn't mirror even as she told herself having Alan there would be a good thing.

"Getting a hotel in Hamilton is going to be impossible with the race. Those rooms are booked months ahead," she warned, feeling the tiniest bit shrewish.

"Don't worry. I've got some connections."

Alan always had connections—people he'd sold houses to and for. Chances are he'd either get a fantastic hotel room, or an actual house for them to use while they were there. Meghan couldn't think of another thing to discourage Alan from coming, so she settled on staring at the phone again.

Letting out a huge sigh, she took out Will's cell number and dialed it and tried to pretend the sound of his voice did nothing to her already raw emotions.

"I'm on board," she said. "When do we start?"

Will closed his cell phone and squeezed his eyes shut before looking up to the sky. "Thank you, God." It was almost scary how happy he was at that moment. Ever since Thad walked down into the cabin with that cast, Will had felt this strange pressing sensation, as if his entire world was going to implode. He didn't know why, but he knew in his gut that he needed Meg on board—and he also knew he'd have to keep his distance. He knew with one look that he wasn't over her, even though he'd tried like hell to be. It didn't help that she was getting married to a complete loser. Meg was the coolest woman he'd ever known and he just couldn't picture her settling down with a guy who wore Italian suits and slicked his hair back. And Will could have sworn the guy's eyebrows had been tweezed. That just wasn't right.

But Meg had seemed happy, hadn't seemed to mind his creepy smiles and hand-holding. Maybe Alan was Meg's type, after all. As difficult as it was to wrap his mind around that, Will knew he had to. He had to stop thinking about her, at least when he was conscious. He couldn't stop the dreams of the two of them making love, he couldn't stop the smile on his face when he first woke up before he realized he was in bed alone. She was engaged to another man and Will was smart enough to know that the burning in his gut was only one thing—jealousy. He'd ruined her life once already and he'd be damned if he did it again.

Chapter Four

Rachel Jenks pulled on a baggy T-shirt and oversized cargo pants, pulled back her hair into a ponytail and walked out the door without looking into her hotel's full-length mirror. She knew what people thought, that she was a bull dyke. She let them think that, because for some reason it was safer than them knowing the truth—that she was a pathologically shy twenty-six-year-old virgin who was in love with a man who probably thought she was a dyke. She lost sight years ago why she'd ever decided that letting people think she was a lesbian was safer than being who she was—an overweight, unattractive woman who never in a million years would lure a man like Thad Westwood.

Like she was going to be able to seduce a man who dated supermodel-type women and who thought *she* wanted to too.

Besides, no one had ever come out and asked her about her lifestyle and she certainly hadn't suggested that she was anything other than a frumpy straight woman. If it hadn't been for a conversation she'd had with some of the crewmembers two races ago, it never would have struck her that people thought she preferred women. If anything, she'd thought she'd been embarrassingly obvious about her crush on Thad. Guess getting Thad a cup of coffee might have been obvious to her, but had escaped everyone else's radar.

"You know, you can invite a *friend* to Bermuda. We're cool with that."

She hadn't immediately understood what the guy had been implying by using the word "friend." By the time she figured it out, the conversation had gone in another direction and she just couldn't bring herself to tell the small group that she was straight. What if she was wrong about what they were saying? Maybe they weren't implying that she was gay, just too ugly to have a boyfriend and didn't want to hurt her feelings. Maybe.

But it became more clear as time went on that everyone on the boat assumed she was a dyke. She didn't set the record straight, could barely utter more than a sentence or two without her throat bottling up in the best of circumstances. They couldn't know the amount of courage it took to leave her wonderfully isolating job as a computer programmer to crew on a sailboat of near strangers. Rachel loved sailing, and so every two years she suffered through a half-dozen panic attacks while she packed for the trip, and drove to Newport for the Newport-Bermuda race. The thought of announcing to the crew that she was straight was simply not an option. She could hardly bring herself to say hello to most people.

And yet, she forced herself to do it, tangling with the butterflies in her stomach, looking forward to seeing Thad so much the butterflies ultimately turned into nausea at the Rhode Island border. Despair couldn't adequately describe the way Rachel had felt after leaving Bermuda two years before having realized, much to her horror, that she was in love with Thad. After that paralyzing revelation, she'd said exactly three words to Thad and they weren't the three that had been tumbling around her heart. "Want some coffee?" He'd said sure and actually smiled at her. That had been it. *Want some coffee? Sure.* Way to go, girl.

When she got home, Rachel called in sick for two weeks from her job. She ate, she slept. She cried. It was on the twelfth day that she stood naked in front of her mirror sobbing that she knew she needed help. She dug out the directory from beneath a stack of pizza boxes and called a first therapist she saw: Abbington, Claire, therapist.

Two years and more than a hundred sessions later, Rachel was fifty pounds lighter and much happier. But as she walked out of that Newport hotel room toward *Water Baby*, she was scared shitless and she resisted the urge to call her therapist. Instead, she took a deep breath, told herself over and over that she was a beautiful confident woman, all the while the butterflies threatened to make her sick.

This year she was going to finally get what she wanted—or at least get the courage to let Thad know she wasn't gay. Big leap forward. So she worked out, lost weight, got a haircut, even painted her toenails pink. Put her in a nice dress and she almost looked like a girly-girl. But Rachel wasn't a girly-girl; she was still herself, still a tomboy, still clueless about what to wear and how to act. Underneath her baggy T-shirts and baggier shorts, she had a nice body. Slightly lumpy, not model-perfect, but not bad. She just didn't know what to do with it.

So Rachel, who'd changed her life and her dress size by four sizes, wasn't quite the same insecure woman who'd been on *Water Baby* two years ago. But she still couldn't stop her palms from getting sweaty or her heart from nearly pounding out of her chest when she saw him for the first time. He was sitting near the helm talking with one of the crewmembers, his bald head tanned and shining in the sunlight. He did the slightest double-take when he saw her, and then didn't really look at her at all. He still saw Rachel the bull dyke and she still loved him so much it hurt.

Meg took a deep breath of the salt air and smiled. God, it was good to be back by the water. Her self-imposed banishment seemed silly now that she was back in Newport Harbor. She walked along the slip toward *Water Baby*'s berth and spotted a few crewmembers already hanging around on the deck. When she reached the boat she felt like she was coming home. She knew nearly everyone, faces she'd seen over the years, looking windblown and ruddy and wonderfully familiar.

"Hey, guys," she said, and was happy with the enthusiastic response. She'd felt a bit strange coming back to the boat until she realized most of the crewmembers on board were unaware that she hadn't been sailing for two years. Though they greeted each other like old friends, most hadn't kept in touch over the past twenty-four months. They were spread about, mostly from the East Coast,

Delaware, New Jersey, Maine, but when they got together, it was as if they'd never been apart.

"Hey, Rachel, glad you're back. Looks like we're the only women this year," Meg said. Rachel was so quiet, Meg hadn't really gotten to know her that well, even though they'd sailed together for two other Newport-Bermuda races.

"I wouldn't miss it," she said, smiling.

Something struck Meghan about Rachel when she smiled—she almost seemed pretty. And no one would have ever used the word pretty and Rachel in the same sentence. "Have you lost weight?"

Rachel's smile broadened. "A little," she said.

Meghan looked at the legs poking out from her baggy shorts. "More than a little," she guessed.

"About fifty pounds, give or take."

"No kidding! You look fantastic."

"Thanks."

"Here comes Captain Ahab," someone joked, and Meghan looked up to see Will heading down the docks.

"Sorry I'm late," he said, sounding annoyed.

"Will's been a bear," Rachel whispered, and Meghan raised her brows with surprise. Will had always been one of the better captains to sail with; easy-going, level-headed, and fair. Even when things got sticky going across the Gulf Stream, which they did every race, Will always kept his cool. One year they'd lost a rudder and had to turn back to Newport. Though everyone was bitterly disappointed, Will never lost it.

"Jeff, get the lines and let's get underway. This wind's supposed to die down and I'd really like to test the new jib in heavy air," Will said, his voice brooking no argument.

Half of the ten-member crew headed into the cabin and out of the way. The crew was divided into two. During the race they'd take three-hour shifts and even when they were "on," most would simply act as ballast to keep the boat sailing as fast as possible.

They practiced tacking and jibing, even though the Newport-Bermuda rarely required a great deal of maneuvering. When the wind and seas were right, it was a straight line to Bermuda, and it fell largely on the navigator, sail trimmer, and helmsman to win a race.

Meghan had never seen Will so intense, had never heard him raise his voice, for that matter. "What the heck is up Will's ass?" Meghan said close to Thad's ear while they were both sitting on the rail. She still had to shout above the sound of the wind and waves crashing into the hull.

"He wants to win," Thad said.

"He always wants to win."

Thad just shrugged and Meghan looked back at Will. She'd seen Will sail a hundred different times but she'd never seen him look so serious as he did at that moment. His eyes scanned the sails with an intensity that was almost mesmerizing, as if he were looking for the smallest flaw in the boat's performance.

"Put up the number two jib," he shouted, and then to Meghan's disbelief, he took out a stopwatch.

"What's with the stopwatch," Meghan shouted as the crew went into action, but Thad was moving so quickly, he didn't answer.

"Move," Will shouted, and Meghan realized he was yelling at her. She scuttled to the other side to release the jib sheet from the cleat as the sail dropped, then winced as the sheet from the new sail was thrown at her and struck her cheek. With amazing speed, the first sail was shoved into the hatch and the second sail hauled up. Meghan scrambled to adjust the jib until the cloth was smooth and filled with the wind, making the boat heel over before the crewmembers had a chance to get to the rail and stop the boat from tipping too far over.

"That sucked, people," Will shouted. "And you were the weak link." That was directed to her. Meghan couldn't have been more shocked if Will had stripped off his clothes and dove into the ocean.

She could only mutter an apology because her throat was closing up and her eyes were starting to sting. What a royal *jerk*, she thought, and wished she was back in her real estate office where the only people who yelled at her were her clients, not people she actually cared about. If Meghan had any doubts about Will's motives for getting her aboard, they were quickly disabused.

For four hours, the crew changed sails, practiced reefing sails, even practiced putting on a second rudder in the event the first broke. Everything was done while Will held that ridiculous stopwatch and wrote down the times in a small notebook he kept at the helm. By the time they were tied up to *Water Baby*'s berth, the crew was exhausted but strangely happy, given the fact they'd just been with a madman for the past few hours.

"Two more days like that and we'll be like a finely tuned machine," Will said, sounding much more like the man she knew. As the crewmembers left, most headed toward the Black Pearl, including Rachel, who quietly followed behind. Meghan had to get back to her office, and watched the others go with growing envy. Alan had said she could take the entire two weeks off, but Meghan insisted that she put some time in at the office, so she definitely didn't have time to tip back a couple of beers before heading back to work.

"What did you think of the practice?" Will asked, and Meghan suspected he knew what she thought. He straightened out one of the boat's bumpers before giving the boat one final look and headed down the dock toward solid land. She tried not to notice how sexy he looked, all bronzed and wind-blown. Hell, how could she not notice? Will was a woman's fantasy and she'd just have to forget that for a while, he'd been more than a fantasy. He'd been a hot-blooded, hard-muscled, free-lovin' man and he'd been hers. She couldn't beat herself up for being attracted to him. He was universally attractive. And he'd done this thing with his tongue that . . . "Meg? The practice?"

"It was different," Meghan said, walking beside him along the wide dock, willing her attraction to disappear. *I'm engaged. I'm engaged. I'm engaged.* "Loved the stopwatch."

"You may laugh if you like, but when you can show people real improvement, they strive to get better."

"I don't know what you did with your easy-going twin, but you can bring him back any time," Meghan said, and was happy to hear Will chuckle.

"We've been practicing for a week now, though this is the first day we've had the whole crew on board. Sail changes have improved by twenty percent and I know that because of that stopwatch. Did you see how well everyone moved? I just wish we could practice in rough seas and a storm. We're supposed to get a thunderstorm tomorrow. I hope it hits while we're out."

"You are insane," Meg said levelly.

"You heading to the Black Pearl?" Will asked, nodding in the general direction of the restaurant where it seemed dozens of sailor were headed.

"No," Meghan said with real regret. "I have to put in a few hours of real work. I'm showing a house tonight."

Will looked at her until she wanted to squirm. "You like that job?" he asked finally.

"It's okay. The money's good. I like finding the perfect house for people. But it's a lot more stressful than I thought it would be. People take it out on me when a deal goes south. I don't like being yelled at."

Will grinned, knowing that Meg was referring to earlier that day. Her heart did *not* speed up. *You're engaged, dammit.* "Get used to it if you're going into snail mode in the middle of a tack," he said.

"Screw you," Meghan said good-naturedly. "Are you going to the Pearl?"

"Nope. Got to head to the school."

"How's that going?" Meghan asked, just being polite. Will's sailing school had never been a serious business venture, but more of a way to make a little money between ocean races. The last she knew, Will was still on the race circuit, more as a crewmember than as a skipper. He was a sought-after helmsman for those boats who weren't captained by the owner. The sailing school helped buy food and pay rent for the apartment they used to share.

"The sailing school's pretty good," he said, then waved to a suntanned goddess he spotted standing at the end of the dock.

"Who's that?" Meghan asked, even though she didn't care. Not really. It was only idle curiosity, a brief wondering about the kind of woman Will was now dating.

"One of my instructors. She's on the Princeton sailing team."

"*One* of your instructors?" Meghan asked as they walked toward the woman, trying not to be relieved the goddess was an employee—because that would make no sense at all since she didn't care if Will was dating her or sleeping with her or anything else with her.

"I've expanded the school a little," he said as they reached the woman, who was even more beautiful close up.

"A little? He's got a fleet of twenty boats now with ten instructors." The girl looked up at Will as if he were a god and Meghan did a mental eye roll. She felt sorry for her because six years ago that was her—minus the goddess looks, of course—gazing up at Will as if he were the one who made the winds blow. Meghan guessed she wasn't even twenty yet. Meghan tried to remember if Will had acted as indifferent to her as he seemed to be acting toward this young woman. Maybe that was his charm.

"It's a small fleet and most of them are Optis for my youth sailing program," Will corrected.

"Still, twenty boats," Meghan said, impressed. "That's so adult of you, Will."

"The Newport Sailing School went out of business,"

he said a little sheepishly. "I just took advantage of their misfortune. By the way, Anne, this is Meghan Rose."

The younger girl's eyes widened. "Wow," she breathed. "You're a legend around here. She's racing the Newport-Bermuda?"

Meghan was a little embarrassed by the girl's reaction, especially given that she'd stopped racing entirely two years before. "I haven't raced at all in two years. Decided to get my feet wet again."

"You sure you don't have room on the boat?" Anne asked, and Meghan had a feeling it wasn't the first time she'd asked.

"Sorry, kiddo."

"Maybe you could stop by the school after the race," Anne said to Meghan. "It would be great, especially for the younger girls, to see someone who's got so many years of experience. I mean, you were around before all-women crews were so prevalent."

"A real old-timer," Will said with way too much enthusiasm.

"She's not *that* old," Anne said, unknowingly making Meghan feel even more ancient.

To the nineteen-year-old girl, Meghan probably looked ancient. "I just turned thirty," Meghan said before realizing just how old thirty would seem to Anne.

Will leaned over to Anne and not-too-quietly said, "She actually looks pretty good for someone who's middle-aged."

"Ha ha," Meghan said dryly.

"Well, I've got to go. Stop by," Anne said, all perky and fresh and too much of a reminder of how Meghan had been when she first started sailing the racing circuit.

When the other woman had gone, Meghan gave Will a none-too-gentle playful punch on the arm and was satisfied to see him wince.

"Hey. It was a compliment. I said you looked good."

"Since when is thirty middle-aged? And please tell me you aren't dating that girl," Meghan said lightly.

Will looked honestly shocked by the suggestion. "She's thirteen years younger than me. Ten years younger is my limit."

"Are you dating anyone?" Meghan asked, being careful to sound as neutral as possible—but she wasn't certain the effort was for her or for him.

"No one serious. Just having fun."

"Sounds great, and as long as the other person knows you just want to have fun, you won't break too many hearts," she said, proud she was maintaining her neutral tone. See? She was over him. He could date as many nineteen-year-olds as he wanted.

"I'm not the one who goes around breaking hearts," Will said, just as lightly.

"For the record, you broke my heart." Meghan was striving to keep her voice even, full of friendly banter, but just saying the words "broke my heart" made her remember what it had felt like to have him reject her so completely.

Will stopped walking and actually seemed shocked by her words. "You left me," he pointed out.

"Only after you refused to talk about the future. See? You've got me so I can't even say the word in front of you. Marriage. Marriage. Marriage."

Will pressed his mouth shut.

"Aha! Got you there." Meghan forced a laugh, forced a smile she really didn't feel.

"Yup. You won, Meghan. You got to dump me and then blame me. Neat plan."

Meghan studied him to see if there was a smidgeon of sincerity in his statement, but he walked away before she could figure it out.

"You dumped me," she shouted after him. Will kept walking, his only response a look to the sky as if he were dealing with a crazy woman.

"You dumped me," she said quietly, but for the first time she wondered if that was how he'd seen it.

Chapter Five

Meghan raced home, thankful for her radar detector, jumped in the shower and found herself surprised when she tasted salt on her skin. Sea salt. She smiled, feeling alive and happy and ready to take on the world. It was remarkable what one day on the water had done for her.

As she dried her hair, she was amazed at how much sun she'd gotten in one afternoon, how much brighter and healthier she looked. She hardly needed makeup. Humming, Meghan threw on a suit and rushed to her car, arriving to the house just in time to meet her clients.

The house was listed as a "starter" home and a "handyman's special," which meant it was a dump. She was showing the small ranch to a young couple who had dreams of owning a house but not enough money to buy anything they really pictured themselves living in. Meghan knew it was going to be a painful process for this couple, who would probably end up renting and saving for a few more years or buying a condo or townhouse.

"It's kind of small," the young woman said, looking

at the house with about as much enthusiasm as a vegetarian looks at a rare steak.

Meghan smiled. "But it's got a big lot, which means you can always expand." That was the line she was programmed to say and she said it even though she agreed with the woman. Small. Ugly. Run-down.

She started pointing out the positives. "You've got a fenced-in yard back there and nice mature plantings. Look at that oak tree. You could put a swing on it." And Meghan watched as the couple looked doubtfully at the tree.

"A lot of raking," the man said.

"I love to rake," the woman said, and Meghan suspected that she was the romantic one in the couple.

The house was livable, but needed a new kitchen, new bathroom, new carpet, new paint. It needed, she knew, someone with imagination and money. Nearly every room was either paneled or covered in the ugliest wallpaper she'd laid eyes on.

The woman hugged herself after the tour, looking defeated and sad. "It just needs so much work," she said. That translated to money. They were at the edge of what they could spend on a house, which meant they'd have to live in the house as is until they could scrape up enough money to fix it.

"Is there anything else in our price range?" the man asked hopefully.

"Not in the areas of Cumberland that you're looking at. I've got a couple of two-families . . ."

The couple shook their heads.

"You could consider a condo. Some of the complexes have amazing amenities. Pools, tennis courts. And then when you want to start family, you'll have a little equity and can buy a single family."

The woman bit her knuckle. "But that's just like living in an apartment."

"But we'd own it," her husband pointed out. "If this is the best we can do, maybe we should just look at a condo."

Meghan felt awful, not only for herself, but for the elderly couple who owned the house who were probably in a more desperate financial situation than the pair in front of her. Not to mention, her own savings were getting a little low. As small as it was, she could really use the commission on this house.

"Think about it. Most of this stuff is cosmetics. New paint goes a long way. There's hardwood beneath the carpeting and even bad hardwood is almost always better than worn, stained carpeting. Try to see past what's here." Meghan laughed at their expression. "I know there's a lot to look past, but truly, this house has good bones."

The man sighed. "We'll think about it."

As Meghan watched them drive away, she felt depression slowly descend on her. That sucked. She waited for her clients to return to their house and told them she'd gotten mixed reviews on the house, that they were a bit worried about all the renovations required. The older couple nodded; they'd heard it a dozen times before and were losing hope that they'd ever sell the place.

"We'll find a buyer," Meghan said, a black cloud hovering over her head.

"I know, dear, don't you worry."

Meghan gave them a weak smile and promised to call if she heard anything.

Meghan drove to her office just to show her face more than anything else. All her enthusiasm for the day had been sucked out of her. The only thing she had left of that glorious feeling she'd had just a few hours ago was her rosy cheeks. She went through her messages, returned a couple of phone calls before Alan came into her cubicle, all smiles.

"Sold that house on Nate Whipple Drive. Six hundred big ones. Let's celebrate."

"Wow, that's great," Meghan said, hating the tingle of resentment she felt. She didn't know if Alan was lucky or just a better Realtor than she was, but he was constantly closing deals.

"I guess your showing didn't go so well," he said, reading her perfectly.

"No. It didn't. Why do I seem to attract the people with the ugliest, rundown houses in town as sellers and the poorest schleps in town for buyers?" It was a rhetorical question, but Alan started to answer it anyway.

"Alan, I didn't really want an answer," she said.

He shrugged good-naturedly, not letting her foul mood ruin his cheerful one. "So, let's go out and celebrate, baby."

Meghan closed her eyes. "Could you please not call me that," she said, knowing she sounded bitchy but not caring because she felt bitchy.

"Baby? You don't want me calling you baby? Okay," he said, bending down to kiss her lightly. "I'll try not to."

Meghan looked at Alan, who despite her meanness was still looking at her as if she could make the stars shine brighter, and let out a sigh. "I'm sorry. I was in a fantastic mood after our practice, but then I showed the Phillips house and that really brought me down."

"This is a business of highs and lows."

"Some of us have more highs than lows," she grumbled.

"Come on, let's go to Stan's for dinner."

Meghan really didn't want to. Being out on the water was tiring, especially with the grueling practice, and she wasn't in the same shape she'd been in the last time she'd been on a boat. Her arm muscles were sore from working the winches and her back ached.

Meghan stretched and watched as Alan's eyes dipped to her breasts. For the first time in a long time she wasn't in the mood. And from experience, she knew Alan was always ready for sex after closing a deal. So, she ignored the look.

"I'm in a real funk tonight. I think I'm tired from today. I really just want to go home and relax." Alone, she thought.

He seemed to mentally back off and grabbed up the latest listings, fingering through them as if he didn't already know every square inch of every house they offered. "How was today?"

"Your enthusiasm is overwhelming," Meghan said dryly. "Actually, it was a lot of fun. Even being yelled at was fun. I didn't know how much I missed it." She watched Alan carefully because she didn't want to upset him, but she'd have to be an idiot not to realize her funk was caused by her job. "It's a different world." An exciting, fun, carefree world that she thought she was completely over. Apparently not.

"It's a fantasy life. Most people have to work for a living," Alan said, and even though she agreed, she didn't like him pointing it out to her.

"It's only for another two weeks. Then I'll be back

here selling houses full time." Depression dropped on her like a ton of bricks.

"Are you sure that it's the racing you miss?"

She acted like she didn't know what he was talking about, made him say it out loud even though that was a little mean.

"Your ex-boyfriend. Bill."

"Will. And don't be an idiot. If you're going to act like this, I'll drop out. Really, Alan, it's not worth so much to me." She smiled. "Though it is nice to know it bugs you, even if your jealousy means you don't trust me."

"Oh, I trust you; it's him I don't trust."

Meghan almost corrected him, almost told him that he was way off base, that he should worry about her. Because Will's indifference toward her, his complete lack of interest had bothered her more than she wanted to admit, which meant she was in danger of falling into her old habit of trying to get him to fall for her. She'd spent four years trying to make him love her, fueled by his indifference. She told herself she was relieved he'd treated her like one of the guys, but part of her was a little hurt that he could be so businesslike with her. Maybe she should quit. Or maybe this is just what she needed to be certain about spending her life with Alan.

But hadn't she been certain not two days ago? *Crapola.*

"Alan, I want complete honesty here. Does this bother you?"

"No," he said after a long pause, coming to her side of the desk and drawing her into his arms. "I just want you to be happy."

"I am," she said, realizing with a small amount of

horror that she didn't know whether that was true or not.

Rachel was not a courageous person. She never considered being on a sailboat in the middle of the ocean during a storm courageous. Walking up to a man you didn't know, or worse yet a man you knew and secretly loved, now *that* was courage. So instead of going directly to the bar, Rachel headed to her hotel room and changed into something a friend had told her made her look like a girl. Rachel wasn't used to wearing clothes that fit her. She'd spent most of her life wearing oversized T's and sweatshirts trying to hide bulges. She pulled on a pair of capris and a light sweater that dipped low enough to show a hint of cleavage, looked in the mirror and grimaced.

Her breasts looked huge. Rachel tugged at the sweater, hoping to loosen it up, but nothing she did could hide what she'd always been so successful at hiding before. "I'd kill for a body like that," her friend had told her with real envy. Rachel gave her reflection a doubtful look. Maybe she didn't look completely ridiculous. For a moment she almost flung off the sweater and put on one of her over-sized T-shirts, then took a deep breath, closed her eyes to her reflection, and marched out the hotel room door. She wore her hair down, which, despite her new style, she rarely did. And she had on lip-stick and mascara, something she'd learned how to apply a month ago at one of those fancy department stores. Rachel's mother died when she was ten and she didn't have an older sister, so she never learned how to be a girl. Her fisherman father was completely overwhelmed with raising two boys and a girl by himself, and Rachel was sure he was grateful she'd never asked him girly questions, even though they burned unanswered inside her.

She was shaking by the time she reached the Black Pearl. It was a warm night, so most of the customers were outside sitting beneath market umbrellas or leaning against the bar the Pearl set up only during the summer months. A quick scan told her that no one outside was part of the *Water Baby* crew. She walked inside, into the tiny, dark bar crowded with people. All around her were men and women laughing, talking, as if it were the easiest thing in the world to do. *You are a confident woman. You are beautiful.* She tried to drown out the other voices that sought to remind her that she was Rachel Jenks, the woman most people thought was a dyke.

Rachel saw Thad almost immediately. He was easy to spot because he was such a big guy, all beef and brawn and about a head taller than most men. Plus the shaven head and white cast didn't do much to camouflage him either, especially not in such a small space. Rachel centered her focus on the cast. It was the perfect prop for someone whose words tended to stick in her throat while her mind worked a mile a minute telling herself what an idiot she was.

"Hey, guys," she said softly, too softly. No one heard her, which gave her the perfect excuse to walk away, face burning red. Rachel almost gave up then and there, but her therapist's voice kept sounding in her head. *You're a beautiful woman who any man would be lucky to find. You've worked hard to get your outside the way you want it, keep working on the inside. Blah blah blah.* It all was such crap when she was confronted with real life. All the words in the world weren't going to change who she was.

Still, she found the courage to stay in the bar and order a drink. Normally she would have gotten a beer without a glass, but she was trying to fem it up a little, so she ordered a white wine, then felt stupid holding that delicate little glass. She took a sip, resisting the urge to tank it down, and pretended to find the dark, black-painted interior of the Pearl interesting. Five minutes. She'd give herself five minutes to gather up the courage to approach him again.

Thad let out a booming laugh at a jab one of the guys made about his arm and the way it had been injured.

"If I was Will I would have broken your other arm," said Tony Robak. Tony was one of the core members of the crew and hadn't missed a Newport-Bermuda in years. "Now we got to deal with Will and Meg pissin' all over each other and bringing us down."

Thad shook his head. "No way, man. That ship has sailed. Meg's engaged to marry some guy in real estate. House and kids for her. She's just helping out Frank. They'll be fine." Thad didn't normally lie through his teeth, but he figured he should at least try to keep the crew's morale up. He shook his empty bottle. "Anyone else need a refill?"

Tony took a deep swig. "I'm empty, too," he said with a grin. "I'll get the next round . . . whoa."

Thad turned instantly to the bar because he

knew what that "whoa" meant—a hot little number was within radar range. "Where?"

"The brunette. Look at those ta-tas," Tony said, and he took a step forward, only to be stopped by a large, hard, white cast.

"Man, what are you, crazy? That's Rachel."

Finally Tony slid his eyes up to the woman's face. "Shit. Think she swings both ways?" he asked hopefully.

Thad gave him a disgusted look. "I'll get you a beer."

"That'll only make her look hotter," Tony said, laughing, and Thad couldn't help but join in.

He was still smiling when he reached Rachel, and she turned at that moment and smiled back. It was the weirdest thing he'd ever experienced with the opposite sex—and scariest. Because his knees went weak, his heart felt like it swelled up in his chest, and his dick actually made a move he was completely not expecting.

"Hey, Rach." Thad told himself it was just Rachel standing there in front of him, but damn if his body didn't see Kirsten Dunst in a wet T-shirt.

"Hey." She stared into her half-full wine glass and she said something else he couldn't quite make out because of the noise in the bar.

"Say what?"

She leaned into him, her soft and absolutely luscious breasts pushing against his good arm, and repeated her question. "Does your arm still hurt?"

Her breath hit his cheek and with her chest still pressing against him, he almost lost his ability to speak. "No." *God, no.* It could have been broken off in that instant and he doubted he would have felt it.

He tried to tell himself he was standing next to Rachel, big, truck-driver-type, total dyke Rachel. Except it was obvious Rachel had gone through some major changes in the past two years. Tony was right—she was hot. She was sexy as hell, she smelled damn good, and she was wearing makeup and a sweater that showed off every delicious curve she had. It nearly broke his heart to think she was gay, though the image that came into his head at that instant was hardly the stuff that would break a man's heart.

"You're looking good, Rachel. Must be love," he said, just to let her know he was cool with the whole gay thing.

Rachel started, horrified that she'd somehow let him know how much she loved him. "Uh, no. No." *As eloquent as ever, Rach.*

He seemed uncomfortable with her, and Thad had never been uncomfortable with anyone as far as she knew. Before she'd gone and fallen in love with him, they'd talked with relative ease while sitting on the boat's rail during races or inside the cabin trying to get a rest while the other shift was sailing. Rachel had quietly hung out with the other crewmembers, never feeling self-conscious—she'd been one of the guys. Other than the last disaster of a race, she'd talked with Thad about sports and some politics, nothing to make a girl's heart race, but it had been enough to make Rachel fall in love. And now he was looking at her in the strangest way and she hated it.

"Well, you're sure to attract someone now, right?" He let out a short laugh, then flagged down the bartender and ordered two beers and a white wine.

It was the first time a man other than a relative had bought her a drink.

"I don't want to attract just anyone," she said, knowing it was a hopeless attempt at flirting. When Thad handed her the wine, she took a deep swallow. "I'm not into girls, you know." The minute she said it, she wished she could call it back, but it was out there, making its way to his ear, entering the canal, making those little bones shake . . .

"Say what?"

"Nothing," she shouted, then downed the rest of her wine. "See you tomorrow." She blindly put her glass on the bar behind her and headed to the door. Outside it was humid and foggy, softening the noises coming from the bar. *Why didn't you just come out and tell him you're into guys?* Because then he might guess she loved him and she wasn't ready for that yet.

She didn't know if she'd ever be ready.

Chapter Six

Newport's heyday as a summer retreat for the wealthy may have been long gone, but the wealthy still came and they owned big boats and bigger wallets. Newport was a unique place in the summer, especially along the waterfront with its incredible views, great bars, and mobs of people hoping to grasp a bit of the Newport mystique.

It was one of the few places that the guy who scraped barnacles off the bottom of boats could stand shoulder to shoulder with a millionaire at a bar, carry on a conversation, and neither would have a clue who was who. And neither would care. The uniform was simple: khakis, saltwater-faded polos, T-shirts, and boat shoes. It looked like a Land's End catalogue, the uniform of New England. Tourists were easy to spot because they were usually overdressed, while the locals and sailors, rich and poor, wore well-worn everything—especially their shoes.

At night, especially in July and August, Newport was transformed from a cold, foggy place that attracted only the hardiest visitors, to a large seaside party that attracted just about everyone. In June, Newport was usually still pretty quiet, but not when the sailors for the Newport-Bermuda were in town. They had money to spend, beer to drink, and seafood to eat. In between getting their boats ready, that's what they did. Most boats arrived with a skeleton crew while the meat of the crew showed up a day or two before the race.

The crew of *Water Baby* had arrived a bit earlier to practice. With Frank paying the tab for hotel rooms and meals, crewmembers didn't have to pay out of pocket for the early arrival. Meghan was amazed at how well-tuned the crew became in such a short time. Sails were hauled down with the precision of a machine with little shouting or argument. She'd sailed on *Water Baby* for years and never experienced the wonderful tension on board this year. When things clicked, it was like watching a ballet, and boy, were things clicking.

Will was a tyrant during practice, but no one seemed to mind because damn if it wasn't working. Meghan didn't know what got under his skin this year, but whatever it was translated into a boat and crew that were true contenders for the St. Davis Lighthouse Trophy. Meghan couldn't stop herself from being impressed by Will, though any other thoughts were stridently ignored. She might notice his biceps, his strong thighs, his flat stomach, his sun-drenched hair, but they were harmless, meaningless, wayward thoughts. She refused to think about the dream she'd had (actually it was more like a memory) of the two of them making love. They had been in a boat in the forward berth and they were slick with sweat and passion. If Meghan had been a boy, she might have had a wet dream because she woke up so aroused it was almost embarrassing and definitely horrifying. Thank God Alan hadn't stayed over that night, because she wasn't sure she could have lived with herself getting aroused by memories of Will then turning to Alan so he could finish what dream Will hadn't.

The dream had shaken Meghan a bit until she reminded herself that few things in dreams matched reality. Alan might not be as physically sexy as Will, but there was nothing sexier than a man who adored a woman like Alan adored her. Heck, Will could strip naked and climb the mast with every appendage he had bulging with masculinity and she wouldn't be fazed in the least. Nope.

"Hey, Meg, could you help me out here?" Will's deep voice penetrated her thoughts and her face heated, which made her embarrassed, then angry at herself, then angry at Will. There, she felt better now.

"Sure."

"I didn't ask you to scrape the bottom of the boat," Will said good-naturedly, picking up on her animosity.

"Sorry. I was thinking about something else."

Will tossed Meghan the new midnight blue race polos with *Water Baby* embroidered on the left side.

"Lacoste. Fancy," Meghan said, holding up the shirt that must have set Frank back more than a hundred dollars.

"I got a bunch more if anyone needs another size," Will said, pointing to an open box.

"I think I need a men's small," Rachel said, moving to the box and rummaging through it.

Meghan listened to the crew talking, the halyard banging against the mast, the little popping noise of the water gently moving against the boat, and didn't even try to stop the feeling of complete excitement that washed over her. Her stomach was filled with butterflies, giving her the same wonderful feeling she'd gotten every time right before a race, except this time it was different. This time she knew it would be her last race. Once she got married, she wanted to have kids right away. Kids didn't really fit into ocean racing, at least not until they were old enough to crew. She couldn't stop the broad smile.

"If I had known you were going to be that happy, I would have told Frank we needed matching shirts a long time ago," Will said.

Meghan tried to be annoyed with him, but she was just too damn happy and ended up grinning anyway. "It's just that it's my last race and we could actually win and . . ."

" . . . And you want to thank me for thinking of you when I needed a trimmer. This doesn't have to be your last race, Meg. You don't undergo a complete personality change when you get married, do you?"

Meghan looked away from his probing gaze. She didn't want to talk to him about her wanting a real life, about wanting a family that did normal things like go to the zoo and live in a house and spend vacations at Disneyland instead of battling the sea. Because not that long ago she'd wanted all that with Will. "I want something different," she said, and wished she'd felt more like she was telling the truth. Man, she'd missed being on a boat, tasting the salt spray, feeling the excitement of twenty boats vying to cross the start line first, the terror of coming within inches of slamming into another boat.

"I think I'd die a slow death if I couldn't get out on the water," he said. "I notice you're looking a little pale."

Meghan gave him a look. "We all have our priorities." She realized she wasn't talking about sailing anymore.

"Don't tell me you didn't miss it these past years because then I'd know you were lying."

"Fine. I missed it. I'm probably going to miss it after the race." Then an alarming thought sneaked into her head: I'm going to miss you, too. She'd spent the last two years telling herself what a rotten, immature, heartless man Will was, and now she had to begrudgingly admit the reality was far different. Will was the same gorgeous, funny, devil-may-care guy she'd fallen in love with. It hadn't been his fault he didn't love her the way she needed him to. And it hadn't been her fault either. It simply was.

Meghan looked around at the other boats, the other crews that were hanging around Bowen's Wharf. The excitement in the air was nearly palpable. In the *Newport Daily News* that morning, there had been an article about the race and the possible contenders. *Water Baby* had been mentioned because not only was it a local boat, but because it was a considered by experts as a long-shot winner. Before their practice that day, Will had pointed out the words "long shot" just to get the crew riled up, and Meghan sat back absorbing it all, wishing she could capture that moment for the rest of her life.

"Hey, Will, do you want us to wear these for tomorrow night?" one of the crewmembers asked, holding up the new shirt. Tomorrow night was the traditional Dark and Stormy Goslings Rum party, so named after the rum drink Bermudans made famous.

"Only if you want to," he said, then turned his gaze back to Meghan. "Are you coming?"

"Wouldn't miss my last Dark and Stormy."

The Dark and Stormy party, hosted by the Bermuda rum-maker Gosling, was held at the New York Yacht Club's Newport "clubhouse," Harbour Court. It was a formerly opulent mansion located on the bay with a lawn that swept down to the water and a marina. The lawn, where the bash was held, had a commanding view of the bay and the Newport Bridge that gracefully spanned the water. It was a spectacular night, unusually clear and warm for a New England June evening, and the yacht club's lawn was crowded with khaki and polo-shirt-wearing sailors.

Will searched the crowd gathered on the lawn and didn't even bother to try to kid himself—he knew he was looking for Meg.

He'd never admit it aloud, but Will knew he was in the midst of the biggest mistake of his life. He never should have let Meg back on *Water Baby*—never, ever to infinity. He was thankful that no one noticed how she distracted him when they were out on the boat, what an effort it was not to stare at her like some lovesick kid in the midst of a tragic unrequited love. How difficult it was to not let anyone know he loved her so damn much, he was dying inside.

He loved her; had, of course, never stopped loving her. All this time he'd tried to tell himself he was fine, he was over her, that his heart still beat whole in his chest. He told himself that if he could screw other women and enjoy it, he must be over her. But he'd been living a lie. He loved her. God-damn it. And seeing her in love with another man, damn, that hurt.

Finally, his eyes stopped their search and focused not on Meg, but on the man she was standing with. Alan. Tall, slim, and wearing the appropriate clothes: a pair of khakis and a blue blazer and boat shoes that looked like they'd never stepped aboard a boat. She was standing next to him, craning her head just a bit because he was so tall, her blonde hair curling and brushing her jawline. God, how he'd loved to kiss that jawline—and every other part of her. She wore a sundress that moved gently in the breeze of the bay. He was about to stroll casually down to them when Thad joined him.

"You seen Rachel?" he asked.

"I don't think so," Will said, stopping and tearing his eyes away from Meg. Rachel was a solid crewmember, but he was pretty certain that in the six years they'd been sailing together, the only words they'd exchanged were "Go get the number two jib" and "Go check on the forward hatch."

"You'd know if you did."

Will finally looked at Thad, who appeared to be pissed off about something. "Why are you mad at Rachel?"

"You see what she's wearing, dude?" Thad asked, jerking his head in the general direction of the Gosling tent. For a moment a woman was partially obscured by the smoke from the barbecue pit. And then he saw who he supposed was Rachel, or rather a pretty facsimile of the woman he'd known for six years. She was wearing one of those white doily-dresses that clung to her very nice curves. Rachel usually wore a baseball cap with her hair pulled through the back hole, but tonight her hair was down and looked all wispy and soft.

"Wow," Will said. "She cleans up pretty good. I never noticed that about her before."

"Me neither. She's friggin' hot now. Lost weight or something."

"Doesn't she prefer the company of women?" Will said, being overly tactful.

Thad scowled.

"You're attracted to a hot lesbian," Will stated slowly, then started to laugh.

"Who wouldn't be? Look at her. Look at her . . ." he sputtered, "dress."

"I think the word you're looking for is 'breasts,' not 'dress.' Rein it in, cowboy. You just have to accept you can't have every woman you want."

"Who the hell said I wanted her?"

Will laughed even louder. "Oh, God, I am going to enjoy this race more than I thought I was."

"Screw you. At least I'm not still in love with my old girlfriend." Thad jerked his head to where Meg still stood with the fiancé. Will pretended Thad had punched him in the gut, making the bigger man let out a sharp thunderous laugh. "Yeah, well, who's more pathetic?" Thad asked.

"I vote you," Will said. "I'm going to get me another drink, then do something stupid. Wanna join me?"

"Think I'll take a pass on that one. I feel dumb enough already."

Instead of heading to the rum tent, Will walked directly down the hill to the couple. They didn't match. He was too tall and too . . . Alan-ish. Any other year, Meg would have been yucking it up with the crew. This year she stood apart looking bored, probably wishing she had another drink and a big sloppy hamburger or spicy rack of ribs. Alan was probably a vegan.

When he reached them, Alan stuck out his hand, offering a handshake that was overly enthusiastic and painfully firm, as if he were overcompensating for something. Like a small dick. But hey, maybe I'm wrong, Will thought.

"You two enjoying yourselves down here?"

"It's a beautiful spot," Alan said. "I was thinking of buying a place on the water. Not this big, of course." He let out a laugh, looking back at the mansion behind them, and Will forced one out too. This guy should not be allowed to buy a house on the water. Hell, he probably didn't know the difference between a seagull and a swan.

"Maybe you could put in a dock so Meg could sail."

"I think I'd get a powerboat, though," Alan said, then seeing Will's expression, held up a hand and quickly added, "No offense."

Will looked to Meg, who had the strangest smile on her face, as if she'd eaten something really nasty and was trying not to let the beaming hostess know how awful it was. "You want a powerboat, Meg?" Will asked, making his voice purposefully pleasant.

"Sure. Get to places a lot faster."

He studied her expression, horrified, until he realized she was taunting him. "Plus that diesel smell is so romantic," he said, and felt his heart swell when she laughed.

"Sailors call powerboats stinkpots," Meghan explained to Alan, whose cheeks turned ruddy with what looked to Will like anger. A chink in the white knight's armor, he thought. "But they are more practical if all you want to do is go from point A to point B," Meg said in an obvious attempt to placate Alan.

"Like flying," Will said, trying not to smile. "Except a lot slower. And more expensive. And noisier."

"Will . . ." Meg said, laughing. "Don't tease."

In that moment, Will knew they were connecting, and Alan knew it, too, because he immediately changed to subject to the last topic Will wanted to discuss.

"Maybe after we're married you can teach me how to sail," Alan said, his eyes on Meg, completely excluding Will from the conversation.

"I'll tell you what," Will said, wishing he had drunk enough rum to push Alan into the bay. "I own a sailing school. I can give you sailing lessons as a wedding present." Will made a little checkmark on his side of the chalkboard, because it was clear Alan did not like that suggestion at all. Meg, on the other hand, apparently oblivious to male mating rituals, gave Will a brilliant smile.

"That's a terrific idea, isn't it, Alan?"

Will could tell Alan thought it was a terrible idea, and frankly, Will had to give the guy credit for keeping his cool. "Sure, baby. That will give us a way to get away from our job pressures. At least until we have a baby."

Will truly wasn't a violent man, but at that moment he had a clear image of himself balling up his fist and smashing it into Alan's face. Instead, he smiled and pretended he didn't care that Alan planned to fuck the woman he loved and impregnate her. "Planning to start a family right away?" he managed to grind out in a semi-pleasant voice.

"Not right away," Meg said.

"On the honeymoon," Alan said at the same time.

Will looked from one to the other, getting a bit of guilty pleasure from antagonizing Alan. And, honestly, he really didn't feel all that guilty. The look Alan gave Meghan was absolutely priceless. He wished he had a camera; he'd blow it up and put it in his office.

"You two should discuss that sort of thing, don't you think?" Will said, full of concern.

"Privately," Alan said.

"Hey, you brought it up," Will said, smiling. He glanced at Meg, who was looking daggers at him. Then he looked at her mouth and realized she was fighting a smile. Without thinking, he winked, and she pulled a frown.

"You do know that Meg's a Buddhist."

"Will, stop it," Meg said, looking as if she'd like to punch him. Will could tell by her expression that she'd had enough of his teasing. He was a smart guy; he knew when to retreat with dignity.

"Just came down to say hello. And, Alan, that offer for sailing lessons still stands. I swear if I'm out sailing the bay and I see Meg on a powerboat, I just don't know what I'll do."

Alan didn't even crack a smile, but Meg did, and that's all he cared about. What a stiff, Will thought. And what the hell is Meghan doing with him?

Meghan watched Will walk slowly back up the hill toward the Gosling Rum tent, a part of her wishing she were with him. He was going to have fun. She didn't blame Alan. He didn't know these people. They'd wandered into a couple of conversations and the poor guy's eyes had glazed over with boredom.

"Are these people actually speaking English?" he'd asked, making Meghan laugh.

"I told you this would be boring for you."

"I know, but I didn't know how boring."

It hadn't been boring for Meghan; it had been exhilarating. They'd been talking about the tactics and new technologies and rankings and ratings and her blood had been thrumming with excitement about tomorrow's start of the race. After they escaped, Will had come down and teased Alan mercilessly. Meghan truly wished she hadn't found Will so funny, but then she's always gotten Will's sometimes maddening sense of humor. He was never out-and-out mean, but he had a way of pointing out people's foibles that was hilarious to those around him who got his sense of humor. Clearly, Alan was not one of those people. Guys who hung around other guys knew how the rules of the game worked. Alan didn't know the rules at all, but he was smart enough to figure out Will was making fun of him. He just wasn't savvy enough to give it back. Poor guy.

"I don't mean to insult you, Meg, but I don't know what you saw in that man," Alan said. It was so unexpected, and so ridiculous a statement, Meghan couldn't come up with a response. What did she see in him? Sure, Alan wasn't a girl, but wasn't it obvious that Will was generally appealing? It was like wondering out loud what women saw in Matthew McConaughey.

Instead, she decided to be nice. "I don't either." Alan smiled and she was glad that she'd made him happy. "Will was just teasing, Alan. You can't take anything he says seriously. Believe me, I know." She put her arm around Alan and was amazed at how tense he felt. "He really bothered you, didn't he?"

"Of course he did. And, frankly, I don't like the way you behave around him. As if everything that comes out of his mouth is the biggest joke. Making other people feel small is not funny." He sounded more pompous than hurt, so Meghan had to dig deep to keep her arm around him.

"I didn't realize," was the best Meghan could come up with. And even that was a lie. She *did* realize. Now, she felt bad about ganging up on Alan. But, heck, did he have to be obtuse enough to talk about buying a powerboat with the captain of a sailboat on the eve of the Newport-Bermuda yachting classic? Meghan let out a sigh, thinking she should have let sleeping dogs lie and never gotten back on a sailboat. Her life would have gone on, she'd probably be at the office, or out to dinner with Alan, oblivious that the world she'd let go was carrying on without her. She might have read an article in the paper about the race and had a moment of wistful envy, and then forgot about it.

She almost wished Will had never stepped into her office that day.

Almost.

Chapter Seven

Rachel sipped her drink and smiled at Tony, who for the first time in six years was actually having a conversation with her. Rachel wished she could feel affronted by his attention, because she knew it was only because she'd lost weight and was dressing like a girl. The reality was, she liked having men look at her as if she were pretty; she just wished it was Thad standing there flirting with her instead of Tony.

"What do you think of Meg being back on the boat?" he asked, nodding down the hill to where Meg stood talking with her fiancé. She'd sensed something was different between Meg and Will, and having a fiancé attend the Dark and Stormy party said a lot.

"She is the best trimmer besides Thad."

Tony tilted his head, studying her. "You mean you didn't know?"

"Know what? That Meg and Will broke up? I figured it out when she showed up with that guy."

"Meg wasn't supposed to crew this year. She's only here because Thad got hurt. Will had to beg her back on the boat."

Tony was an okay guy, but he was more than rough around the edges, especially after he'd had a few drinks. At first she liked the way his eyes kept straying to her breasts, but she was beginning to find his fascination kind of creepy. The more he drank, the longer the looks were getting. She wasn't a big fan of gossip, either, having been the center of speculation for years. "I really can't picture Will begging," she said, looking around for someone to talk to so she could escape Tony.

"He dumped her, so he must have been desperate to go back with his tail between his legs," Tony said with relish.

"She dumped him," Thad said, his tone even. "And he asked her to help out and she said yes. End of story."

"That's not what I heard," Tony said, as if he knew, which Rachel figured he didn't. Tony was a crewmember, but not Will's friend.

Rachel turned subtly toward Thad, effectively cutting Tony out of the conversation. "At least you didn't get so hurt you're off the boat," she said. She felt as if her entire body were being pulled toward Thad, and she had to mentally chastise herself against literally throwing herself at him. That's what she wanted to do, to feel his arms wrap around her, to touch her lips against his, to take his hand and put it on her breast. That's what she wanted. Instead, she took a sip and looked nervously away. When Tony left, she hardly noticed, because her entire focus, whether he knew it or not, was on Thad.

"You all ready for the race tomorrow?"

Small talk. She didn't want that with Thad. She nodded and took another sip of her sweet drink and swallowed hard. "You still dating that girl from the last race?"

Thad gave her a confused look. "What girl?"

"The blonde, at least I think she was." Rachel knew exactly what she had looked like, how she sounded, what she wore. And she also knew the way Thad had looked at her, the way he'd been so easy with her, casually throwing his arm around her, bringing her to him a dozen times for a kiss. Every time he'd done that, it had killed her a little inside. And then she'd felt foolish feeling jealousy over a man who didn't even know she existed.

Thad narrowed his eyes in thought. "I don't remember a blonde," he said, shrugging his shoulders helplessly. "Let's see, there was a redhead, black, pink—you ever meet the girl with pink hair? She was a trip and a half. She had more tattoos than a hooker, but man, she could really . . ." He stopped, and a tiny bit of red touched his cheeks. "I remember a brunette. Nope. Can't remember a blonde."

By the time he was done with his list, Rachel was laughing out loud. "You brought her to this party. Last time," Rachel said, wondering why she would bring up another woman—a model-pretty woman—with a man she desperately loved.

"Oh," he said, drawing out the "O." "Sandy. Yeah, I remember now. God, no. She was a pain in my ass."

"Oh?"

"Too needy, if you know what I mean. High maintenance."

Rachel didn't have a clue, only hoped she wasn't needy the way Sandy was. "High maintenance?"

"You know. Take me out, Thad. How do I look? You don't like my dress? Don't you ever think about the future? Don't you want to have babies with me?" he said in a high-pitched voice that made Rachel laugh again. His smile slowly disappeared and he stared at her, making her blood suddenly slow, her body uncomfortably warm.

"You're really pretty when you smile like that," Thad said in the easy way he said everything.

"Thanks." It was all she could manage at the moment, and she was glad she managed that.

"What about you? Are you with any . . . one right now?"

I've never been with anyone. I've never been loved or held. Or kissed. "Not right now," she said.

He seemed uncomfortable all of a sudden, and Rachel wanted to blurt out that she wasn't gay, that she was in love with him, that she wanted to pull him into the nearest dark corner and strip him naked and run her hands all over. She couldn't do it. It would sound so ridiculous coming out her mouth, because she wasn't completely certain that he thought she was a lesbian. Maybe he just wasn't interested. Maybe that was why no man ever approached her.

She looked away and watched Will walk back up the hill. He'd been talking with Meghan and her fiancé and she wondered if he was all right with that. "Meg and Will seem to be handling everything well."

Thad raised an eyebrow, looking diabolical and sexy. "You think so? I give them a day into the race before they're at each other's throats."

Rachel laughed and Thad gave her another one of those looks. He shook his head and let out a chuckle.

"What's so funny?"

"Me. I'm laughing at myself."

"Care to let me in on it?" Rachel asked, proud that she sounded flirtatious.

"Maybe someday. Shh, here comes the captain. Pretend you think we're going to win," Thad said in an overloud whisper for Will's benefit.

"You're both fired," Will said.

"You didn't hire us. We work for free, remember?"

Will smiled. "Oh, yeah." He looked toward a man in his fifties who fairly oozed wealth and privilege. "Bob Sanderson was giving me shit earlier today about *Water Baby*. Said she was sitting in the water like she was loaded with lead. You didn't notice anything, did you?"

Thad shook his head. "Dude, you are so easy. Sanderson is yanking you good, my man. He's scared. He came within a breath of winning that trophy last race against *Spiral*. He thought he had a lock when *Spiral* wasn't racing this year. And now he's seen us practicing and he's thinking he's got a new enemy."

"They suck," Meghan said, walking up to the small group. She'd left Alan talking real estate with one of the wives of another boat, slipping away like a kid sneaking out of a room filled with old aunts. "Did you see them out on the bay yesterday? They looked really disorganized out there. He's got a bunch of new crewmembers and they look like a bunch of newbies."

"Yeah, but he's got one of the best navigators around," Will said.

Meghan gave Will a hard look, not quite believing he'd said that. She'd noticed two things about Will this year: he was pathologically intense about winning, and he was incredibly unsure of himself and his crew. Will had always had enough confidence for two crews, and the uncanny ability to not get upset when they failed. "Will, you're one of the best navigators in this race and you know it," she said.

"Damn right," Thad added, giving his friend a shove and causing Will's newly freshened drink to spill over a bit. Will brought his hand up to his mouth to lick off the spilled rum and at that moment, he looked at Meghan, who was staring at Will licking that rum and getting more turned on than she had in. . . . She didn't want to think about that. Meghan looked away, horrified by the rush of lust she'd felt. It was as unexpected as it was unwanted. Holy crapola. She prayed, prayed, prayed that Will hadn't seen the heat in her eyes. He knew her too well, he would have recognized that look—he always had.

"Plus you've got all that new equipment," Meghan said as if nothing had changed in the last few seconds, but she couldn't quite make her eyes reach his. *You do not lust after Will. You do not.*

"It's the same old equipment," he said, low and slow. "It just works better now."

He'd seen the lust. Of course he had. She might as well have worn a neon sign with the word LUST stamped on her forehead. Damn and double damn.

"I thought you threw out all that old crap," Thad said, and Meghan could only be grateful that Thad didn't have a clue what was happening between her and Will. She could feel Will staring at her, willing her to look at him and acknowledge that strange bolt of lightning that had passed between them, but Meghan kept her eyes firmly on Thad.

"I don't think that's what he meant," Rachel said,

laughter in her voice. Meghan looked at the woman she'd known for years and didn't really know, shocked and more than embarrassed that she'd somehow caught on to Will's innuendo.

Escape was the only plan of action she could think of. She looked around and saw Alan still talking to the woman, the animation on his face making Meghan smile. Poor Alan had never been so far out of his element as he was today. Thank God he found someone to talk to, she thought. She didn't want to disturb him and told herself she was being selfless, even though she was bullshitting herself. "Rachel. Come with me to the ladies room." She didn't wait for the other woman to say a word, just walked away, wincing when she heard Will's low chuckle.

When they were out of eyesight of Thad and Will, Meghan stopped and rubbed her temples.

"You all right?" Rachel asked.

"God, no." When Rachel laughed, Meghan smiled. "I didn't know it would be so difficult. You know we broke up, right?"

Rachel nodded. "The fiancé and all."

Meghan gave her a sheepish grin. "Well, I haven't seen Will in two years. I'm sure you know we weren't very happy with each other sailing back from Bermuda after the last race. I gave Will The Ultimatum and he basically said, see ya later."

"I'm sorry."

Meghan waved her hand at Rachel. "Don't be. I've moved on. I have a great job. A *real* job," she said, making Rachel laugh again. "I met Alan who actually loves me and wants to spend the rest of his life with me. But seeing Will again. . . . It's so strange. It's as if no time has passed, as if the last two years were two days. I should still hate him, but I don't. And I want to, believe me."

"I could sort of tell," Rachel said with endearing shyness.

"I'm over him," she said with force, knowing deep down it was a lie. She wasn't nearly as over him as she thought she was. For the past two years, anger had helped her along the way, but now that the rage and hurt had dissipated, she found herself actually liking Will. He was a likable guy. A likable guy with a gorgeous face and a body that would make a nun drool.

"Oh, I'm sure you are. You're getting married, right? To another guy."

Meghan nodded. "It's so nice to have someone who wants the same things I do. Alan and I are at the same place in life. We both want a home and family and Will isn't ever going to want that kind of life. I have a feeling Will is going to be eighty and still living his bohemian life. He'll be a gorgeous eighty-year-old, but he'll still be twenty years old inside."

"Alan seems nice."

"He is," Meghan said. "He's the nicest guy I've ever dated. That's why I'm marrying him."

"Because he's nice?" Rachel asked doubtfully.

Meghan let out a chuckle. "Nice goes a long way when you're not used to it. Nice is better than sexy."

"If you say so."

"I do." She forced her mind toward Alan, wonderful, loving, solid Alan. "Here's the deal. Don't say a word of this to anyone on the crew—not that there's anything to tell—and I won't tell anyone you're madly in love with Thad." It was a shot in the dark, but after a couple of Dark and Stormies,

Meghan figured she'd go for it. She'd noticed the way Rachel looked at Thad, the way she blushed when she saw him. And now that she looked back, the two had spent a lot of time together during the races. She never given it a second thought because she assumed what everyone else had falsely assumed—that Rachel wasn't interested. "Guess your secret's out."

Rachel's expression was almost comical.

"I was right! I knew it."

"Please don't say anything," Rachel said, looking as though she might actually cry.

Meghan grabbed her arm. "I won't. Of course I won't if you don't want me to. But why the big secret? Don't you think you should let Thad in on this?"

Rachel shook her head vigorously.

"Is he the reason for your miraculous change? I've got to tell you, you look pretty hot tonight. And I feel safe telling you that because it's obvious you're into guys. Right?"

Rachel let out a little moan. "Right," she said. "I don't know why I let everyone think . . ."

Meghan said, "Maybe it was safer that way. As long as everyone thought you were gay, you could use that as an excuse as to why you weren't going after Thad. Not that there's anything wrong with being gay," Meghan added with a chuckle.

"That's what my therapist said, that I was using that as a defense mechanism. A million times I practiced going up to him, but I couldn't. I'm really, really shy," she said, full of misery. "I'm seeing a therapist for that. But it's not working."

"Are you kidding? You're like a different person.

And you're funny. You've actually said at least three full sentences per practice session."

"Maybe I'll run for president," Rachel mumbled as they continued walking toward the yacht club.

"I really do have to pee. You don't have to come with me."

"I'll go, too," Rachel said.

"Doesn't it sort of make you mad that all the guys made that assumption about you?"

To Meghan's surprise, Rachel shook her head. "I have a mirror in my house," she said dryly. "My Dad was a fisherman and he really didn't know how to have a girl. I was already a tomboy so it made it easier for him that I was never a girly-girl. I dressed in big, baggy everything. I still want to. I'm a total tomboy. You have no idea how hard it was to walk out of my hotel room wearing this," she said, looking down at her dress as if it were a burlap bag instead of a sexy sundress.

"You look amazing," Meghan said. "You just have to get used to the new you. If you want, I can help. I'm not a total girly-girl, but I did have lessons in makeup and clothes from my big sister. And for the past two years I've worn a skirt at least once a week. I even wear heels." She wrinkled her nose.

Rachel smiled. "I'll take any help I can get."

"Does that include help with Thad? I could drop a hint or two that you have a boyfriend."

Rachel took several thoughtful steps before responding with a small smile. "I'll let you know."

Meghan sipped her third drink, feeling wonderfully warm and happy. The sun had just sunk below the horizon, giving the few clouds in the sky of bit of gold leafing around the edges. Block Island was a dark silhouette in the distance; the white sails of the few boats still out on the bay looked pink in the fading light. Meghan glanced up at the moon and smiled to see Venus shining brightly nearby. When was the last time she even noticed the sun setting?

"Pretty night."

Meghan turned to see Will standing next to her and suddenly and completely unexpectedly, she wanted to cry. She swallowed down the lump in her throat and looked out to the bay, watching as a schooner pulled in its sails as it got ready to head into Newport Harbor.

"I missed this more than I thought I did," she said.

"I missed you."

In the four years they'd dated, Will had never said anything as poignant and heartfelt as those three words. Stunned, Meghan turned to Will, who smiled slightly and shrugged. Meghan searched for a flippant answer, but found none. "Me too, I guess. When I wasn't trying to come up with ways to kill you." Oh, well, flippant after all.

They both stood in silence for a long time, staring out onto the bay in the fading light. Will stood close, too close, and Meghan could feel the heat of him. She willed herself to walk away, to say goodnight and search out Alan, but her feet felt like lead. "Why didn't you . . ." she stopped with a silent groan. She really didn't need to know why Will hadn't come after her, why he'd let her go rather than spend the rest of his life with her.

"You scared the hell out of me, Meg. You always

did." He shoved his hands in his pockets. "You still do, I guess."

"Yeah," she said sadly.

She could feel Will looking at her and dug deep not to turn toward him. She was afraid of what she might do if she looked at him and saw something there that she'd never seen before. She could feel his pull, like a magnet drawing her toward him and she refused to be sucked into his world again. If she looked over and thought she saw love in his eyes, she knew she couldn't trust herself. But he never really told her before and he sure as hell wasn't going to do it now, not with Alan less than a football field away. She was engaged. She'd moved on and fallen in love and was planning a life with another man. Will was just going to have to deal with it.

"Too bad Frank couldn't be here," she said, desperate to change the conversation. "I'm surprised he didn't make it."

"He wasn't feeling quite up to it," he said, a strange edge to his voice.

"Did I tell you I stopped by his house?"

Will stiffened. "No, you didn't."

"Nancy answered and told me he was out. She didn't even invite me inside. Is she mad at me or something?"

"Well, you did break her surrogate son's heart. I think she's a little pissed about that one."

Meghan snorted. "You broke your own damn heart, Will, and you know it," she said lightly.

"It still got broken."

Don't do this. Please, please don't make me fall for you again. I've got Alan now. Meg turned to him, pretending to be annoyed, trying to keep things light.

"You are full of crapola. People with broken hearts don't date every woman they meet." She lifted her head in triumph.

"Whatever Thad told you is a lie," he said, accurately guessing where she'd gotten her information. "Well, an exaggeration. And everyone deals with broken hearts in their own way. Some people have sex, some people latch on to the first thing that smiles at them and get married." She gave him a look to tell him his teasing had gone a little over the line. "And what the hell are you doing grilling Thad about my life?" he asked, in an obvious attempt to go on the offensive.

She stuck out her jaw. "Thad was letting me know that you weren't lying around pining away for me. I think he thinks he was being a loyal friend."

Will took a couple of steps toward the bay and for a moment Meghan thought he was walking away. She wasn't certain if she was relieved or disappointed. Maybe a little of both. But when he turned back to her, Will stood in front of her, the expression on his face unreadable in the fading light.

"I never got a good-bye kiss," he said, and Meghan wished the sun was still up so she could clearly see his eyes.

"You got it, you just didn't know it was the last one."

"After four years I think we deserve a good-bye kiss," he said, his voice going low and sexy and making her want to run. She just wasn't sure she wanted to run into his arms or back up the hill toward the crowd.

Will moved a step closer, Meghan a step back. "What are you afraid of?" he asked in that same low tone.

"I'm not afraid of you, Will. I could sleep with you and remain completely unfazed."

"Liar."

Meghan let out a puff of air, angry at his arrogance and at herself for being momentarily sucked in by him. He never would change. He was all about the hunt, but never quite knew what to do with the girl once he'd caught her. "Will, leave me alone. I can't believe I actually . . ."

His mouth was on hers, gentle, warm, and horribly intoxicating.

"Please," he whispered against her mouth. "Please."

Meghan wanted to turn away. She wanted to punch him—hard—right in his treacherous mouth. Instead, she let out a small sound and brought her hands up to clutch at his shirt, about a millisecond before she came to her senses and pushed him violently away.

"You are such a *jerk*," she said, her voice low and savage. "Alan could have seen that. You are the most insensitive ass I've ever known." She wiped at her mouth viciously. "I quit."

If Meghan hadn't been quite so angry with herself, she would have appreciated the look of abject horror on Will's face.

"No, no. God, Meg, I'm sorry." He reached out to grab her arm in an attempt to stop her from leaving, but she jerked her arm away.

"I don't care how sorry you are. That was wrong."

"I know," Will said. "Damn it." He nearly shouted it, and Meghan prayed the wind drowned him out. "I'm drunk," he said, sounding slightly desperate.

"No, you're not."

Will could not believe what he'd just done, what he'd nearly told her. He'd been so close to begging her to love him, to telling her that he hadn't gotten over her, that he never would. He wished he was drunk so he could blame the rum, but two drinks over three hours wouldn't have done the trick, even on an empty stomach.

"You can't quit, Meg. I'm sorry. I never should have touched you."

"You keep doing this do me," Meg said, sounding as if she might cry.

"I'm an ass."

"And a jerk."

"A huge jerk. I promise I won't touch you again. I won't even look at you if you don't want me to. But don't quit. We need you."

In the dim light he could see her shaking her head. "I'm really mad at you, Will."

"Don't quit."

He heard her let out a sigh and knew he had at least convinced her not to quit the crew.

"The only reason I'm not quitting—the *only* reason—is the rest of the crew. I owe it to them. You," she said, pointing a shaking finger at him. "can go to hell."

He watched her walk up the hill, probably looking for Alan, feeling guilty that for an infinitesimal moment she'd responded to his idiotic kiss. He turned back to the bay, hating himself, hating that he was hard for a woman he could never have, but who had forever ruined him for other women. Why the hell hadn't he known this was going to happen when he let her walk away? He looked up to the few stars that had broken through the nighttime sky, wishing he could call back the last ten minutes of his life. She'd never trust herself to be alone with him again.

He'd truly had his good-bye kiss.

Chapter Eight

The night before the race, Meghan lay in her bed alone and unable to sleep because, after all, a person as rotten as she was didn't deserve to sleep. Or eat. Or breathe.

She let out a groan and flicked on her reading lamp and stared at the ceiling. She wasn't certain who she was more angry at, herself or Will. The one thing she did know was that Alan did not deserve the woman she'd become that night. She could not forget the hurt look he gave her when she'd told him she wanted to be alone that night. It hadn't escaped her—and probably not him—that they hadn't had sex since Will had walked into the agency more than a week ago. The first few days she'd had a legitimate excuse—she'd had her period—but after that she just hadn't wanted to. For the first time in her life, she'd pushed a man she loved away and she didn't know why. At least she didn't want to know why.

The drive home from Newport had been agony for Meghan, who could swear she still felt Will's kiss, even though it had been light and not at all passion-filled. Instead, it had been worse; a kiss of desperation, of terrifying need. Will had never kissed her like that, like if he didn't he'd die. And even though she'd pushed him away and gotten all mad, Meghan had participated even if it was for just a second or two. The worst part was that she hated him for kissing her and she hated herself for wanting more.

That was the crux of it.

Now she was beleaguered by guilt and confusion and Alan didn't deserve any of that.

"I'm tired," she'd said, and that was true enough. "I really just want to go home. Tomorrow's a huge day."

"Did something happen tonight?"

Meghan felt as if she were going to be sick. "Will really pissed me off," she said honestly. "If it wasn't for the rest of the crew, I would have quit."

"What happened?"

"Just an argument. Nothing, really. He just rubs me the wrong way."

"Well, I can certainly understand that."

Meghan had closed her eyes and leaned her head against the cool, hard glass of the car's window. Why couldn't Will have a girlfriend? Why did he have to be so nice? *I miss you.* Will had never been a manipulative person, which meant whatever he said was sincere. She wished he had been drunk. She wished a million things.

Meghan looked at the clock. One in the morning. Too late to call Alan and hear his voice. She needed to hear his voice, to pull her back into this world.

The sailing world was a fantasy, a vacation, and it was more intoxicating than a Dark and Stormy.

Will and she had been good together before she'd started wanting more. They'd hardly fought, the sex was great, the laughter endless. They'd done just about everything together except talk about the future. And when they did, it was more about the future of the boat, the next race, whether or not they were going to head down to Key West in the winter or sail the Med. It wasn't such a bad life; in fact, it was pretty darn good until Meghan saw thirty looming in front of her like a hurricane flag warning whipping in the wind.

Then she'd met Alan and it seemed as if everything she'd started to want had been magically handed to her. Meghan was beginning to think she'd become one of those people who were never happy where they were, one of those annoying grass-is-always-greener-on-the-other-side kind of people.

Meghan let out a groan, hating the thought of stepping onto *Water Baby* and seeing Will. She'd never been awkward with him. She'd never been awkward with Alan, either, yet she had been tonight.

"I'm going crazy," she said aloud, pressing the heels of her hands against her burning eyes.

Rachel was drunk. Really drunk. She knew this because in the back of her foggy brain a small voice was telling her that. But it felt so nice. She wasn't shy. She wasn't a bull dyke. She was a sexy, beautiful, funny, intelligent woman. Just one who couldn't walk straight. And Thad was standing next to her, so close their arms were touching, and it was so intoxicating she felt as if she might actually lean into him and stay there. Oops. She was already doing that. Nice. Very nice.

"You okay?"

God, she loved his voice. All low and sexy. "Sure." She grinned up at him and swayed a bit. "I think I had too many Stark and Dormies." She shook her head and giggled. "I guess that's proof then. Dark and Stormies." She enunciated each syllable of the drink. "Yes, officer, I'm fine to drive."

"Do you need a ride?"

"I didn't drive. Took a taxi. I could call one." She let her voice drift off hopefully. Damn, she was getting good at this girly stuff, because Thad was smiling down at her and then he offered her a ride back to the hotel. And once they were there, who knew? It was such a lovely, lovely thought.

"Let's go," Rachel said, grabbing his good arm and pulling him toward the front of the yacht club. Drunk was good. Drunk was doing what you wanted and not giving a flying fuck.

Thad led her to his Jeep and she leaned on him a bit more than she had to, loving the sensation of her breast pressing against him. Everything felt wonderful and electric, her entire body humming with lust and love and rum.

"Here we are." Thad seemed a little uncomfortable, Rachel thought. Stiff and unfriendly. And here she was a friendly girl who was drunk enough to do just about anything. She might just lean over and kiss him right now, right on that beautiful mouth of his. If only her head would stop spinning. Really, it was making her feel a bit queasy, like ten-foot swells—oh, she shouldn't have thought of that—heaving waves, up and down, spinning her head.

"I think I want to . . ." *Kiss you.* "Throw up." And she did, right on his lap.

At Sea

Chapter Nine

Meghan stepped aboard *Water Baby* and nearly slipped on the deck, which was slick from a recent washing, and she said a quick prayer it wasn't a foreshadowing of things to come. Despite everything, Meghan wanted desperately to win this race. All around the wharf other crews were gathering, making last-minute equipment checks, milling about the marina. The less serious racers were standing by hibachis eating hot dogs and hamburgers, hanging out on the deck and throwing crumbs to seagulls.

"Hey, Rach," Meghan said, seeing her friend huddled near the helm, arms wrapped tightly around her knees. She looked a bit green, not at all like the stunning woman she'd been the night before. She hadn't changed into her *Water Baby* polo yet, and instead was wearing a too-big T-shirt which she'd pulled over her knees making a little tent. "Too many Dark and Stormies, I take it?"

"Don't even mention liquor," Rachel said, as if the mere act of speaking would do her in.

"Has Will seen you yet?"

"Yes," she said, and held her head with her hands, obviously holding it on. "He's not very happy with me right now. Neither is Thad."

"Oh?"

"I threw up on him last night."

"Charming."

"Yeah. He was thrilled."

"She ruined the only pair of good khakis I own," Thad said from the companionway. He was smiling, so Meghan figured he wasn't really angry with Rachel.

"I said I was sorry," Rachel mumbled. "God, am I sorry." A new wave of pain and nausea must have hit her, because she suddenly got a terrified look on her face and began breathing in short little gasps. It was nearly noon, so Rachel must have really done some major drinking if she was still hungover. The hot sun overhead and the gentle sway of the boat probably wasn't helping much, either.

"Need a bucket?" Thad asked, chuckling.

Rachel shook her head, clutching her stomach, and swallowing almost frantically. "I'm okay," she said, finally. "Other than the fact I'm a complete idiot."

"Welcome to the club," Meghan said dryly, and turned away before Rachel could ask for an explanation.

"I think I'll hang out near the head just in case," Rachel said, getting up gingerly. She gave them a sheepish grin. "I'm not really a big drinker."

"No kidding," Thad said. Thad heaved himself out of the companionway, giving Rachel a wide berth.

"Don't worry, I only hit my targets once," Rachel said, glaring at his mock fear.

"Where's the crew?" Meghan asked. Usually the crew met early at the boat to get ready for the start.

"Most are still having an early lunch at the hotel, including Will," Thad said. "He was up almost all night, by the way, trying to figure out the latest satellite pictures of the Gulf Stream using that new computer program. The man is obsessed this year."

"What's up with that, anyway?"

Thad shrugged, but he looked away, making Meghan think he knew something she didn't. "He's just sick of not winning. And with all the money Frank's spent on the boat, he feels he ought to come through with a win."

His explanation made sense, but Frank spent a boatload of money on *Water Baby* for every Newport-Bermuda. If there was a new gadget, he bought it, leaving it up to Will to do all the research on a new item, even though some of the stuff wasn't allowed under race rules. One such gadget was a computer program to help predict what the Gulf Stream would do, computing sea levels, current speeds, and wind, because everyone who'd ever sailed the Newport-Bermuda knew one thing: The Gulf Stream could make or break a boat. He could use the program up until they sailed, but not when they were under way.

The Gulf Stream was like an intense, fast river with swirling currents stretching along the Atlantic from north to south that could throw you up toward Europe and away from Bermuda, or bring you south toward Bermuda so fast, the captain sometimes had to fight to slow a boat down. Winning the Newport-Bermuda was all about how and where the boat hit the stream. Miss a meandering curve south, and the crew might as well count the race as a vacation. And everything depended on satellites being able to see the stream. If it was cloudy, hitting the stream right was anyone's guess, so sailors prayed for clear weather and a swift curving doughnut of current that would whip the boat through.

That was Will's job, and this year it seemed to be weighing far heavier on him than it ever had before. It was almost as if he had something huge at stake, other than merely wanting to win.

Meghan knew the basics of navigation, but she never really wanted to know more than that. A boat's success depended on good navigation and a sail trimmer who knew how to capture wind when there was none—or stop the boat from being battered in a storm. Will and she had been a terrific team, but they'd never won the Newport-Bermuda.

"Here they come now," Thad said, nodding toward the end of the dock.

Meghan had to smile at the sight of seven men, all in matching polos, walking toward the boat, with Will at the lead. He wasn't the tallest man of the bunch but there was something about him, a larger-than-life air that told even a casual observer that he was the captain of the boat. Even though her stomach clenched at the thought of seeing Will after their kiss, the excitement of the race was just too intoxicating to dwell on her personal problems. The air was electric; it seemed as if the entire harbor was thrumming with anticipation of the start of the race. On one part of the pier, TV news cameras had set up and were interviewing one of the boat captains, though Meghan couldn't tell which one. A few TV vans, their satellite dishes set up, were parked nearby, adding to the general excitement.

"Someone's getting their fifteen minutes," Meghan said to Thad.

"Bob Sanderson. Bastard."

"God, that's going to feed his ego. That's all he needs."

"Won't do much good when we kick his ass," Thad said, then grimaced when they both heard the sound of Rachel being sick down below. "Poor kid."

"You're being awfully understanding given the fact she vomited on you last night," Meghan said, trying to gauge how Thad felt about Rachel.

Thad grunted, then moved with amazing grace to the dock, his broken arm held high. He met Will with a nod toward the TV crew interviewing Sanderson. "Think he called them?"

"Probably," Will said. "I got to tell you, the last thing I'd do if I were him would be to call attention to myself right before a race I was going to lose." Will laughed, but his laughter faded when he spotted Meghan standing on the boat. "You ready?" he asked tonelessly.

Meghan nodded. "As ever."

"Though I can't attest to Rachel's readiness," Thad said. "She's hanging big time."

"That's okay. I don't really need her until we get into the open water." Will looked toward the Atlantic and Meghan followed his gaze. Though it was clear and sunny where they were, Meghan could see the eerie gray bank of clouds on the horizon that told of a thick fog lingering out on the Atlantic. The Newport-Bermuda almost always started in the sun, but within hours, every boat was enshrouded in fog.

Water Baby had a ten-member crew that was divided

into two shifts. During the key parts of the race, the crewmembers were all on deck lending a hand. But with low winds and calm seas, half the crew hung out below deck, sleeping, playing cards, or cooking. Some boats actually had televisions and air conditioning. But *Water Baby* was stripped down as far as the racing committcc would allow under the rules of the race. The race was grueling, sleep difficult, and eating a matter of filling one's stomach. Once they were under way, food consisted of quickly made sandwiches and MREs, those dehydrated meals the military ate, eaten out of plastic containers.

Three of the crew were college kids who helped Will with his racing school; another was a doctor and old friend of Frank. Not only was Alex a longtime friend of Frank, he was a damn good sailor and it had made practical sense for a man with severe diabetes to have an MD on board.

Every crew needed a loudmouth, and Tony Robak filled that role nicely. Tony also was one of the best helmsmen around, so when Will had to work on the navigation equipment down below, Tony took the helm.

"Everyone here?" Will asked.

The race's first warning gun was set to sound just before one o'clock and it was getting close to the time they'd begin setting up for the start, the mad dash across the start line. The start of any sail race was not meant for the faint of heart. Even though starts for long ocean races were not as critical as for short races, these sailors didn't seem to know that. It was a small victory to be the boat who timed going across the start line so they were the first across.

Will was a terrific starter, mostly because he had

a good crew who knew how to stall a boat that was going too fast, or make the most of a weak wind to push the boat faster.

"Looks like Sanderson is heading out," Thad said, nodding toward Will's nemesis. He'd never said it aloud, but everyone who knew Will knew he got almost as much joy beating Sanderson and his *Hurricane* as he would getting the Lighthouse Trophy. Last race, *Hurricane* crushed *Water Baby* and Will's reaction when the final times were calculated was not a pretty thing to witness. Though he'd been overly gracious in front of Sanderson, of course.

"Okay, ladies," Will said, "let's launch."

"What about Frank?" Meghan said. Frank had always been on hand to watch the start of the race, even after he'd lost his leg and couldn't be on board.

Will stopped dead, as if the thought hadn't occurred to him. "He's . . ."

"Watching from Beavertail," Thad said. "He didn't want to deal with the parking and the crowds this year. You know, the whole wheelchair thing."

"Of course," Meghan said, feeling disappointed and sad. Frank had always been around for the Newport-Bermuda start and she couldn't believe he hadn't come this year to wish them well. "What's his cell phone number? I'll call him and wave when we go by."

"Doesn't have one," Will said, unnecessarily tightening up the boom. "Wave anyway. I'm sure he'll see you from his van. He'll have his binoculars."

Will had acutely felt Frank's absence this last week with all the meetings and festivities that the old guy had loved so much. That morning, Will had called Frank and spoke with Nancy, who'd said Frank was sleeping and she didn't want to wake him. Thad hadn't lied to Meghan. The plan all along had been for Nancy to somehow get Frank into their van so he could watch the start from Beavertail. A week ago, he'd been enthusiastic about the plan, but this morning Nancy had seemed uncertain whether the old guy would be up for it. "I know he wouldn't miss it for the world," she'd said. "But his nurse isn't very happy with the idea. He's had a couple of rough days."

"How rough?" Will asked, his entire body tensing.

"Oh, he's fine for now, Will. Don't you worry. I'll keep him alive so he can hold that trophy." She'd laughed, but Will wondered after he'd hung up if she'd forced out that small chuckle just to placate him.

"You'll call me if something changes." When she didn't answer him right away, he said, "Call me, Nancy." She'd agreed reluctantly.

For a while after he'd hung up, he had a horrible feeling that Frank had died and Nancy was lying because she knew how important this race was to them both. He'd actually bought a paper that morning just to look at the death notices, feeling only slightly relieved when he hadn't seen Frank's name. Nancy wouldn't do that, would she? She just might, thinking she was sparing him. He nearly gave into the impulse to drive to Jamestown to see Frank for himself.

"I really miss Frank this year. It's not the same without him," Meghan said, unknowingly throwing some salt into his open wounds. Just then Meghan's cell phone rang. "I'll shut it off when we get out," she said, right before she flipped open her phone.

Will listened intensely until he realized she was

talking to a client, not her fiancé. The gist of the conversation seemed to be that someone wanted a house and she was telling them to call Alan the Tool. When she hung up, she was smiling. "I think I might have finally sold a house."

"Congratulations."

"I've got two more calls to make. Is that okay? Then I promise to shut off my phone."

"Go crazy," Will said. The first call she made was to the homeowners, telling them about the offer and recommending they accept it. The second call was to her boyfriend, and Will had to fight the urge to rip the phone from her hand, especially when she softened her voice.

"Great. Thanks, Alan. Wish me luck." There was a pause and Will could just imaging all the bullshit he was handing her, all the stuff that perfect boyfriends say to make women happy. Meghan smiled gently, then turned away so he couldn't see her, but he could still hear her. "Me too."

I love you. Me too. Crap.

When she snapped her phone shut, Meghan still wouldn't turn his way, even when Will asked her if she was ready. How the hell could she love that guy? How could a woman who'd once loved him love a guy who was the complete opposite of him?

"Come on, ladies. Let's go get a trophy."

The crew let out a manly whoop. As soon as *Water Baby* navigated the slips and boats moored in the harbor, Tony popped his head out of the companionway with a big grin on his face.

"For you, madam," he said with a flourish and presented Meghan with a tray full of clams on the half-shell already drizzled with lemon and hot sauce.

"Oh, my God, I forgot all about that," she said, laughing. It had been a tradition for years that at the start of every ocean-going race that Tony crewed, he would give Meghan a plateful of clams, which she shared begrudgingly with whomever wanted some. Thankfully for her, Rachel was the only person on the crew who loved raw clams as much as she did. Meghan and Rachel could slurp down a tray full of them and didn't care a bit that most people thought raw quahogs swimming in their own juices was about the most disgusting thing a person could put in their mouths.

"I don't think I can stomach them today," Rachel said, still looking a bit green. "Maybe I can force down one. Or two."

Meghan couldn't remember anything looking quite as wonderful as those clams.

"Looks like a pile of snot," Will said.

Meghan ignored him and handed a clam to Rachel, who slurped it down with relish. "It was good, but I think that's all I can handle right now."

"More for me," Meghan said happily. In a matter of minutes, the clams were gone and she was feeling supremely satisfied.

"I don't know how the hell anyone can eat that and actually enjoy it."

"And you call yourself a New Englander."

"I call myself sane," Will said, making Meghan laugh.

There, that was better. A bit of banter helped to put them back on track. No more strange looks from Will, no more kissing, just happy talk between two old friends.

* * *

Fifteen minutes later, Will headed into the wind and let the boat bob silently for a few seconds, breathing in the scene before him of boats heading out to the starting line, of seagulls hovering in the air, of powerboaters hanging around to see the start of the race. It was like a water-going party for many of the entrants, but for Will, it seemed as if every race he'd ever entered, every moment he'd spent on the water with Frank by his side was coalescing to this single moment, this single race. The anticipation was palpable and Will could hardly contain the feeling of euphoria that hit him at that moment. This was it. Raising his face to look at the top of the mast where a wind indicator swirled, he shouted, "Raise the jib."

With great flourish, the crew raised the crisp white sail, which opened and snapped in the stiff westerly breeze. The boat heeled slightly to port side and for the next four hours, Will forgot everything except that he was at sea in the race of a lifetime.

Two hours into the race, the crew of *Water Baby* found themselves flying on a reach with a southwesterly wind into one of the thickest fogs they'd seen during a Newport-Bermuda—and that was saying a lot. Meghan loved sailing in the fog, the sense of tearing blindly ahead, the soft mistiness of it. Even with radar, it was always thrilling to hear the booming sound of a ship at sea putting out a warning to all that it was bearing down on them. Meghan hung out in the cockpit, her hands on the winch that connected the sheet to their largest jib. The huge sail lay smooth and taut, propelling the boat at twelve knots. Even though the wind was fairly steady, Meghan was ready to make tiny adjustments to keep the boat going at top speed.

"We're flying," Thad said from his place on the rail. When the boat was heeling over in a stiff wind, most of the crew who wasn't on critical duty sat on the edge of the boat to keep it from leaning too far into the water. *Water Baby* cut the cold Atlantic waters.

"Thirteen knots," Will boomed from his spot behind the helm. He'd be there for another hour before Tony took over, giving him a rest.

In the galley, Tony was boiling water to throw into the MREs, which didn't smell half as bad as they tasted.

"I'm hungry," Meghan said to no one in particular. She turned to Will. "What's on the menu, sir?"

"Filet mignon with a side of lightly herbed red potatoes and fresh summer vegetables, perfectly steamed," he said, grinning.

"Beef stew served in Tupperware," Tony corrected, tossing one of the covered containers to a crewmember from the companionway. Tony heaved himself onto the deck and began handing out the rest of the containers.

"It's not even Tupperware," Thad complained. "It's that disposable stuff."

"Weighs less than Tupperware," Will said.

Eating on a boat was tough at any time, but with the winds this strong, it was all they could do to shove the stew down as quickly as possible and pray they didn't need to tack or change sails.

"I think I ate too many clams," Meghan said, even though the smell of the stew was making her mouth water. She followed Will into the cabin, still clutching her unopened container, to check out the latest satellite picture of the Atlantic.

"Man, it looks dead out there," he said. "Nothing really going on, even in the stream. It's going to be a slow race, I think."

"Is that good or bad?" asked Cal, one of the college kids, as he came out of the head.

"It depends. The bigger boats like big weather. The smaller boats do well in light air. And us? We're in the middle so we just have to work like hell to keep ourselves in contention. We'll know better where we stand tomorrow morning."

At Cal's look of confusion, Meghan explained that every morning of the race each boat called in their position. That way everyone knew where they stood in the race. "Don't forget, though, we could cross the line twentieth and still win the trophy on corrected time."

"Or we could cross first and some thirty-footer could take the trophy ten boats behind us."

"Or you could be a huge boat and kick everyone's butt so badly and win it all anyway," Meghan said. She glanced at her watch, noting they had another two hours before they had to go back on duty. She was tired and looked longingly at the forward berth when Tony called down.

"I could use some rail meat if you all are done chatting."

Meghan caught Rachel's eyes and made a face before heaving herself up and heading topside. The wind seemed bitingly cold after the warmth of the cabin, so Meghan reached down and grabbed a knit hat.

"Winds up to twenty-five knots," Tony said. "Good thing we have a real man on the helm."

"Just keep her sailing in a straight line," Will said dryly, smiling when Tony snapped to and saluted.

"Cold," Meghan said. "My lips are numb." She smacked them together a couple of times. They felt really weird, but she figured it was just the cold wind. It sure didn't feel like June at the moment.

Meghan took her place on the rail, her feet dangling off the side. She tried not to look at the jib, which wasn't trimmed perfectly, but was doing its job. She flexed her fingers, which felt as if they were falling asleep, and her feet were tingling from the cold.

"I feel kind of funny," Meghan said.

"You look funny, too," Will said, eyeing the hat.

"I'm cold," she said. "My face is numb, my hands are numb and I can't even feel my feet."

"You have been landlocked for too long," he said, nudging her a bit with his shoulder. "You can lean on me for warmth."

He had the devil in his eyes, so Meghan laughed.

"I might even try to steal another kiss."

"Go ahead and try," Meghan said, more as a warning than an invitation. "I'll sic my fiancé on you."

Will's smile instantly disappeared.

"Is it the word 'fiancé' that bothers you so much or . . ." Meghan stopped, because a wave of nausea hit her so quickly she couldn't talk. "Oh, God," she managed, before tucking her head over the side and vomiting.

"Seasick?" Will asked.

Meghan hadn't realized he was holding her until he spoke.

"I guess. I can't believe I would be. The seas aren't that bad and I've never been seasick on the rail." She let out a puff of air. "I feel better now, but I think I need to brush my teeth."

Meghan moved toward the companionway.

"Maybe it was a bad clam," Will called out.

"No such thing," Meghan said as she tucked herself into the cabin and immediately felt the heaving of the boat in her stomach. Whenever she was in the cabin for a long period of time during rough seas, Meghan would always get a bit queasy, but this instant nausea was unusual for her. Maybe it was hitting her so hard because she hadn't been on a boat for two years. Swallowing, she moved to the front berth to get her ditty bag and pulled out her toothbrush and toothpaste. But before she had time to put the paste on the brush, she was bending over the small toilet in the head. "Man," she said aloud. "Maybe I *did* have a bad clam." She shook her head and spit into the sink, praying that she wouldn't get sick again as she brushed her teeth. Her head hurt, she realized, and she looked through her bag for some sort of pain reliever. As she put her head up to look in the mirror, the entire bathroom swirled around her.

"Oh, shit." Swallowing desperately, she tried not to throw up again, but her stomach heaved painfully. Dimly she heard Tony yell that he needed everyone on the rail. "I'm okay. I'm okay," she said softly in an effort to make it true. She hung her head over the toilet, her entire body was bathed in sweat. It wasn't until she tried to walk toward the companionway that Meghan realized something more serious than seasickness was going on. Her legs weren't fully cooperating with her effort to reach the stairs—and it just wasn't a lack of sea legs. It was as if they were attached to a different body and she only had limited control over it.

As she tried to move to the opening, she saw

Tony at the helm, his image swirling in front of her. The boat slammed into the waves and suddenly tilted over. "Jesus, Meg, I need everyone on the rail. Even your pitiful weight will help."

"I can't," she said, though she knew it came out muffled, as if she had cotton in her mouth. She tried to reach for the companionway railing but couldn't get her arms in the right position to grab it. "Will," she shouted. "I need help."

She heard Tony call for Will, who was down into the cabin in seconds. "What's wrong?"

"I think I'm really sick. I'm sorry."

"Seasick?" he asked, looking down at her in disbelief.

"No. Sick sick. Something's wrong. I can't walk." She sort of slumped against one of the back berths.

"What do you mean, you can't walk?" Will said, alarm nearly paralyzing him.

"I mean, I can't walk. My legs aren't working right. It's weird."

In their four years together Will had learned one important thing about Meg: She'd have to be half dead not to be on deck during a race. He stuck his head out the companionway and gave a shout. "Doc. Come down here now. Rachel, take over at the jib."

"Rachel's no good," Meghan said, her voice sounding as if her tongue weren't working quite right.

"She's good enough for now," Will said, trying to tamp down the growing concern. He didn't know what was wrong with Meg, but whatever it was seemed serious.

"What's up?" Alex said.

"She's throwing up. Says she can't walk."

In an instant, Alex's demeanor changed, and the

concern in Will's gut grew tenfold. Alex sat next to Meghan and studied her. "Your face numb?"

She nodded sloppily, as if her head weren't on tight enough.

"You feel tingling in your hands, feet. Tongue?" Meghan kept nodding.

"I feel like a rag doll."

Alex turned to Will. "She's got PSP," he said. "How many of those damn clams did she eat?"

"What the hell is PSP?"

The older man pulled Will toward the bow where he could have more privacy.

"Paralytic Shellfish Poisoning." At Will's blank stare, Alex grabbed his shoulders with both hands. "It's potentially fatal."

Chapter Ten

Will backed away from Alex in disbelief. "You can't die from eating bad clams." You could get sick, he knew that. You could throw up, maybe even end up in the hospital because of dehydration, but people didn't die. Did they?

"PSP is caused by a bacteria found in red tide. There was a scare near Long Island earlier this week and they banned all shell fishing. If those clams Meghan ate were harvested before the ban, she could be in real danger."

Will pressed his hands against his forehead. "She ate a shitload of those damned things. Oh, God."

"She may not in danger but we can't take the chance. This thing moves fast." Alex squeezed his eyes shut. "She could be dead within hours if we don't get her to a hospital. If this thing progresses aggressively enough, it could paralyze her, including her lungs."

"Oh, my God." He looked back at Meghan, who was still lying drunkenly on the berth. "You have to do something," he said, keeping his voice low and savage.

Alex just shook his head. "Unless you have a respirator on board, I can't do anything. That's worst case. She could recover within hours, too. She's young and healthy. It all depends on how much bacteria she ingested." He shook his head. "Nothing I can do, buddy. She'll either get better, or worse. It's good that she threw up. She probably got rid of a lot of the toxins. It's a good sign."

"Rachel had at least one of the things," Will said. "Could you check on her?"

As Alex walked by, he lay a comforting hand on the younger man's shoulder.

Will thrust himself up the companionway. "Come about."

"What?" Tony asked. "Why?"

"We're heading back to Newport. Meghan's sick. Real sick. Come about," he said. Tony didn't have to question Will again, and immediately turned the wheel and Gary pulled the jib tight. They were heading into the wind, which meant the sail home was going to be long and tedious, full of tacks, with waves pounding against the hull. Will could almost feel the boat slowing beneath his feet, plowing into the waves.

With the boat turned, Will headed back down into the cabin and grabbed his ship-to-shore radio, putting it on the frequency for the U.S. Coast Guard.

"This is Will Scott of *Water Baby.* Our position is forty degrees north by seventy-one degrees west. We have a gravely ill crewmember on board and request immediate assistance."

"This is Petty Officer John Kay, Mr. Scott. What is the nature of the illness?"

"Paralytic Shellfish Poisoning. We have a doctor on board."

"Okay, Mr. Scott. We can't send out a helo because of the low ceiling," the officer said, referring to the dense fog. "We've got a . . ." the petty officer paused as if checking what boats were available, " . . . a four-hour-plus ETA." Will could hear the regret in the young officer's voice, as if he knew he might be signing the death warrant to someone.

"That's too long. You've got to get someone here faster. We may not have four hours."

"I'm aware of that, sir," the officer said grimly. "I'll do my best to reroute, but right now that's the best we can do. Stay by the radio."

"You have to get someone here sooner," Will said, feeling himself starting to lose it. Meghan could not die. He wouldn't allow it.

"I'll do my best, sir," the officer repeated.

Will hung up the radio, grabbing the stair rail so tightly his arm shook. This was not happening; it was insane to think this woman who laughed during gale force winds would be felled by a goddamn clam.

"What are you doing, Will?" Meghan demanded, as she tried to sit up. "Why'd you come about?" She was like a rag doll and her limbs flopped ineffectually. Will's heart did another dive: She was getting worse. "I feel funny," Meghan said, and giggled.

Will felt the back of his eyes prick as he kneeled beside Meghan and laid his hand on her forehead.

"Do I have a fever?" she asked.

"Doesn't feel like it."

"See? I'm fine. I just have to get my arms and legs working again."

"Very funny."

"I'm so sorry, Will."

He swallowed hard and stared at the bright blue canvas of the berth. "Don't worry about it. It's just a race. We'll win next race."

"Next race," she repeated. "But this is my last year."

"You can race again. Married people are allowed, you know."

She smiled and his heart nearly ripped in two. If she died, he'd just go crazy. He was the one who convinced her to race, the one who begged and bribed her, when she'd been perfectly happy with her new life. He should have left her alone, let her have her dream of a house and kids and a man who would never put her in this kind of danger.

"We're getting you to a hospital."

"I don't need a hospital for food poisoning. I haven't thrown up that much and I'm not dehydrated."

Will swallowed hard. "It's not the typical food poisoning, kiddo. It's real serious stuff. I called the Coast Guard and they're coming to get you."

"You're kidding." Meg was silent for a long time. "You can't *die* from this. Can you?" she asked, suddenly losing her bravado.

"Not if we can get you to a hospital, which we're doing."

His eyes scanned her features for any sign of panic. "They'll be here in a few hours. Maybe even sooner."

"Then you can still race. You don't need me. Rachel's pretty good at trimming a sail and Thad could help her out."

He didn't give a rat's ass about the race at the moment. "It doesn't matter."

"Tack around," she demanded. "The Coast Guard can find us and you can finish."

"Do you really think I could keep racing knowing you were in a hospital somewhere?" Will wondered fleetingly if he would have kept racing if it had been any other crewmember who'd become inflicted. It didn't matter, Meg wasn't any other crewmember, she was his . . .

She was his.

"Frank's gonna be pissed off big time," she said.

Will didn't even care about that. He didn't care about anything but making Meghan safe, getting her off this cursed boat. "Yeah, well, he'll just have to deal with it, I guess," he said, not even feeling the smallest twinge of guilt. "Anyway, the crew can't win with both of us off the boat."

Meghan smiled. "You're coming with me?"

The thought of being apart from Meghan right now was making his heart ache. "Of course I'm coming with you."

"Can you call Alan for me? Let him know what's happening?"

The pain in his heart took a spike. Of course she'd want to have her fiancé there. Of course. "Sure."

"He's number two on speed dial. My mother is number one."

"What number am I?" he asked, just to make her smile. He really didn't expect to be on her phone at all.

"Big fat zero," she said, then giggled. "Man, I really do feel weird. Maybe it's a good thing you called the Coast Guard."

Will let out a shaking breath. "You breathing okay? That's one of the things to look for."

Meghan took a wonderfully deep breath for him. "Seems to be working just dandy."

"That's good," he said, pressing a kiss to her forehead.

"You're being so nice to me."

Because I love you, you idiot. "I'm always nice to you. I'll be right back, I've got to talk to the crew and let them know what's going on, okay? Then I'll call Alan for you."

"'kay."

When Will reached topside, it was to a boat driving into the wind, heeling sharply, and struggling against an oncoming sea.

"How's she doing?" Tony asked, moving aside to give up the helm to Will.

"You've got to man the helm until the Coast Guard gets here."

"You called the freakin' Coast Guard?" Tony said is disbelief and alarm. "What the hell's wrong with Meg?"

Will called to the rest of the crew and explained the urgency of the situation. Most of them had never heard of PSP and were shocked to discover it could be fatal. Tony turned white when Will said Meg was sick from PSP, because he knew instantly how she'd gotten that way.

"I got those clams from the same distributor I always do," he said, as eight pairs of eyes turned to him. "This is a friggin' nightmare. How's Meg doing?"

Shouting from his spot near the mainsail, Alex explained Meghan's condition, reassuring the crew that she would likely recover. "But we can't take any chances. If it advances quickly, she'd going to be in real trouble."

"I've got to call the restaurant and warn my people," Tony said, looking as if he might be sick. "And no one touch the clam chowder I brought along."

If anyone was disappointed not to finish the race, not a word was said about it, but went back to their duties in solemn silence. The only sounds were the sails snapping, the waves pounding the boat, and Tony's shouts into the phone telling his manager to throw away every clam in the restaurant.

When Will returned to Meghan, she seemed to be the same, and he let out a silent sigh of relief.

"I don't know why you had to come about if the Coast Guard is coming. These waves are pounding *Water Baby*," Meghan said almost sullenly. "My head hurts enough without this." At that moment, the boat slammed into a wave, forcing Meghan to flail her arms ineffectually to stay on the berth.

Will knew she was right, but he'd felt so damn impotent when Alex had made his diagnosis, he wanted to do something to get Meghan help faster. At the moment, they were tacking away from the mainland in an effort to make headway to the west. Four hours of this seemed like a maddeningly long time.

Again he stuck his head out of the companionway. "Tack to the rhumbline," he shouted. "It'll be an easier sail."

Tony nodded his agreement, and within moments Will could feel the boat turning so they moving with the sea pushed by the westerly wind. They were still in dense fog, which was going to make the Coast Guard's job more difficult, and Will prayed the fog would lift as they sailed south. By the time the Coast Guard arrived, it would be night and finding the boat in the fog more difficult. As the boat smoothed out and ran with the waves, Meghan seemed to relax.

"Gonna win," she said, smiling, and Will just wanted to cry. "It's crazy to stop the race, Will. I could understand it if everyone on the boat were sick, but it's just me."

"I told you already we can't win without you," Will said, a bit harsher than he wanted to. He forced a smile when all he really wanted to do was scream in frustration that he couldn't do anything to help her and all she was worried about was the damn race. "Listen, I'm going to try to call Alan. I don't know if we'll get a signal from here. It fades pretty quickly once you get off shore unless you have a booster."

"I do," she managed to say.

"You sure you don't want to talk to him?"

"With the way I sound, it'd just scare him. I don't want him to get worried."

Will stared at her and wondered whether she fully comprehended the gravity of the situation. Stepping toward the bow, he shut the door that divided the main cabin from the forward berths and called Alan.

"Hey, baby." Just the way the guy answered the phone was grating, and Will had to force himself to remember this was a man Meg loved.

"Alan, it's Will."

"Oh, hey, Will. How's everything going? I watched the start of the race on the news. Couldn't see you, though. Sorry I couldn't make it, I had a client . . ."

"Meg's sick. That's why I'm calling you. We've called the Coast Guard and they're picking her up."

"What?"

The signal either sucked, or Alan was panicking.

"Meghan's sick," Will repeated.

"What's wrong?"

"She had some bad clams and has something called PSP. It's potentially serious and we need to get her to a hospital just in case."

"Bad clams?" the other man asked, sounding dumbfounded. "I never understood how she could eat those things. I don't know how many times I told her she'd end up getting sick eating them, but she insisted . . ."

Will gripped the phone hard. "I don't know which station is sending a boat so I don't know where she'll end up. Right now we're east of Gardiners Island, so she might end up in Long Island or Jersey. I just don't know."

"Just how serious is this?" Alan said, his voice moving up in pitch the more agitated he got.

"It's potentially fatal, but Meg seems to be holding up fine." Just saying the words aloud made Will physically ill. "That's why we've got the Coast Guard on the way. We have a physician on board and he's done everything he can for now." Will didn't bother telling Alan that nothing could be done to save her if the disease progressed quickly.

"You've got to be fucking kidding me. From eating clams? Who the hell gave them to her? I swear, if anything happens to her, I'll sue your ass and everyone else involved until you're living on the street."

"You do what you have to," Will said, wishing he could reach through the phone and strangle the guy.

"I want to talk to her."

"Her tongue is numb so she's real hard to understand. She wanted me to call you."

"I want to talk to her. Now."

Will let out a sigh and went back into the main cabin. "Alan wants to talk to you," he said, holding the phone against her ear.

"Hey," she said. She was silent for a long time, listening to whatever it was The Tool was saying. "I've been eating clams my whole life," she said, her words coming out as if she'd just started learning to talk. "I said I've been eating them my whole life."

Meghan shook her head in disgust. "You talk to him. He's too upset."

"Alan. It's Will again."

"What the hell is wrong with her? She sounds like she's been drugged."

Oh, for God's sake. "It's the poisoning. It made her tongue numb. She can't walk well, either."

"Tell him I'm fine," Meghan said, and Will smiled because her speech was so difficult to understand, no one would think she was "fine."

"She says she's fine," he said, winking at Meg, who smiled.

"She's not fine. I knew I shouldn't have allowed her to go on this race. That was my instinct. I should have followed my instinct instead of letting her get on that boat with a bunch of useless weekend warriors."

Will felt his blood grow hot. "You're upset right now."

"You're goddamn right I'm upset. My fiancée is on a boat in the middle of nowhere, sick, maybe dying and I'm supposed to be calm?"

"Of course not," Will said. *But you don't have to be*

such a prick. He used every bit of willpower he possessed not to hang up on him.

"Let me know where she's being taken."

"Will do."

"And Will, if she dies, I'll blame you and I'll make you pay. That's a promise."

Will felt his self-control threaten to snap, not because of the man's ridiculous statement, but because it wasn't the first time someone laid a death on his shoulders. He squeezed his eyes shut as he closed the phone, trying to rid himself of the memory, but it came anyway.

He'd been ten years old, coming home from school and slightly confused when he saw his father's battered old car in the dirt driveway that led to their one-bedroom house. Will had liked the little place at first, and his father had called it a bachelor's pad, even though the red cottage was little more than a shack. It had a tiny kitchen, a living room big enough for their worn-out couch that served as Will's bed, a bathroom with a shower, and one small bedroom. But the yard was big and filled with huge trees that Will thought would be perfect for a treehouse. Best of all, that house was only two streets away from the bay and he could actually catch a glimpse of it from the house's only door.

Will lived with his father because his mother took off when he was three. He couldn't remember her face, but sometimes he'd have a dream about a woman and he thought maybe it was his mother. His father didn't have a single picture of her and if he did, Will had never seen it. The only thing he kept was the note she'd left behind. He'd put it in a frame and wherever they lived, hung it in the kitchen. Dad wouldn't talk about her, never mentioned that she existed, and if it wasn't for that note with its loopy writing, Will wouldn't have known she existed. His mother was a phantom, until that day he came home from school and his father was sitting at the table with a half-empty bottle of whiskey and a newspaper clipping in front of him.

"Hey, Dad."

His father shoved the clipping toward Will. "Mother's dead."

That's when Will realized that even though he tried not to think about it, he'd always held out hope that his mother would come home for him, that she'd scoop him up and say she was sorry for that awful note she'd left behind and kiss him. Even though he was ten and way too big for that stuff, he thought about it sometimes, way back in his mind where he let things like that lie. He reached for the clipping and read the obituary that someone had sent to his father and felt his heart sort of squish and shrivel up inside him.

"Car accident out west. California," he father said, and that's when Will realized his father had been crying, that the red-rimmed eyes weren't caused only by the liquor. "She never wanted this," he said, waving a hand around their dump-of-a-house.

Will stupidly said, "She never even saw this place."

Rage filled his father's face as he stood up violently, the chair he'd been sitting in crashing to the linoleum floor. "She never wanted me. And she sure as hell never wanted you. You're the reason she left me. I wouldn't get rid of you, so she left.

And she wouldn't be dead right now if she'd stayed. She wouldn't have left and she wouldn't have died."

Will stood there, frozen, scared out of his mind. He'd seen his father angry before, but this was different. There was a kind of madness in his eyes and for the first time he was afraid his father was going to hit him. He stood still, barely breathing, wishing he could disappear, as slowly his father's eyes cleared and the madness was gone.

His father looked around the room, his bleary eyes finally spotting the chair he'd been sitting in lying on the floor. He picked it up and sat down, burying his head in his hands. "She's not coming back now. Not now."

Will watched his father sob for a few seconds, loud, ugly, embarrassing sounds, before running outside, running, running until he got to the small beach near his house. He stared out at the bay, at a single-sailed boat gliding through the water, feeling the cool air buffet his fevered skin. And he wished with all his heart that he was on that boat, sailing away from this place, away from the horrible truth that his mother hadn't wanted him and his father probably didn't either. He stood there forever watching that boat as it nearly sailed out of view.

"You sail?"

Will had turned and saw Frank for the first time, standing on the beach behind him.

"What did Alan say?"

Will was dragged away from his memories by the sound of Meg's voice, and he let out a shaky breath. "Well, I don't think I'm up for a conversation with your mother. Is there anyway I can call your father directly?"

Meghan laughed. "He was upset, huh?"

"He said he shouldn't have allowed you to go on the race," he said, knowing that would irk Meg.

"Not his choice," she mumbled.

"But once you're married. All that obey bullshit. You're just going to have to get used to it."

Meghan rolled her eyes. "They don't say 'obey' anymore. At least I don't think they do. Anyway, Alan knows he can't control me. And he never said anything about me not going on the race. He encouraged me to."

Will had his doubts, but he wasn't about to argue the point at the moment. "Don't you think your mother should talk to, say, Rachel?"

"Will, just call her. She doesn't hate you anymore now that we're not dating." She smiled smugly at him.

"Shit." He dialed her mother, dreading the chirpy hello he was bound to hear. "Hello, honey." Yup, there is was.

"Mrs. Rose, it's Will Scott."

"Oh. Will. Where's Meghan?"

"That's why I'm calling you. Right now, Meg's fine." He turned to Meghan and said, "Tell her you're fine."

"I'm fine, Mom," she said.

"That wasn't Meg," her mother said.

"She's sick and we're getting the Coast Guard out here to bring her to the hospital."

"Oh, my God."

"She ate some bad clams and she's sick and Dr. Youklis thinks it would be good to err on the side of safety and get her to a hospital."

"Oh, my God, what did you do to her?"

"Well, I didn't force-feed her bad clams, if that's what you're implying," Will said, anger surging through him at her accusatory tone. What the hell was with all these people accusing him of killing the woman he loved? He was a good, decent guy who'd never hurt anything intentionally in his life.

"Mom," Meg called out. "I'm fine. Will didn't feed me clams." Meg started laughing and could tell by the look on Will's face she was lucky he didn't strangle her.

"Let me talk to the doctor," Meghan's mother said, and Will sighed.

He called up to Alex and explained the situation. After the good doctor outlined exactly what Will had told her, Meghan's mother seemed somewhat pacified.

With the phone back in his hands and a headache pressing against his eyes, Will explained again that he wasn't aware yet where Meghan would end up.

"Call me when you hear anything. Have you called Alan? As her fiancé, he really should be aware of the situation."

"I've already talked to him," Will said, taking a small delight in the fact that she was the second call.

"Oh. Good. I'm sure you've met him." She let the sentence hang like a question, and he could fill in her unspoken inference: I'm sure you've met him and found him to be as wonderful and charming as I have.

"Yes."

"Well, then. You understand things."

"I've always understood things, Mrs. Rose." Will glared at Meghan, who was laughing at his pain. "We'll be in touch." He snapped the phone shut and tossed it onto the opposite berth as if it were contaminated.

"One thing I never did understand was why your mother hates me so much," Will said. Maybe he was doomed to be hated by all maternal figures. Equally baffling was why she liked Alan so much, but he kept silent on that mystery.

"She didn't think you were husband material. And she was right."

Will didn't have the strength—or the ammunition—to fight that point. Will had always thought of himself as married with kids and living in a house with a dog and a white picket fence. Someday. He'd never planned to just go on forever, young and free and happy. Except he wasn't happy anymore and he knew why, but now it was too late. He was husband material, all right, but only if Meg was the wife part of the deal.

"I'm going topside for a while." He looked at his watch. It had only been an hour since he'd called the Coast Guard and they had at least another three hours before Meg could be taken aboard and more hours before she actually reached a hospital. "How are you feeling?"

"About the same," Meg said. "I can still move my arms and legs, they just don't do what I want them to do. Watch this. I'm going to scratch my nose."

"Is it itchy?" Will asked, smiling down at her.

"Yes."

He watched as she almost drunkenly tried to find her nose, and he would have been scared to death if she hadn't started giggling. "Here. Let me. Where's the itch?"

"On the side." She waited. "The other side." Then she closed her eyes in bliss. "That's the spot."

"I always was good at finding your spots."

Her eyes snapped open. "You were okay."

He kissed her nose. "I'll be back down in a few. Call me if anything changes."

"Bye," she said in a small voice, and he wondered if she was really frightened beneath all those giggles.

"I'll be right back."

She smiled at him and he marveled briefly how he'd existed the past two years without seeing that smile every day. And he wondered how he'd live the rest of his life without it.

Chapter Eleven

It was happening again. The heat, the raw lust was raging through him and all he was doing was sitting across from her as she struggled to keep the boat going at top speed. What the hell was going on with him?

Thad was a guy who found certain women hot and he got turned on easily enough like any normal guy. But this wasn't normal and he was getting a little freaked out by it. Maybe he had a thing for lesbians and didn't even know it.

Maybe he could convert her, like Tony suggested. Tony, who was having trouble steering the boat on a pure reach because his eyes kept wandering to Rachel's chest. It wasn't because she was wearing anything revealing. She was dressed pretty much like she always had been with nylon pants and a rain slicker. Like all of them, she was wearing a PFD, which was hardly figure-flattering for a woman.

But they knew what was underneath now: a luscious, sexy woman.

"Tony, keep your eyes on the job," Thad said.

"What for? We're quittin' anyway. What's the point?"

Thad knew there really wasn't a point, but he didn't like Tony staring at Rachel the way he wanted to but had too much self-control to. "You never know. It doesn't hurt to keep us going as fast as possible." To demonstrate, he adjusted the mainsail a hair.

"I don't know why we can't just let the Coast Guard pick Meg up and then go on our merry way. We can still win without her. Or at least just finish the race."

Will showed his face in the cockpit at that moment and Tony's face turned ruddy. Thad had known Will a long time and he'd never seen the murderous expression in his friend's eyes that he saw now.

"Because I'm going with her. Because if she's going to die, I don't want her to be alone," Will said, his voice low and harsh.

"She's not going to die," Rachel said, and her soft voice made Thad feel another ridiculous surge of lust. God sure was having a fun time with him with this little joke. She sounded so sure of herself until she asked, "Is she?"

"Probably not. But I don't want to take any chances. You still feeling okay?"

"I'm perfect," she said, as if she wished she was the one below. "I never thought I'd be happy to be hungover."

It was growing dark and was time for a shift change. Normally, the crew would have changed to a larger jib because the wind had died down with nightfall. But no one mentioned doing it and Will didn't even seem to care whether they had any sails up at all. He kept looking at his watch and grimacing, then staring down the hatch as if deciding whether or not to check on Meg. Thad had a pretty good feeling that Will had never fully gotten over Meg, and now he was sure of it. The man he knew would have thrown a crewmember on the Coast Guard boat without slowing down, then headed toward the finish line as fast as he could get the boat to sail. This year especially, Will had been almost maniacally driven to win the race. Thad knew it was all about Frank and getting that Lighthouse Trophy in his dying hands, and he couldn't have dreamed up a scenario where Will would stop a race.

Thad watched his friend stare out onto the darkening horizon, not bothering to look at the sails, not checking their position, not studying the Gulf Stream data he had, and realized he was so in love with that women in the cabin he could barely think. Knowing Will as he did, Thad had a feeling Meg would never know how much Will loved her.

"Everyone get something to eat?" he asked, as if remembering he still had a role on the boat.

"I think so." Thad then boomed the question out to the crew. "Yup."

"When the Coast Guard gets here I'm putting you in charge, Thad. Bring the boat back to Newport. No need putting the crew at risk for a race we can't win."

No one argued with that, because it was true. Maybe they could win without Meg. Maybe. But there was no way in hell they could win a Newport-Bermuda without Will's navigation expertise. Hell, they'd probably end up flying toward Portugal on a northward current.

Thad left the mainsail and moved to sit next to Will. "How is she, really?"

He watched Will swallow hard. "She's the same. Can hardly move or talk, which is scary as shit. But she's not getting any worse."

The doctor jumped into the cockpit and went down below and Will stared at the companionway until he reemerged two minutes later, walking directly over to the two men.

"I may be crazy, but I think she's over the worst of it. From what I know about PSP, it progresses rapidly. I don't see any progression and I'm fairly certain her coordination is getting better."

"What do you mean, 'fairly certain'?"

"Subtle changes, Will. She's not out of the woods yet, but I don't think it's going to progress to a point where she'll need a respirator. Another hour or so and I'll know better."

Alex went back on the deck to sit with the rest of the crew and Will let out a long sigh that could only be relief. "Another hour," he said, mostly to himself.

"Then what?"

"If she's better, we're changing that goddamn jib and moving our asses out of this dead air."

Thad grinned.

"Good news?" Rachel asked, and his smile faded when he looked at her face. If she wasn't the most beautiful woman on this earth, he didn't know who was. How could it be that for six years she hadn't been anything but Rachel, and now she was Rachel-the-Goddess? It was more than her losing a few pounds, because it wasn't like she was a twig now. She was still a big woman, just big in all the right places. Like her ass. And her breasts.

And her heart.

Thad cringed inwardly at the thought, knowing he hadn't really given a crap about any woman's heart in a very long time. Oh, yeah, God was up there having a good ol' laugh.

Meg felt her nose itch, so she did the Bewitched wiggle, hoping that would ease the tickle. No such luck. *Think, girl, think. Move your arm, bend your elbow, take your index finger and . . . ahhhh.* She scratched her nose a bit awkwardly, but was thrilled that she'd actually been able to accomplish the task.

Then she tried to clap her hands, laughing when she missed the first time. It was the weirdest feeling she'd ever had in her life, not being able to control her own limbs. She moved her leg up and down, then crossed them at the ankles, then reached up and poked her eyes instead of her nose. Oh, well.

Meg was still slightly nauseous, but her headache was much better. Slowly she pulled herself up to a sitting position. The cabin swirled a bit for her, but after about five seconds, her vision cleared. So far, so good. If she could get herself up the companionway steps and poke her head out the opening, Meg knew she could convince Will to cancel the Coast Guard and get this tug moving. She could feel the boat cutting sluggishly through the sea and it was driving her crazy. The crew was chatting above her head, Tony was manning the helm, and she could just make out Will's silhouette against the nighttime sky sitting next to Thad. And all the while the rest of the fleet had probably found some good air and were flying toward Bermuda and that Lighthouse Trophy. No f-ing way she was going to let that happen.

Meghan pushed herself up, clutching an overhead rail with all her strength as another small wave of dizziness hit her. Suddenly that song from *Santa Claus Is Comin' to Town* was playing in her head: Put one step in front of the other and soon you'll be walkin' 'cross the floor. Put one step in front of the other and soon you'll be walkin' out the door. She started to hum the tune as she took a couple of baby steps. Thankfully, her legs were starting to do what she told them to. She wouldn't be running any marathons, but she was actually walking, something not two hours ago she couldn't have managed. With a wild grab, and a lucky one if she was honest, Meghan gripped the railing on the steps leading to the companionway and willed herself to walk up the first two. When her head was finally showing, she started laughing at the pure joy that she wasn't going to die.

"Hey, Will," she called out. "Let's get this tug boat moving. What do you say?"

Chapter Twelve

Will stared at Meg, his relief at seeing her standing in the companionway so profound he couldn't speak for a few long seconds.

"Come on, Will, get the number one jib up," she said, in a voice still slightly slurred, but so close to normal that Will smiled.

"Doc," he called, his voice booming into the foggy night.

Alex jumped down into the cockpit, his eyes widening when he saw Meg standing in the doorway. "It's safe to say the worst is over," he said, turning to Will, who couldn't get the grin off his face. "She won't be any good on the boat, though, for at least part of the race."

"Says you," Meg said with spunk, but Will knew with one look that Meg wasn't as well as she was pretending to be.

"Hold off on everything, guys," he said, as he moved down the companionway, helping Meg down on the way. She was shaking with the effort to appear normal and her skin was bathed with sweat. She sagged against him right before he set her on the berth, and his heart skipped a beat. "Little liar," he said gently.

"I am better. Just not all better," she said, a mutinous look on her face. "Cancel the Coast Guard, Will."

Will got down his haunches so he was eye level with her and studied her face, looking for any sign that she was worsening. Just because she had the willpower to haul herself up the companionway didn't mean she was getting better; it simply meant she was one stubborn woman.

"Scratch your nose," he demanded.

Meg screwed up her face in concentration and he just about lost it right there. He loved this woman so much, it hurt, literally hurt his heart to watch her struggle with something so simple. But she did it, first try, and smiled triumphantly.

"I couldn't have done that two hours ago. Heck, one hour ago." She proceeded to name body parts and drunkenly point to them with a fair amount of accuracy. When she got to her lips, she pressed her index finger on her sexy mouth and looked up and Will, God knew he didn't want to, but he stared at her mouth then stared into her eyes, and he bent his head. With restraint he didn't know he had, Will laid the gentlest kiss on her lips, pressing so lightly he hardly felt the contact because he was so damn afraid she'd push him away and hate him. He would swear he didn't move, but she must have, because before he knew it, they were kissing, really kissing, and she was letting out those sweet little sounds that had haunted him in his sleep for two years. Sounds he never thought he'd hear again.

Will pulled away before he did something stupid, like push his tongue into her mouth and pull her closer and drag her into the forward berth so he could see a little more of her.

"I won't apologize for that," he said.

Meg looked away. "Must be the fever."

"You don't have a fever."

Her brows drew together as if she didn't like his response.

"Meg."

She finally looked at him, and her eyes were so sad, it nearly finished off his broken heart.

"We're friends. Old friends. You might have died and now you're better. I kissed you because I'm glad my old friend isn't dying," Will said, knowing he should be nominated for sainthood because he was trying to make her feel better about their almost-innocent kiss.

"I don't remember you being so nice," she said softly.

"I wasn't. I'm not." When she laughed, he smiled, wishing he didn't love her as much as he did. If he didn't, he'd pull her against him and ravish her the way he wanted to. But she was feeling guilty again, he knew it, and her next words only confirmed it.

"I should call Alan. Do you think I'm talking well enough not to scare him?"

It was Will's turn to look away, because he couldn't stand to see the look in her eyes when she talked about the man she was going to marry. "Sure." He looked around for the cell phone, finding it lying on the berth where'd he'd thrown it after talking to her mother. "You'd better call your mother too and let her know that my evil plot to kill you was thwarted."

Meg let out a small laugh and held out her hand for the cell phone, before withdrawing it. "I'm better, but I don't think I can dial the right speed dial number and I'd hate to call the pizza guy."

Will pressed the one and handed the phone to Meghan. "It's not going through. Can I use the satellite? I promise I won't take too long. I know how expensive they are to use."

Will grabbed the satellite phone Frank rented for emergencies. "What's the number?" he asked, and punched in the numbers Meg dictated to him. He didn't want to listen, so he went up to the cockpit and asked the doctor to give Meg one more exam before he called off the Coast Guard and started racing again.

"She's talking to her fiancé and her mother right now. I don't want to make any calls until you take a look at her. But she's definitely improving."

"She's talking to her fiancé," Alex said, his voice strangely toneless, and Will raised his brows in question.

"Not that I'm a voyeur or anything, but I get a pretty good view of the cabin from my spot on the rail."

"Just an innocent kiss between friends," Will said, feeling his face heat.

Alex chuckled, and said under his breath as he made his way to the cabin, "Wish I had friends like that."

Maybe some women would be touched by the hysterical concern Alan had showed when she called to tell him she was feeling better and continuing on with the race. But Meg had never in her adult life been talked to as if she were a child who was incapable of making a decision. It was their first heated argument, the first time Meg had considered that she might be about to marry an ass.

"You are not to finish that race. If you do, I will not come to Bermuda. That's a promise. What the hell is wrong with those people? You're sick and should be in a hospital," he'd said, getting that high-pitched voice he got when he was riled up. She'd never heard it directed at her before. It was as grating as a fingernail on a chalkboard, and she told him that.

"Your cute comments are not going to change the fact that you are acting irresponsibly," he said, his voice clipped as if he were making an effort not to scream at her.

Meghan had taken a deep breath to calm down, because she knew he was upset because he was so worried and that was endearing. Sort of. "I know you're worried, Alan, but treating me like a child is not going to work. Making threats is not going to work either. I think if you just take the time to calm down, you'll realize that continuing on with the race is the best course of action. We can win this thing and now that I'm getting better, there's no reason to quit."

She'd heard his breath coming in short spurts, like a bull staring at a red cape. "I don't care about the friggin' race. If you continue on, I'll have to seriously consider our future together."

Meghan felt the blood drain from her face. "You can't be serious. That is unfair *and* irrational. You don't mean it, Alan."

"I'm angry," he said, and she could tell by his tone that he was about to soften his not-so-veiled threat. "And you don't seem to give a damn about me and how I feel. How would you like it if our positions were reversed?"

He was calming down, and Meghan let a sigh of relief. "I'd respect your decision because you're an adult."

"Then respect my decision now," he'd said, the pitch of his voice going up a notch.

"Okay," Meghan said with utmost patience, "You're not getting my argument. You're supposed to respect *my* decision to stay in the race because I'm a thinking, intelligent adult."

After a long silence, he'd said, "If you don't come home now, I think we have a problem."

Meghan felt her face heat with anger. "Then I guess we have a problem."

He clicked off without saying good-bye.

"Jerk," she said to the silent phone.

After she ended the call, she wondered if perhaps she *was* being foolish to stay in the race. Chances were the Coast Guard was more than halfway to the boat; she could just get on and get to a hospital. Maybe she could convince Will to stay on the boat and keep racing, especially now that it was clear she was getting better.

But if she was getting better, why get off the boat? Why disappoint the crew who had been looking forward to this race for two years?

She dialed her mother, happily surprised she was coordinated enough to do that. She was definitely getting better. Screw Alan.

"Will?"

"It's me, Mom."

"You still sound strange to me. But better. Please tell me you're getting better."

"I am and I'm staying in the race."

"You sure?" her mother asked, and Meghan smiled. Her mother had never been happy about her bohemian sail-racing lifestyle, but she'd never been heavy-handed about her unease.

"I'm sure. I don't know how much help I'm going to be for the next day or so, but if I get off the boat Will says he will too and then the race is over. I don't want to do that to the crew."

"Why would Will get off?"

"To be with me. He's been really sweet about the whole thing."

"Oh, God," her mother said, and Meghan could hear the dread in her voice.

"Don't 'oh, God' me, Mom. Could you do me a favor? When I called Alan, he was a little crazy about my staying on the boat. Could you run some interference for me, say you support my decision because you know I'm an adult and can make decisions for myself?"

Her mother let out a soft laugh. "He didn't try to strong-arm you, did he?"

"He practically threatened to break up with me if I finished the race."

"He didn't," her mother gasped.

"Yup. Guess he didn't realize he's not the boss of me."

"No one's ever been the boss of you, dear. Not even when you were little."

"I know you tried," Meghan said, and nodded to Alex, who'd just come down the steps to the cabin. "Anyway, I've never heard Alan so upset or so . . ."

"Unreasonable," her mother supplied.

"Exactly. I suppose I understand his concern and I know it means he loves me, but right now I'm too mad at him to appreciate the reasons why he was such a jerk."

Her mother let out a long breath. "I'll call him if that's what you want."

"Let him stew for a little while. You should have heard the way he was talking to me."

"He was just worried. That shows how much he loves you." Her mother could defend just about anything Alan did.

"If he loved me, he'd understand how important this race is to me."

"I didn't even know it was that important to you and I'm your mother."

"Maybe I didn't realize either until it was nearly taken away. I'm lovin' this, Mom. I really needed to get back out on a boat."

There was a long pause. "Will is . . ."

"Keeping his distance," she lied, refusing to think about that kiss.

"Okay. I'll wait until tomorrow morning before I call him. Do him good to suffer a bit, right? Anyway, it's late."

Meghan looked at the clock. It was nearly midnight.

"Bye, Mom."

"Bye. I'm so glad you're feeling better."

"Me too."

Meghan shut off the satellite phone and looked to Alex. "I'm even better than the last time you were down here," she said, then demonstrated by clapping her hands together. "See?"

Alex got all doctory in front of her and made her go through a series of exercises, including some small motor skills, before pronouncing her on the mend. "I can tell Will to cancel the Coast Guard. But you have to stay below until the morning. You're still not coordinated enough to get topside safely."

"Sure." Meghan felt as if she'd just been handed a winning lottery ticket.

Alex called up to Will, "Hey, Skipper, call off the Coast Guard and let's get this boat moving."

The crew let out a collective shout and within seconds Will was in the cabin and reaching for the radio to cancel the rescue. After he'd taken care of the Coast Guard, he turned to Meghan, a grin a mile wide on his face.

"You do know that we are going to win this race now. I feel it."

Meghan rolled her eyes. "You always feel it," she said.

Will laughed. "You'll see," he said. "Now get some rest in the forward berth and get better. I have a ton of work to do to get us back in this thing and you're in my way."

"Guess the coddling is over," Meghan said.

"Damn right." She could feel Will watching her as she made her way slowly to the front of the boat.

"Hey, kiddo."

She turned to look back.

"Glad you're better. Right?"

Will had never been a man of many words, but the way he looked at her at that moment sent a small shiver down her spine. She wasn't sure she liked the way things were ending up, all topsy-turvy with Alan being a jerk and Will being the hero. Then again, Will had never been a jerk, never said a mean thing to her.

He simply hadn't loved her.

* * *

The next morning Meghan pulled herself rather easily up to the cockpit and let a feeling of elation wash over her. The ocean air was still blustery, the seas moderate, and the wind jamming from the west.

"Wow," Meg said. "Where the hell are we?"

"I'll know better in about ten minutes," Will said. That was when all the boats started calling in their positions. "We've been in this wind all night. But everyone else could have been, too. We had some ground to pick up after the clam debacle." He glared at her in mock anger. "But I think it actually helped us get into the wind. Boats to the east aren't getting this. We're flying along a low pressure system."

Meghan automatically turned to look at the sails, smiling at Rachel, who gave her a look of helplessness that she'd been assigned to the jib.

"Tell me you're well enough to take over."

Meghan flexed her hands. "I'm a lot better. I'll take over for an hour."

"Half hour," Will said. "Rachel, I need you on the mainsail anyway."

Rachel happily gave up the line to Meghan and took over for Thad, whose one good arm was beginning to shake from overuse.

"Tony, take over at the helm for five minutes while I call in our position," Will yelled, then heaved himself down to the cabin to the navigation station. Meghan watched as he pulled out the global positioning system and marked a chart laid out on the galley table. He turned on the radio to the right frequency and waited for the boats to start calling in. Within minutes, Will was furiously writing down positions the other boats called in. Then he marked all the positions on the chart and stared hard at the table for a long moment before sticking his head out the companionway.

"We're ahead of *Hurricane* by at least fifteen miles," he shouted, and the crew roared its approval. *Hurricane* and *Water Baby* had almost identical ratings, so beating Sanderson was key to winning the Lighthouse Trophy. Under the race's rating system, *Water Baby* would have to cross the line within two minutes of *Hurricane* in order to beat them on corrected time. The fact that they were ahead of the other boat was the best news possible, especially because *Water Baby* always handled the Gulf Stream better.

"How the hell did we get ahead of them?" Meghan asked.

"Clearly it was the fine jib trimming," Rachel said, pretending to be offended by Meghan's disbelief.

Meghan laughed. "I wasn't commenting on your skills as a trimmer and you know it. I mean we lost all kinds of time. How'd we get it back?"

"We hit this low, which we wouldn't have if we hadn't slowed down. Everyone to the east of us is sitting in ten knot winds and we're flying along this front with twenty-five knot winds. I told you, Meg, this is the year."

He moved to the helm, practically lighting up the dull morning around him with his pure joy. It had been a long time since Meghan had seen anyone as happy as Will was at this moment.

"See? The clams saved the day," Meghan said.

Will gave her a dark look, only making Meghan laugh aloud.

Just then, Meghan heard a tearing sound above the noise of the wind and the sea and looked up to see a huge rip in the mainsail. "Crap."

"Bring 'er down," shouted Will, even though the two college kids were already on the job. To an outsider it might have looked like complete mayhem on the deck, but it was well-tuned, finely honed and choreographed mayhem. Tony jumped into the cabin to get the spare mainsail and within minutes the torn sail was down, the new sail up, and they were sailing at top speed. Meghan couldn't help but think that all that monotonous sail-changing practice that everyone was groaning about before the race had paid off big. The boat hardly slowed down before the new mainsail was pulled up.

Meghan looked again at Will. God, he was amazing standing at the helm, the wind whipping his hair, his eyes hard and intense on the sails in front of him. And in those eyes was a look of fierce happiness. He looked over to Meghan and smiled and her heart did a crazy little flip that was as startling as it was unwanted. She vowed then and there to keep her eyes where they belonged: facing forward into the wind.

Chapter Thirteen

"The Sox won," Rachel said, referring to her beloved Boston Red Sox.

"Oh, yeah?"

Rachel frowned. "Ever since they finally won the World Series, no one seems to care whether they win or lose."

"We care. We just don't live and die over every game anymore."

Rachel shrugged and tried to come up with another safe topic to talk about, even though all she could think about was how much she wished she hadn't gotten so drunk the night of the party. If she hadn't, maybe she'd have gotten that kiss in and who knew?

Sure, Rach, you'd be talking about wedding plans and how many babies you were going to have together and whether you were going to live in Maine or Rhode Island. If she had gone through with that kiss, Rachel figured that Thad wouldn't be sitting next to her at all, and suddenly she was glad she'd thrown up instead of thrown herself at him.

They sat next to each other on the rail, close

enough so their shoulders knocked together when the boat chopped into a wave. Below, a few of the crew were trying to get some needed sleep. Will would not let anyone get to the point of exhaustion, especially with the stream coming. It was promising to be a faster race than expected and he needed his crew in top form.

"Remember the time it took us more than a week to cross the line?" Rachel asked.

"I remember you refusing to go below to sleep," Thad said.

"I'm sorry, but the stench of unwashed male bodies wasn't something that makes a girl want to sleep." There, she sounded normal, like a normal woman flirting with a man. "If I remember correctly, you were the ripest of the bunch."

"I was the only one who washed up in the sea water," Thad said, and Rachel's cheeks burned red because she remembered that suddenly, the way Thad had stripped down to birthday suit and poured a bucket of water over his head. She remembered every gorgeous detail of his body, the way the water ran in rivulets down his torso, the way he shook his head like a dog and a drop touched her lip and she couldn't stop herself from darting out her tongue to taste it.

"Oh, yeah," she said, her voice soft. Thad gave her a sharp look and she looked away, praying he couldn't read the lust in her eyes. All she had to do was sit next to him and she was aroused. It was a sickness, an obsession. And this year, she was going to do something about it.

"I'm in therapy, you know," she said abruptly.

"Oh?"

"It's all self-esteem stuff. Beauty on the inside

first. It's a package, you know? You can't lose weight and get in shape if you still hate the person inside."

Thad grunted. "Makes sense. But you don't really hate yourself, do you?"

"Maybe not hate. Dislike, I suppose. I am painfully shy."

"Not when you drink," he said, grinning.

"Ha ha. Wouldn't you say that's a problem if I can only be myself when I drink too much?"

"Not if you're as hot as that when you do," he said, then looked sharply out at sea as if realized what he'd just said and regretted it.

"You think I'm hot?" she couldn't stop herself from asking, from demanding that he say it again, because it felt so nice to hear, especially from Thad's lips.

Thad shook his head. "I shouldn't have said that."

"I won't sue for sexual harassment, if that's what you're worried about."

"No. It's just that . . . I shouldn't have said that."

Rachel took a deep breath. "You know, Thad, you're a nice guy, but as stupid as a brick."

Thad watched as Rachel heaved herself up off the rail and headed toward the bow to sit next to Tony. And damn if it didn't look as though she was flirting with him. Did lesbians flirt with men? Did they want men to think they were hot? Did they lean into you when they were drunk and look at you with drowsy, sexy eyes? Thad closed his eyes and was beginning to think maybe Rachel was right—he was as dumb as a brick. All the years of assuming Rachel wasn't into guys may have been a product of her incredible shyness.

Thad leaned back to try to catch her attention,

feeling his gut clench when he heard her laughing over something Tony said. Tony could be a class A jerk, but he was amazingly lucky with women—unless he was all talk. Guys like Tony liked to talk and Thad had wondered on more than one occasion if Tony was telling tales. But he didn't like him nuzzling up next to Rachel, not with her hair pulled back in a ponytail and her cheeks flushed from the wind.

"Hey, ladies," Will called just as the sun was setting. "Water temperature's just gone up ten degrees. We're in the stream."

Three hours later, the only thing on anyone's mind was whether or not the boat could sustain the kind of punishment it was getting without breaking apart. The sails were reefed in an effort to slow the boat down as it pounded relentlessly into the powerful waves the Gulf Stream was famous for. Pushed along by twenty-knot winds, the boat slammed into waves, jarring the boat and the bodies on board until everyone felt as if they'd been in a two-hour barroom brawl. In the darkness Will could barely make out Meghan, but he could hear the clicking of the winch and knew she was constantly adjusting the sails in an effort to get the most of the current and the wind without putting the boat and crew into danger. He was only letting her take one-hour shifts now, which were still exhausting her. The sound of the hull hitting the waves was deafening and could be frightening for anyone who'd never done it. As seasoned as this crew was, Will could sense a feeling of, perhaps not fear, but deep concern as wave after wave pummeled the boat. No boat had ever broken up during the Newport-Bermuda, but he had watched one split in half off Hawaii. It was an image he'd never forgotten.

To make matters worse, a clap of thunder resounded seemingly over their heads and the wind, already blowing, wailed down upon them.

"Reef the mainsail," Will said calmly, and watched as the crew jumped and tied down the sail, leaving little more than a large triangle of Kevlar. The click-click of the sails being adjusted was music to him above the howling of the wind.

"Jesus, we're flying," he whispered, his hands gripping the large wheel as he felt the sting of rain against his face. Meghan's hands flew back and forth, making small adjustments. Will knew she wasn't in racing shape, knew her arms must feel like they were about to fall off, especially given her weakened condition. But he needed her now and she doggedly stayed at her post, her eyes on the jib, her arms shaking with the tension of constantly adjusting the sails to maximize their performance.

"You okay, Meg?" he called out.

She nodded, not even bothering to turn to him. She probably didn't have the energy to talk. Will watched the sails, watched the sea, and watched Meghan struggle as best he could in the darkness. They were just an hour into their shift; half the crew was below trying to get some sleep. Even as exhausted as they were, sleeping in this kind of sea was nearly impossible. Around him, the sea and sky had blended into one black maw. The only thing that distinguished water from the horizon were whitecaps foretelling the rough seas. It started pouring, rain beating down on them in torrents, making visibility worse. He could hardly see the jib, and wondered how the hell Meghan could. The click-click continued, and he figured she was making adjustments by instinct because she sure as hell couldn't see anything.

Everything was a roar: the sea, the rain, the wind. He called out to one of the college kids to secure a line that was dragging in the water and couldn't even hear his own voice. Instead, he hand-signaled to the kid, who limberly scuttled down to the railing that was slicing through the water and grabbed the line, securing it.

He looked up and saw a huge wave right before it hit. "Hold on," he screamed, right before the front of the boat plowed in the mammoth wave, stopping the boat for a split second before it washed over the boat, soaking the crew and pushing with such force, if they hadn't been tethered to the boat, he would have lost half his crew.

"Everyone okay? All accounted for?" he yelled, and Tony did a quick head count.

"All here," he called, then something changed in his expression, something horrible and paralyzing. "Will, Meghan."

It was only a split second in time before he saw her lying on the deck by his feet struggling to get up, but in that split second when he looked where she'd been and didn't see her, he just about died. And when he did see her, trying to reach her station, so exhausted she could barely sit up, never mind man the jib, he lost it. Really lost it.

"Tony. Take the helm."

He didn't know how he got her down to the cabin, didn't remember undoing her safety tether, picking her up and dragging her to the bow and throwing her onto the pile of sails where some of the worn-out crewmembers slept. But she was there, looking up at him, her blond hair plastered to her face. The hull continued to slam into the stream's square waves, but the violence of the storm was over.

"Don't you ever do that again," he said in a harsh whisper, his eyes darting to the sleeping crew. His voice shook; hell, his entire body shook.

"I just got knocked over by a wave," she said calmly, as if he was the lunatic.

And of course, he was. He stood there panting, looking at her, loving her desperately, and feeling so angry with himself he wanted to scream.

"I'm okay," she said. "I'm a little weak. That's all."

Will wiped the rain off his face. "I'm sorry. I overreacted." He held out his hand to lift her up and she took it without hesitation, a slight smile on her lips.

"Some day you're going to explain to me what just happened, right?"

Will looked down at her face, at her oblivious expression, and all he could think of was that he wanted her to love him as much as he loved her. A little cruel voice reminded him that she had. She had.

"I thought you'd gone over. I thought you weren't tethered."

They heard a shout from above and Will gave himself a mental shake. He was in the middle of a critical point of a critical race and he was below lamenting his love life. What the hell was wrong with him?

"You stay below for twenty minutes and rest," he said, pushing her back down, this time gently and with a smile. "You're no good to me exhausted and I need you."

"Yes, sir," she said, but he could tell she didn't

want a rest; she wanted to be up on that deck with the sails under her control.

"Twenty minutes."

When Will left, Meghan sat amongst the sails feeling slightly bemused but surprisingly not angry. She didn't like being manhandled and ordered about, and Will had just done both. But for some reason she couldn't explain, this time she didn't mind. Maybe it was the crazed look on his face, or maybe it was the gentle way he'd pushed her down to the sail bags the second time and told her to rest. She didn't know why she'd reacted so differently to Alan's demands that she leave the race. Meghan respected Will's decision-making on the boat almost without question. Perhaps that was it. Will *was* the boss of her on the boat. She supposed if he'd tried the same tactic on shore, she would have reacted completely differently.

Meghan pushed the heels of her hands against her eyes. She did not want to think about Alan right now and how in the past week she'd kissed Will twice and not made love to Alan at all. The boat slammed into a wave and she winced, waiting to see if whoever was at the sails was slowing the boat down. If they hit another wave like that, she was going topside and to hell with Captain Will. She almost hoped the boat did slam into the next wave. Behind her, Gary was snoring loudly, as he always did; he was famous for his ability to sleep through just about anything, including the jarring waves in the Gulf Stream.

Meghan knew she'd never sleep, so she lay down and stared blindly at the ceiling listening to Gary's snores, the boat and the infrequent noise of the crew. If Gary was sleeping, that meant Will or Tony was at the jib and that worked for her. They were both terrific trimmers. She had to admit she needed this break. Her arms felt like noodles and they ached, a product of her illness and being out of race-shape. Despite everything, Meghan smiled because she realized that she wouldn't want to be anywhere else at this moment. Not at home, not snuggled up with Alan, not anywhere but here in the bowels of a sailboat going fifteen knots in a bumpy Gulf Stream.

Meghan let out a tired sigh. Alan wouldn't break up with her simply for disobeying him. He wanted the best for her. He'd been worried. He simply hadn't gone about it the right way. How could she blame Alan for being upset with her when in the last two weeks, she'd turned into another person? He didn't know the woman who would win at all costs, who loved the wind and rain lashing in her face, who swam naked in a warm salty sea. The Meghan he knew—the Meghan she now was, she insisted silently—was quiet and steady and . . . boring. She loved the new boring Meghan and she loved her new boring life.

Unfortunately, old Meghan seemed to be in charge of her at the moment and was laughing her ass off at new Meghan.

Chapter Fourteen

When the sun came up on the third day of the race, *Water Baby* had left the Gulf Stream and was heading toward Bermuda at a discouraging three knots.

"No wind," Will said, stating the obvious. The water was molten, the seas calm, making last night's gale seem impossible. That was one thing Will loved about the Newport-Bermuda race; it was never the same. The only thing a sailor could count on was that.

"We're in Bermuda high," he said, popping his head up from the navigation station. Light winds could help *Water Baby*, because she was one of the smaller boats in the fleet. This was when having a good trimmer and top crew made all the difference. A boat that found wind or used what they found to the best advantage was the boat that won. Will had a gut feeling that they had hit the stream just right, but as he looked out at the calm seas he felt slightly sick. Boats had languished in the doldrums for days and Will had a horrible feeling that Frank didn't have days. The fact that Frank hadn't made the starting line had weighed heavily on his mind.

"I don't think we have to worry about *Hurricane* anymore. Our next big worry is the *Bravado.* She was fifteen hours ahead of us yesterday and if she's increased that lead, we're dead."

Thad poured a breakfast MRE into his mouth from a plastic bowl and chewed before answering. "They need eighteen hours to beat us, right? Stop worrying."

"Stop worrying, he says."

Meg was back as trimmer, looking far more chipper than she had the night before. Light wind was where Meg shined; she could outsail anyone he knew when the air was this calm.

"Danny," Will called to one of the college kids. "Climb the mast and see if you can spot me some wind." The kid was up in a minute, standing on the mast's spreader and gazing at the horizon in every direction.

"We're in the wind," he called down. "No boats, either."

Will hoped that was good news. In some races, they didn't see a boat the entire race. They were 200 miles north of the island—two-thirds through the race—but unless they hit some good air, they wouldn't reach the finish line for at least another thirty hours or more. Not knowing where they stood in the pack was maddening. It would be another hour before boats started calling in their positions.

An hour later, Tony took over on the helm and Will headed below again to study the weather conditions and was assaulted by the accumulated smell of lousy MREs and unwashed male bodies. "I never said you couldn't bring along some deodorant," he yelled out.

"Why ruin the fun?" Thad called down.

Will took his place at the nav station to study the weather information. What he saw was discouraging. A strong high was sitting over the island and looked like it was going to stay there for a while. Wind was light and variable and that meant his already tired crew was going to have to work like dogs to keep the boat going.

At eight o'clock the first boats started calling in, and Will wrote down their positions on a chart. *Hurricane* was nearly an hour behind them, and that was terrific news. All he had to do was out sail them in light wind and he'd have them beat. He listened for *Bravado*'s position, marking it down when they finally called in.

"Holy shit," he whispered. "Six hours. Six goddamn hours we gained."

Will heaved himself up to the cockpit, a huge grin on his face. "We gained six hours on *Bravado*," he called out. "That means they're stuck in some pretty rotten air. They're coming in slightly more east of the rhumbline than we are. Whatever we do, let's stay out of that air."

The crew let out a whoop. Will could almost taste victory. He never felt as confident as he felt at the moment and he was tempted to call Frank and let him know. More than tempted.

"I'm calling Frank on the satellite," he said to no one in particular.

"Dude," Thad said, gripping his arm. "Don't."

Meghan watched the curious exchange. "Why shouldn't he call Frank with the good news?"

"Because until we win, I think we should just be cool," Thad said with quiet authority.

Will sagged a little. "You're right," he said. "It'd kill him if we told him we were going to win and didn't."

"Don't you think you're being a little dramatic?" Meghan asked, and watched as Will and Thad exchanged another look.

Will shrugged. "You know Frank. He's more obsessed about this race than I am."

"Well, I'm calling Alan," she said, just to be difficult.

"Why would you call him? He doesn't know a sailboat from a rowboat."

Meg adjusted the sail two clicks. "For your information, Alan is extremely interested in anything I'm interested in," she said smugly, even though it was a blatant lie. The only thing that interested Alan about the race was how much it was going to impact her house sales, but Will didn't have to know that.

"Anyway, I'm sure he's worried about me."

Will gave her a blank look, then acted as if he finally understood. "Oh, yeah. That almost-dying thing. He was worried about that?"

"Ha ha."

"Because the only thing I heard was him mumbling about commissions or some such."

"You are so funny," she said dryly. "As a matter of fact, he was so worried, he told me he'd break up with me if I didn't leave the race. See? He cares."

Will looked slightly dumbfounded. "You're kidding."

"That's how a man acts when he's in love. He says crazy things he doesn't mean because he's so worried. If I remember you correctly, the first thing out of your mouth when you learned I was slightly better—still not out of danger, mind you—was 'Set the jib!'"

Meghan was kidding, but it was obvious Will didn't find her banter funny. "Watch your sail, Meg. It's luffing."

Meghan turned back to her job, feeling slightly guilty for allowing the sail to buckle. "I'm still calling Alan," she said, sounding to herself like a petulant kid.

"Because he's so interested in the race," Will said, grumpily baiting her.

"Exactly. And because he's so interested in me," Meg grinned.

"Go get some breakfast, Tone, I'll take over on helm."

Tony went below, leaving Thad, Will and Meg in the cockpit. The rest of the crew was hanging topside. In this light wind, there wasn't much to do except wait for something to do.

Meg wasn't sure why she wanted to bug Will, but she did. Shc took out her cell phone and turned it on, hoping she'd get a signal. "Damn," she said when no signal bars showed up. "I don't suppose me wanting to talk to Alan could be classified as an emergency," she grumbled half-heartedly.

"Not quite. He'll live without hearing your sweet voice for a day."

"My, my. Such hostility," she said. Just then the faintest breeze picked up and for the next two hours, her only thought was the sail in front of her.

By noon, that breeze had disappeared, leaving the crew baking beneath an unrelenting sun. The sails hung listlessly, the halyards banging lightly like wind chimes against the mast from the slight movement in the sea.

"This sucks," Tony said, staring out at the calm ocean. He looked up to where a crewmember was hanging out halfway up the mast hoping to see some air. "At this rate we're going to be here for days."

"There's a potential for a small weather system tonight, but we haven't a chance in hell to get to it in this wind. The front's cutting across south of us. Maybe we can capture the edge of it," Will said doubtfully. "It's time for a shift change soon. You guys can get some shut-eye. I'm sure as hell not going to need you on the rail."

Will looked around at the crew, noting only one member of his shift was missing. "Hey, Thad, go down below and wake up sleeping beauty, will you?"

Thad gave Will an intense look that was meant to convey he wasn't all that happy with his assignment. He really didn't want to be alone—even if it was nearly impossible to be alone on his boat—with Rachel. He didn't like the way his body reacted, he didn't like the way he couldn't seem to keep his eyes off her, and he especially didn't like the way Tony looked at her the same way. But he headed below anyway without a comment.

The bunks were empty, so Thad continued toward the bow, stopping dead when he saw her lying on the sail bags, curled up and content. Her cheeks were flushed from the sun and wind and sleep, and her hair was a dark curling mass around her. Thad started to kick one of the sail bags she was sleeping on to wake her up when he happened to look at her mouth. Damn. He'd never noticed how soft it looked, how incredibly feminine, and at that moment there was nothing he wanted more than to have that beautiful mouth pressed against his. She wasn't a complete knockout, her jaw was a bit too square, her legs a little thick, like an athlete. Rachel was no delicate flower, that was for sure. But there was something so blatantly feminine and sexy about her at the moment, he felt an unwanted rush of heat to his groin.

Thad squatted down and smiled at Rachel, then reached out an index finger and touched one velvety cheek. She opened her eyes slowly, and he was startled to see they were the most beautiful violet-blue eyes he'd ever seen. He'd never noticed her eyes before, or her mouth. But man, he was noticing them now.

"Timc to wake up," he said, his voice low and gruff.

"Wow. I was just dreaming about you," she said sleepily and stretched out, arching her back. It was an innocent enough gesture, completely uncalculated, but his penis almost instantly came to attention and his eyes couldn't stop their sweep to her breasts.

"A good dream?" he asked when he figured he could talk.

She smiled, unknowingly seductive. "I was kissing you," she said, and her cheeks turned pink. He would have thought she'd look away, because he knew how shy she was, but she kept staring at him with those incredible eyes.

Thad backed up a bit. "Kissing me?"

Rachel reached up a hand and put it behind his neck, looking uncertain and scared as hell. "Like this," she said, and brought him down for the sweetest kiss he'd had since he was a teenager.

"What are you doing?"

Rachel's heart was beating a mile a minute. She couldn't quite believe what she was doing, and decided she could only blame the incredibly hot dream she'd been having a moment before the star of her fantasy woke her up. "I think I'm kissing you," Rachel said.

"You think?" he asked, a smile in his brown eyes.

Rachel nodded, then kissed his mouth the way she'd imagined doing it a thousand times in her dreams, moving her mouth against his, flicking her tongue out to touch his lips.

Thad pushed her gently away, his eyes filled with something Rachel, in her hysterical mind, would have sworn was pity. "Rach, what are you doing?" he repeated.

"I can't be that bad a kisser," Rachel said good-naturedly, even as her stomach clenched in horror. She'd made a horrible, irreversible mistake. He thought she was ugly, he wasn't attracted to her at all. He was being nice and overly polite and . . . Oh, God.

"I know you're kissing me," Thad said with patience. "I just thought." He let the last word dangle there and Rachel swore his cheeks, already ruddy from the sun, turned a bit brighter red.

Rachel rolled her eyes. "I'm straight, you idiot."

"Oh, my God."

"Yup."

He looked at her as if he'd never seen her before and Rachel wasn't sure she liked that look or not. And then he smiled, his teeth gleaming in the gloom of the cabin. "All this time you've been straight?"

Rachel nodded with a sick look. "And madly attracted to you. Sorry. Can we kiss again?" she asked.

"Um," he said, looking back toward the companionway.

"Never mind," she said quickly, all her insecurities flooding back in force. "I just had that dream about you and here you were with your lips and everything and I thought I'd find out what it was like to kiss. Kiss *you*, I mean. It's not like I haven't kissed a hundred men. Maybe a thousand. Because if that was my first kiss and you rejected me, it would be devastating to a girl like me who everyone obviously thought was a lesbian and the whole time was mad . . ." She stopped, thankfully not so stupid she could completely humiliate herself by confessing she was in love with him. " . . . mad enough to think a guy would want to kiss her back." She sat back, arms crossed, and stared at nothing. "You can go topside now."

Next to her, Thad's smile grew until he was grinning like the idiot she'd just called him. Then he realized she was majorly pissed at him and probably hurt and he was just trying to wrap his mind around the fact that the hottest woman he'd ever seen wanted to kiss him silly.

"Rachel, come here."

"I will not participate in a pity kiss," she said, moving even farther away from him and making the sails crunch beneath her.

"Pity has nothing to do with it."

"Yeah. Right."

"Oh, for God's sake, Rach, give me a break. I've known you for years and this whole time I thought, well, you know what I thought. This just takes a bit of getting used to. And for the record, I feel like a real jerk for thinking that."

He got this intense look in his eyes that Rachel didn't recognize. It was either anger or passion; she didn't have the experience to know which one.

He gripped either side of her head and gave her a gentle shake. "I'm sorry for not seeing you until now. You're beautiful, Rachel. You know what I wish right now?"

She bit her lip and his eyes darted to her mouth. When he let out a small growly moan, she felt a power that she'd never in her life experienced. "What?" she whispered.

"I wish we weren't on this boat because I want to show you just how beautiful I think you are."

Rachel smiled and he shook his head. "Hell, Rachel. I think I'm the dumbest, blindest idiot I know."

She relaxed and she let the tiniest of smiles touch her lips. "I agree," she said.

They heard Will yell from the cockpit and pulled apart as if they'd been doused with freezing water. Thad was a decent enough guy, and Rachel knew he'd never embarrass her in front of the entire crew. But he wasn't a saint. He pulled her to him and kissed her silly, then pushed away and practically leaped into the cockpit.

Rachel thought if she were to be struck by lightning at that very moment, she would die happy. *You are a beautiful, confident woman.*

Chapter Fifteen

Nancy stared out the master bedroom window at a soft fog moving slowly across the bay from Newport. As she watched, the fog took on a menacing feeling, as if when it finally reached the island, it would enshroud everything in its path and suffocate each and every thing. She tried to shrug off her malevolent thoughts, but behind her, the man she'd loved for more than forty years was slowly dying. It hit her that morning when she came in to see him and saw a man she didn't recognize. For a moment before she'd stepped into their bedroom, she'd forgotten what the disease had done to Frank, forgotten he wasn't still the strapping, ruddy-faced guy with a booming voice and irrepressible good humor.

There was an old man sleeping in a hospital bed and that man was Frank, but it didn't look like Frank or smell like Frank or even sound like Frank.

Nancy turned away from the window and looked over at him, feeling so sad and so alone. Funny, there had been times in their marriage when she'd thought she'd be okay alone, when she'd even looked forward to it. But she hadn't really thought about what it truly meant to be alone until now. Alone was not sharing a funny news story, not talking about little things, like what to have for supper or when they should start picking the zucchini. Alone was staring out a window for hours, turning around and having no one there to tell how beautiful the sunrise was that morning.

Frank was dying, slowly winding down, his organs failing one by one. He didn't have long, the hospice nurses said. A few more days before he slipped into a coma, and when that happened it would be hours. Hours of listening to his breathing grow slower and slower, until finally, he'd be gone forever.

As sad as she was, Nancy was smiling when he opened his eyes and focused on her.

"Any news?"

"Good morning to you, too," she said, cheerfully. "No news. You know Will is going to call as soon as they reach Hamilton."

"Not if he doesn't get that trophy. He'll be too afraid to call me," Frank said, letting out a hoarse chuckle.

"True."

"Wish he'd hurry up about it," he said, and Nancy knew he'd tried to make light of it, but failed miserably. "It's for Jack as much as for me, you know."

"I know."

"Got to tell him we got the trophy when I see him." They often talked about their long-dead son as if he were just in another town, living his life.

"I have a feeling Jack will yell at you for being so obsessed about a sailing race for most of your life," Nancy said in mock anger.

Suddenly Frank got a panicky look on his face. "What day is it?"

"June 20. Monday."

Frank let out a small sigh. "Thought we missed his birthday. Strange that I would think that, with his birthday in August. I know what month it is. Isn't that funny?"

Nancy looked down on Frank and grabbed his hand, squeezing lightly and trying not to think about how fragile he seemed. He'd always had such strong hands. "It's not funny. He's just on your mind with the race and all."

"But I know what month it is, for God's sake," Frank said, clearly disgusted with himself and a little bit frightened.

Nancy was a little bit frightened, herself. Frank was always so self-assured, so confident, and now she found herself looking at a scared old man. She wanted her husband back.

Frank must have seen something in her eyes because he gave her hand a squeeze this time. "It'll be all right, Peaches," he said, using her old pet name. He hadn't called her that in decades.

"I know, Frank. It's just . . ." and her throat closed before she could say it. *I don't want you to die. I don't want to be alone.*

"I know. I know."

Nancy forced a shaky smile, then crawled onto the narrow hospital bed, lay next to her husband, and listened to him breathe.

Chapter Sixteen

"Okay, what's up with you?" Meghan asked Rachel, who'd been grinning and chuckling to herself for about an hour. It was beginning to get slightly irritating for a person who was pretty unhappy at the moment, given her personal life and the fact the boat was still stuck in the doldrums. They sat side-by-side on the rail, feet dangling over the side of a boat that rose and fell slowly in the calm seas. The water was a brilliant blue, the sky cloudless, the wind nonexistent. If it hadn't been for the fact they were in a race, it would have been a lovely thing sitting there beneath the sun if Meghan had been so inclined to appreciate anything beautiful at the moment. On the horizon, one of the larger boats sat in the same still air, its owner probably cursing and looking behind as *Water Baby* slowly but surely moved closer. At least she wasn't the only miserable one.

Water Baby was only about one hundred miles from Bermuda, and if they found any wind at all, they'd probably cross the finish line sometime the next day.

Meghan looked over at Rachel's happy face and gave her a friendly nudge. "You look like a kid who's sneaked a piece of candy. Give it up."

"He knows," she said, ducking her head slightly in embarrassment.

Meghan's irritation with the world vanished. "You mean Thad?"

Rachel nodded and smiled.

"He knows you're straight or he knows you're in love with him?"

Rachel looked around crazily to make certain no one heard Meghan, even though she'd asked the question in a near whisper. "He knows I'm straight," she said, then after a moment added, "We kissed."

"What? When? Where?"

"This morning right before our shift. He came down to wake me up." She frowned slightly. "I kissed him, actually."

Sensing that Rachel was about to dive into a pit of insecurity, she asked, "Did he kiss back?"

The smile was back. "Mmmm hmmm."

"And?"

Rachel shook her head, again looking behind her to make sure no one was nearby.

"And? And?" Meghan said, just to tease the other woman.

"He said he couldn't wait to get on shore."

"Woo hoo," Meghan said just above a whisper. "Good for you."

Rachel should have grinned again, but instead she looked as if she might be ill.

"What's wrong?"

A shrug, a look out to the horizon, a shake of the head.

"Isn't that what you wanted?"

Rachel bit her lip and squeezed her eyes shut. "It's just that, I'm not really that experienced. You know, with all that kissing and, you know, sex stuff."

Meghan let out a small gasp. "You're a virgin." She could tell by Rachel's expression that she was right. "And Thad doesn't know. Of course Thad doesn't know. You're too embarrassed to tell him, right?" Rachel kept nodding. "But you have to, and you're dreading it, right?" Meghan stopped talking, stunned by what Rachel had told her. "Are you, um, saving yourself?"

Rachel laughed aloud. "God, no. I mean, not on purpose." She let out a frustrated sigh. "When I said I don't have much experience, I mean it. I really have no experience. I never dated in high school or college. I'm in therapy because of my shyness and my lack of self-esteem. I'm better and because of that I lost some weight. It goes hand in hand, you know. Anyway, it just never happened. And I don't mean the virginity thing, I mean dating and all that."

"Wow."

"Yeah." She was quiet for a moment before admitting, "It was my first kiss. The first real one anyway. I'm not going to count spin the bottle, but I was the booby prize there and the boys didn't want to kiss me."

"Oh, Rach, that must have been awful."

She shrugged. "It sort of got easier not to care what men thought. You saw the way I dressed. The way I still want to dress. Then I met Thad and it hit me that I was going to die and never have experienced anything. I wasn't going to have someone love me, I wasn't going to get married and have children. I was going to eat and sit around until I was dead and my obit would be two sentences long.

Rachel Jenks, born, lived for a while and died alone. Funeral tomorrow."

"You really thought about that stuff?"

"Almost every day."

Meghan put her arm around Rachel and gave her a little squeeze. "I'm so proud of you," she said. "I can't believe you got the courage to kiss him first. How did that happen?"

Rachel's cheeks turned pink. "I was having a dream."

Meghan started laughing. "And then the man of your dreams showed up."

"Something like that. I think I surprised him a little."

"I'm sure that's an understatement. Listen, don't rush into anything. Thad's a nice guy and I know he'll be okay with the virginity thing. Just be honest with him."

Rachel turned to look at Meghan. "The way you're being honest?" The second it was out of her mouth, Rachel blushed and apologized. "See?" she joked. "Therapy really is working on me."

Meghan wasn't offended. That much. "I'm just a little confused right now. Especially since Alan is being such a jerk about my staying on the boat after I got sick. He actually threatened to break up with me if I didn't quit."

"And he thought that was going to work on you?"

"He doesn't know my competitive nature."

Rachel furrowed her brow. "How is that possible?"

"He's never seen me on a sailboat. Honestly, that's the only thing I get real passionate about."

"Then why did you quit?" Rachel asked quietly.

Good question. Meghan looked at the aqua water

gently pushing against the boat. "I quit Will when he quit me and I guess sailing went with it."

"But here you are."

"Here I am."

"Maybe it's none of my business, but since you know all about my life it's only fair that you tell me a little bit about yours. Do you still love Will?"

"No. God, no," she said quickly, then sighed. It was Meghan's turn to look behind them to be sure they had privacy. "I still have feelings for him, but I don't know if I'd call it love. Right now is not a good time to ask me, because Alan is being so ridiculous and Will has been strangely nice on this trip. I need to talk to Alan. It's so frustrating not having cell phone access out here. Knowing Alan, I'm sure he regrets his threat. He's an extremely mellow person. Solid."

Rachel smiled. "Sounds like love to me."

"Ha ha. I'm just angry right now, I'm hundreds of miles away from him, and I'm sailing. This isn't me anymore. Call the last two years therapy for a life that went in the wrong direction."

Rachel didn't look convinced.

"Will broke my heart, Rach. I can't put it out there for him again. I just can't."

"Okay. I know all about broken hearts."

Above them, the mainsail let out a small snapping sound and Meghan felt the tiniest of breezes against her face.

"I just felt some air," she called to Tony, who had the helm for Will.

"We got some ripples to starboard," the crewmember on the mast yelled down.

The crew headed the boat slightly to starboard

and they adjusted the sails, which still hung discouragingly limp.

Will stuck his head up from the companionway. "Looks like we're catching that front," he said, as Meghan scuttled to the cockpit. "It moved in a little faster than I thought it would. Looks like we'll be seeing Bermuda tonight and crossing the finish tomorrow morning."

"Will," Meghan said, feeling excitement wash over her. "I think we might do it this year."

He grinned and she couldn't help but smile back, even though she'd promised herself to keep an emotional distance from Will. "I know the big boats aren't going to beat us. And everyone behind us who could beat us on corrected time isn't going to hit this front for another two hours." Suddenly the boat heeled over as the wind picked up and Will let out a shout worthy of a battle cry.

The crewmember on the mast scrambled down. "Some really nice air coming toward us," he said.

The mood on the boat lifted with every increase in speed *Water Baby* made. Ahead of them, the larger boat had disappeared on the horizon, benefiting from the front even more than *Water Baby*. But it didn't matter. That boat would have to beat them by more than twelve hours into Bermuda, and that just wasn't going to happen.

Thad came down from his spot on the bow, his eyes on the horizon behind them. "Will, you have any idea who the hell that is?" he asked, jerking his head toward a sailboat barely visible in the distance.

"Shit."

Meghan ran down to get the binoculars and jerked them to her face. "Damn," she whispered. "I think it's *Hurricane*."

"You're kidding. How the hell did he make up all that time in that lousy air?"

Meghan shook her head and handed over the binoculars, watching as Will searched for the boat. "It *is* Sanderson," he confirmed, shaking his head. "I just don't know how he made up that time. He's a damn good sailor but he doesn't have the crew or the boat that I have. I must have missed something," he said, then pulled himself down into the cabin and sat at the nav station. "I just don't get it. There's nothing out there. I know his equipment and his crew's a bunch of hacks compared to us."

"He's got to pass us and beat us over the line by more than two minutes," Meghan said, for some reason desperate to reassure Will. She'd sailed with him for years and had never seen the look of desperation she now saw on his face. "I don't see how they can possibly overtake us. Not this close to the finish line."

"I don't know how I missed something," he said, staring at the equipment in front of him as if it would offer up an explanation. "What time is it?"

Meghan looked at her watch. "Half past five. Want to change shifts now?" she asked. He nodded in an odd jerking way, as if he were so tense he could hardly move his head. She lay her hand on his shoulder, finding it rock hard with tension. "Will, we're going to win. And even if we don't, you'll do it next race. There's always a next race. That's what you always say, right?"

He looked up to her and she nearly shrank back from the look in his eyes. "There is no next race," he said, his voice raw-sounding.

"What do you mean?"

He just shook his head and moved around her to

the cockpit. "Tony, I'm taking the helm. Gary, let Meghan take over."

Tony gladly gave up the wheel, but Gary seemed less than pleased, knowing that letting Meghan take over as trimmer was a comment on his skills. Meghan looked back and was shocked to see *Hurricane* closer. Will saw her expression and looked back, swearing beneath his breath.

"Let's just sail our boat," Meghan said, turning to the sail and trying not to give into the temptation of looking behind them.

By nightfall, *Hurricane* had not gained any ground on *Water Baby*. Meghan was exhausted, having stayed as trimmer for two hours longer than normal. Her arms were aching and her stomach screaming for some food. Even the MREs would taste good about now.

"Two-hour break, Meg. This is it. Crunch time and I need you."

"Geez, Will, I can hardly lift my arms to eat. I really don't know if I *can* do it."

"You have to do it," he said, his voice brooking no argument. That, however, never stopped Meghan.

"Where'd the guy go who was willing to give up the race to save my life?"

"He left when he saw *Hurricane* on the horizon," Will said so grimly that Meghan had to laugh.

Meghan scarfed down some barely edible chicken and dumplings, then headed for the bow of the cabin to catch an hour of sleep on the sail bags before her shift started again. Night had fallen, and the moon was just a sliver, not giving enough light to illuminate *Hurricane*, but a quick look at the radar told Meghan the boat was still far behind. Just as she was about to drift asleep, every muscle in her poor body aching, Will plopped down three feet away.

"I hate night sailing," he said about two seconds before he started snoring.

When morning dawned, pink and warm, Bermuda was in sight—and *Hurricane* was several boat lengths ahead of *Water Baby*. Will couldn't believe his eyes when he thrust himself onto the deck after another two-hour sleep. Each time Tony and Gary took over, *Water Baby* lost ground.

"What the hell happened?" he asked, his voice low and harsh so the crew with Sanderson wouldn't hear him. "You should have woken me up. *Damn it.*" That he said aloud, not caring whether or not Sanderson heard him. Not caring if Frank heard him back in Rhode Island. He was incredulous that *Hurricane* had glided past them in the early morning hours and the crew he had counted on so heavily had let it happen without letting him know.

"We didn't see him until it was too late," Tony said, his tone defensive. "They took our wind and we just stalled."

"They never should have gotten close enough to steal our wind," Will bit back. "Meg. Get your tail up here," he called down to a drowsy-looking Meg. Will knew she was exhausted and still not at one hundred percent after her illness, but at the moment the only thing he really cared about was getting *Water Baby* moving.

"I'm coming," she said, not even bothering to hide her irritation with him. When she popped her head out of the companionway and saw *Hurricane*, all irritation disappeared—at least with Will.

"Holy crap," she said. "What the hell happened? You two fall asleep?"

Disgusted, Gary threw down the line and without a word, headed below. Tony just grinned. "You may have the helm, el Capitano," he said with a flourish.

Will was amazed at how quickly things began turning around as soon as Meghan took over the jib and Thad took the mainsail with the help of Rachel. Wind was light, and that's when Meg shined. A few clicks on the winch and he could feel the boat pick up a knot. "Come on, come on," he whispered, his eyes darting from the sails to *Hurricane*, who still had a lead. But he couldn't tell how much of one.

"Brad, try to figure out how far ahead she is," he said.

The college kid screwed up his face and said, "A hundred yards?"

Will nearly crushed his teeth searching for patience. "In time. How far ahead is he in time? Look, when they pass that buoy, start timing."

Everyone on the crew was silent as they watched *Hurricane* pass the buoy, then waited in agonized anticipation for the time.

"Three minutes, twelve seconds," Roger said.

"Shit," Will spat. "Goddamn finish line is less than twenty minutes away." Will felt as if he were going to be sick. He was exhausted, mentally and physically, and waking up to find *Hurricane* ahead of them was almost more than he could bear at the moment.

The crew sailed on in tense silence, with only the sound of the waves against the boat and the frantic clicking as Meghan adjusted the sails again and again. With wind as light as this, it was constantly changing speed and direction, forcing Will to make small adjustments to the helm that forced Meghan to change the sails. It was well-choreographed and Will knew there wasn't another person on earth who could anticipate his moves better than Meg.

"Okay, Brad, when *Hurricane* passes that channel marker, start the count."

Again and again, Brad stood beside Will with his digital stopwatch, measuring *Hurricane*'s time against *Water Baby*. And every time he did it, they had gained ground. By the time the final marker was in site, they were within two minutes, thirty-five seconds of her. To beat the boat on corrected time, *Water Baby* had to cross the finish line within two minutes and twenty-two seconds.

Will adjusted the helm, and watched Meg, whose arms had started to shake from the strain, make tiny adjustments to the jib. "Bring in the mainsail a bit," Will said, surprised how calm he was.

A horn sounded. *Hurricane* had crossed the line. Next to him, Brad pressed the stopwatch. "Here we go, ladies," Will said.

It seemed as if *Water Baby* slowed to a crawl, as if the wind died down, as if there was no way in hell their boat was going to ever cross that finish line.

"Give me the time," Will said softly.

"One minute ten," Brad said, his eyes staring at the watch intently. The St. Davis Lighthouse loomed on the shore, its beacon cutting through the soft morning air.

"Come on, come on," Will whispered.

"Two minutes," Brad said.

No one on the boat moved, as if the slightest movement would slow the boat down.

"Two ten. Two eleven."

The horn sounded. "What was the time?" Will asked, feeling strangely detached.

"Two minutes, twelve seconds."

"It appears we have ten seconds to spare, ladies," Will said, then let out a shout. The rest of the crew joined in, two college kids getting so rowdy they nearly tumbled off the boat and into Bermuda's spectacular blue-green water.

Within minutes, Thad was carrying up bottles of champagne, a concession Will had made at the last minute even though it only added unwanted weight to the boat.

Will grabbed a bottle and took a deep swallow. "Wc won't know for certain until we get the official time, but no matter what happens, you are the best crew in this race on the best boat. Thank you." The crew let out another cheer.

Will handed the bottle to Meghan and pressed it into her hands. "We couldn't have done this without you, kiddo. I want you to know that."

Meghan grinned up at him, her eyes sparkled with unshed happy tears, and he allowed himself for just a second to forget she'd never be his again. She was sunburned, her skin flushed and dotted with dried salt spray, her hair a curling mess and he could only think that she'd never looked more beautiful. Hell, no woman had ever looked as beautiful as Meghan did at that moment, smiling so widely that when she took a swig of champagne, most of it dribbled down her chin.

He wiped her chin ineffectually with his index finger. "We're a good team," he said, and was slightly mystified when his felt his throat close.

Meg handed the champagne back to Will as if he'd just offered her cyanide, and almost maniacally said, "I think I'll call Alan with the good news. We get cell service here, right?" Call Alan, think of Alan, not Will, standing here grinning at you, looking at you as if . . . he'd never looked at her that way before. She gave herself a mental shake. The man had just won the most important race of his life, there was no way in hell the look he'd just given her was anything but pure joy of victory.

Still, she backed away as he suddenly grown horns and sprouted cloven hoofs.

"Why don't you wait until we have something a bit more official," he called to her, but Meg just waved a hand at him. She had to get away, and not because of the way he'd looked at her, as if he loved her, which was ridiculous because why would Will love her after all this time? She had to run away because she didn't like the way her heart had nearly jumped from her chest and she was desperately afraid that the thing she should be most afraid of was her feelings for Will.

Alan, think of Alan. Your fiancé, the man you want to marry, the man who loves you. The man you . . . Meg squeezed her eyes shut. She should be up on deck celebrating, not thinking about this crap.

Meghan found her cell phone and turned it on, breathing heavily as if she'd run a hundred yards instead of just a few feet. She was more than tired and she was still recovering from an illness that could have killed her. Sure. That explained the rush of heat she felt between her legs when Will told her they made a great team. It wasn't the words, it was the sound of his voice, the way he'd looked at her. The way she'd looked at him.

This was bad. Very, very bad. And the only remedy was to hear Alan's voice.

After turning on her phone, she grimaced when she saw she had six messages. Calling her voicemail, she heard all of Alan's frantic and maddening messages. She especially loved the one where he threatened to break up with her if she didn't call in an hour. Even if they hadn't had cell service at sea, she probably wouldn't have had the chance to call him. His apology was weak at best, she thought, skipping ahead to the last message. She winced when she heard Alan's voice again.

"I think I'm going to skip Bermuda, baby. Work's crazy and we just can't spare another agent. You'll probably have more fun without me, anyway."

What the heck did that mean? she wondered, feeling a wave of guilt over how relieved she was that he wasn't coming to Bermuda. She'd better call him to make sure he wasn't canceling because he was still angry with her. Alan had never been a high-maintenance guy. Then again, she hadn't ever made him work very hard for her. Maybe this was a good thing; knock him off balance a bit.

She rang his number and got his voicemail. "Alan, looks like we won. Too bad about work," she said, feeling another tsunami of guilt hit her because she wasn't sorry at all. Not a lick. "Call me when you can. Um. Hope everything's okay."

She rang off feeling as if a weight had been lifted from her shoulders. Now she could celebrate the win—if it turned out they truly had won—and her only worry would be how many Dark and Stormies she could stomach.

Among the messages were two from her mother, asking her to call as soon as she reached the island. Meg pressed the speed dial for her mother.

"Hey, Mom."

"Meghan. You were on the news. Well, not you, but *Water Baby*. They mentioned your boat as one of the top runners."

Meghan grinned at her mother's enthusiasm. After all, she was the one who got Meghan interested in sailing all those years ago. She'd got caught smoking in school and sailing was her mother's frantic attempt to get Meghan into something wholesome and safe.

"I think we won, but we won't know for sure until later this afternoon. You should have seen the finish. We're just seconds ahead of *Hurricane*. It was incredible."

"Oh, my God, that's so wonderful. Have you called Alan with the news yet?"

Meghan frowned. "He left several insane messages on my voicemail. I called him and left a message. He's not coming to Bermuda, so he's probably still having a hissy fit."

"He was just worried."

"I think he's pathologically worried. I'm going to have to talk to him when I get back."

"He's really not going to Bermuda?"

"No. He said work was too busy," she said, and as she repeated it, realized how ridiculous an excuse it had been. He'd been talking about Bermuda since the day she'd decided she was going to crew. He probably was still angry, and for the life of her, Meghan couldn't garner up enough energy to care. She'd wanted to party with the crew and not worry about what she said, what she ate, how she dressed. With Alan in Bermuda, she'd have to worry whether he was having fun and then she wouldn't have any fun. "To be honest, I'm glad he's not coming. It's going to be crazy here in the next week, especially if we are the winners."

"Afraid Alan would cramp your style?" her mother guessed with precision.

"Sort of. Yes. Alan can be a bit of a stick in the mud sometimes. It's what I love about him." She suddenly felt as if she were lying, just saying the words her mother wanted to hear.

"Meghan, you do not love Alan because he's boring."

Actually, she did. "You're right. Anyway, I'll call you when the results are more official. Bye, Mom. Love you."

"Bye, honey. *Be good.*"

She knew what her mother meant—stay away from Will. It struck Meghan a little odd that her mother didn't mention him at all in the conversation. She usually managed to insert some insult about him into every conversation she had. "I'm always good," she said, even though she knew it wasn't true. She was about to dial Alan again if only to get thoughts of Will out of her head when Rachel called down into the cabin.

"Hey, Meghan. The champagne's almost gone. What the heck are you doing?"

She snapped her phone closed. "Save some for me," she said, and heaved herself back on deck.

The crew had taken the sails down and they were motoring in to Hamilton Harbor. Ahead of them, *Hurricane* had done the same. While the *Water Baby* crew was jubilant, the *Hurricane* crew was subdued, which was rather reassuring. Poor slobs, Meghan thought as she took a swig of champagne. She lifted the bottle in a mock toast.

"To the *Hurricane.* If they didn't suck so bad, we

wouldn't have won," she said, then doubled over laughing. Boy, was she tired, she thought giddily.

Then she straightened and lifted the bottle up again. "To Will Scott. The best damned captain a boat has ever seen."

The crew shouted their approval and Will smiled, flashing white teeth against his bronzed skin. He was grubby, needed a shave and a shower, and his hair was sticking up like a man who'd gone mad with too much gel. And Meghan couldn't help but fall a little bit in love with him again. Just a little, she told herself. Enough to fill, say, a thimble. A big collector's one.

"And to Thad," Rachel said. "If he hadn't broken his arm, we wouldn't have the best trimmer in the fleet on our boat." Another cheer went up.

"Hey," Thad said, pretending to be wounded. "That sounded more like a toast for Meghan."

"Okay, ladies, if the lovefest is over, let's get this tank in the slip and get to shore. We could all use a good shower and a good nap." That got one of the biggest shouts of all.

The thought of a hot shower and a soft bed was enough to make a grown woman cry, Meghan thought.

The crew had already left for the house Frank had rented, leaving Will alone to await official word that *Water Baby* had won the trophy. Everyone agreed they'd won, but Will refused to call Frank until he got the official ruling from the racing committee. And when it came, he flipped open his cell phone and speed-dialed Frank's number, his heart pounding hard in his chest.

"Hello."

"Nancy. I need to talk to Frank."

The long pause scared him half to death. "He's sleeping and I really don't want to wake him up. Unless . . ."

"We won."

Will heard a gasp and he knew Nancy was fighting back tears. "Oh, Will, you did it. Frank will be so happy. Give me a minute and I'll try to wake him."

Try to wake him? Will gripped the phone, swallowing down the ache in his throat. He couldn't be too late, he couldn't.

Then Nancy was back on the line. "Okay, Will. He's awake. Go ahead."

"Frank," Will shouted. "We did it. We got the Lighthouse."

"Who the hell is this?"

Will laughed aloud, because it sounded so much like Frank and he'd been so damned scared he'd been too late. "It's Will. We got it, Frank. We got first place. I'm coming home in a week and you can give it a kiss."

"You got the trophy?"

"We beat Sanderson by, get this, sixteen seconds. Sixteen seconds. It was so sweet. You should have seen his face. I would have taken a picture for you if he hadn't been so pissed about it. Meghan was terrific. The whole crew was terrific."

Will struggled to hear Frank's response, but all he could make out was some rustling, then Nancy came back on.

"He's so happy, Will. He's overcome. Thank you. This meant so much to him." Will could hear the tears in her voice.

"I know. Listen, I've got to tell the rest of the crew

that the win's official. They're all waiting at the house. I wish you and Frank could have been here."

"I know."

Will took a deep breath. "How is he?"

"Not great. Not good." She let out a soft laugh. "He's better now, that's for sure."

"I'm not going to get that trophy for another five days," Will said, leaving the question unasked: will he make it?

"I don't know, Will. He's failing. The doctor said he doesn't have long. But this has made him so happy, Will. You have no idea."

"Tell him I'll be on a plane with that trophy as soon as I get my hands on it."

"I will. And thanks."

Will rang off, wishing he had the trophy in his hands at that moment. He'd be on the next flight to Providence. But at least Frank knew *Water Baby* had won and the promise he'd made to his son all those years ago was fulfilled.

At that moment, Sanderson walked up to him, hand extended. "Damn good race, Will," the older man said. He had a grimace on his face, as if congratulating Will was ripping out his gut.

"Thanks. Your crew sure made it exciting at the end, there."

"Didn't think you guys were going to pull it off. We were nearly four minutes ahead of you. How the hell did you do it?"

Will smiled, loving every second of this conversation, and again feeling the absence of Frank by his side. The old man would have relished this scene, would have replayed it every day for the rest of his life. "Had the crew jump out and push from behind," Will said, flashing a smile. "How else?" He sure as hell wasn't going to tell him his secret weapon was a five-foot-five woman with the tenacity of a pit bull.

Sanderson practically snarled, but congratulated him again, and Will finally let the joy of victory wash over him. They'd won the St. Davis Lighthouse Trophy. He walked out of the Bermuda Yacht Club, where the racing committee was holed up, and out into the bright Bermuda sunshine, feeling as if he could have anything in the world, anything he wanted, even the thing he wanted most—Meghan Rose.

Back on Land

Chapter Seventeen

Frank rented a huge house above Horseneck Beach, which had enough beds to hold the crew and a couple of extra for any guests who might decide they couldn't make it back to their hotel or boat. It was a typical Bermudan house, painted pink with its tiered pristine white roof designed to catch rainwater. Outside, a sparkling pool was located just before a stone walkway that led down to a pink sand beach. Meghan didn't know how much something like this cost to rent for two weeks, but she did know it couldn't have been cheap.

The house had six bedrooms and slept the entire ten-member crew. It was almost as if Frank had somehow known they were going to win and had gone all out to make the crew happy.

By the time Will had returned with the official results, nearly everyone had managed to sneak in a quick shower, and the crew was shiny-faced and smelled far better than when they'd stumbled off the boat that morning. They'd had a quick toast and then one by one headed for the nearest bed, falling into one of those deep sleeps you only get when you're thoroughly exhausted.

Meghan woke up slightly groggy but with a smile on her face. She'd been so tired when she'd fallen into the soft bed, she hadn't even taken a look out the window. But now she stretched, feeling wonderfully rested and clean. She padded over the cool tile floor, stepped out onto the small terrace off her room and looked out, past the palm trees, to the stunningly green-blue waters below them. The sun was getting low and the air was soft and moist and thick with the smell of oleanders. It was a distinctively Bermuda smell and feel. For all her life, the scent of the oleander, which seemed to cover the entire island, would transport her back to Bermuda, to when she was young and single and . . .

She turned away, suddenly not wanting to remember how Bermuda made her feel, what it made her remember.

She and Will had spent hours exploring the island on the back of two scooters, two young people with nothing more important to do than lie on a beach, drink dark rum, and make love. They always found a place, even when there wasn't a place to be alone—or close to being alone.

Despite herself, she let out a laugh, remembering the time she'd come and nearly screamed and Will had put his hand over her mouth, his eyes shining with silent laughter, so an elderly couple admiring the view wouldn't see them six feet away behind a bush. Will could make her laugh and he could make her come, and he did it without even trying. He could turn her into an idiot who tried to make him love her the way she loved him. It'd had hurt so much then, and damn if it didn't still hurt. Especially now, with her skin moist from the humid air and her senses filled with the scent of oleander, and Will in the same house. Her real estate office and Alan seemed very far away at the moment and the thought of going back to her "real" life was slightly terrorizing.

That's when a thought hit her, like a soft blow to her heart: she had been living a lie the last two years. She'd been trying to mold herself into something she wasn't, like trying to squeeze her toes into those pointy shoes she was supposed to wear. She wanted to be barefoot or wearing comfy boat shoes, she wanted to wear cargoes and T-shirts. She'd felt like she'd come home these past few weeks and it had been wonderful.

Then she thought of Alan and her heart wrenched. Would he fit into this world, would he want to?

Did she really want him to?

"No," she whispered, and felt tears prick her eyes. Funny, but all it had taken was two weeks away from her well-planned life for her to realize she'd been living a lie. She shook her head, wondering if Bermuda, the salt air, and Will had somehow intoxicated her. Meghan took a deep breath, almost tasting the sweetness in the air, and was fiercely glad Alan had decided to stay home.

On the terrace below, she saw Thad step out and was about to call down to him when Rachel walked up behind him and wrapped her arms around him. He captured her hands in his and pulled her tighter against him. Meghan smiled and stepped back into the room, not wanting the couple to know their private moment hadn't been so private.

"What's the smile for?"

Meghan let out a gasp. "I could have been

naked," she said, a hand to her chest because Will had scared the hell out of her.

"That's what I was hoping for, but . . ." He gave her a little shrug and that boyish smile she'd fallen for all those years ago.

"Will, stop the flirting stuff. Please."

"I'm getting to you, aren't I?"

Meghan gave a dramatic roll of her eyes. "I'm engaged," she said, because technically she still was and because she did not need any more complications at the moment. To say she was in a state of complete confusion was an understatement. "Do you want a wedding invitation as proof?"

"Wedding, schmedding. This is Bermuda, kiddo. Anything goes. Or have you forgotten?"

Meghan wished with all her heart that Will didn't look so disarming at that moment. He'd showered, of course, and shaved and combed his dark hair back from his face, but his stubborn curls had fought for a place back onto his forehead. Will was not a guy who fussed with his hair. He washed it, combed it, and basically let it do the rest. The result was breathtaking and he really hadn't a clue.

"I know it's Bermuda. Believe me."

Will plopped down on the bed and put his hands behind his head, his feet resting on the tile. "Remember the time . . ."

"I'm sure I do. Will."

He sat up, looking as innocent as Lucifer.

"Please stop."

Will's expression changed suddenly, got serious and regretful and something else she didn't want to guess at. "I can't help it," he said, and Meghan felt her heart stop.

"Yes, you can. You can turn off the charm just as

quickly as you turn it on. I ought to know, because as soon as I said the 'l' word, it disappeared completely."

Will threw up his arms in mock surrender. "Here we go again."

"Tell me I'm wrong."

"Do you love him? I don't get it. He's the complete opposite of me. Is that the attraction?"

"I take it you're talking about Alan. His complete oppositiveness," she screwed up her face, knowing she'd just invented a word, "was the only attraction. I'm pretty sure that was the only thing about him I was immediately taken with." She said it all lightly, as if she was lying, but she knew, deep down, that she *had* fallen for Alan because he was as far away from Will as possible.

"I think that *is* it," Will said. "Which only proves you have deep, unresolved feelings for me."

Meghan knew he was only messing with her head, but she hated the truth behind those words and was afraid he knew they were correct as well.

"The only thing unresolved in our relationship is the punch in the head you deserved."

Will grinned and Meghan tried real hard not to smile, but her frown muscles were out of shape and her lips curved up on their own accord.

"Thad and Rachel are an item, you know," Meghan said, just to change the subject.

"It's this Bermuda air," Will said, giving her such a goofy look she had to laugh. "So, when does Prince Charming arrive from the exciting world of real estate?"

"Do you always have to put him down?" Will gave her a blank look. "He's not coming. Apparently it got really busy in the office."

"Really."

Meghan didn't like the not-so-hidden innuendo of his tone.

"Really. He wanted to come but couldn't. Poor guy. He was looking forward to this trip. Sort of a pre-honeymoon," she said, just to be mean.

"Gee. Too bad. I could have married you two here on the boat, given I'm the captain and all."

"I don't think it works that way. Besides, we're planning a big wedding. Lots of family and friends. You're not invited, of course."

"Of course." Damn if he didn't smile. Meghan knew she shouldn't be having so much fun antagonizing him, but she was. Maybe it was seeing love blooming between Rachel and Thad. Maybe it was the scent of oleander making her remember things she wished she'd forgotten.

Or maybe it was her heart's maddening beat every time she looked at a man she thought she'd gotten over a long time ago.

Meghan snapped her cell phone off again, feeling frustrated and angry that Alan was ignoring her. She, more than anyone, knew how many times Alan checked his voicemail. He'd gotten the message she'd left and he hadn't called her back. She could only think he was trying to punish her for finishing the race. It boggled her mind that Alan could be so obtuse; it was so unlike the man she thought he was.

"Hey, what's with the scowl?" Rachel asked as she met Meghan coming out of her room.

"Alan," she said, as if that explained everything.

"He still hasn't called, I take it."

"No. And I'm not going to let it bother me."

"Nor should you," Rachel said, smiling. Rachel had become overnight one of those highly irritating in-love people who was constantly smiling. It was especially bothersome to a woman who was in the midst of a fight with her current boyfriend and fighting an attraction to her ex-boyfriend. "Tonight is for celebrating."

"Some of us have more to celebrate than others," Meghan said, and watched as Rachel blushed scarlet. "How's the romance going, anyway?" As if she had to ask.

"Pretty good," Rachel said, suddenly going shy on Meghan.

"Only pretty good?"

"Okay. Very good. You ever have a crush on someone and then find out they're not nearly as nice as you thought they were?" Meghan nodded cautiously. "Well, Thad's better."

"Yeah, yeah, love's grand. Just wait until you want to have a life. Or better yet, wait until you start talking about babies."

Rachel shook her head sadly. "Bitter, bitter, bitter."

"You're damn right I'm bitter," Meghan said, laughing. "I'm officially not the person you should be talking to about relationships. Apparently my judgment sucks."

"So I can't blame you if things go south with me and Thad."

"No," Meghan said, following Rachel to the noise of the celebrating crew. After a good rest and shower, they were ready to party, and more than a few were already visibly intoxicated. The rum was flowing, and Meghan immediately saw that some of the younger crewmembers had actually managed to scare up some women to come to the party. Meghan was not surprised to see Will leaning up against a wall chatting with one of them. "Sure. Pour salt in the wound," she muttered, glaring at him.

"What?" Rachel asked.

"Nothing. Where'd all the women come from?"

Rachel looked around the room. "I only see two."

It felt like a harem to Meghan. When Will looked her way, Meghan turned toward the makeshift bar, which was manned by Thad.

"Aren't there any two-armed men who could be doing that instead?" Meghan asked, smiling.

"I don't mind. What'll you have?"

"A beer, I guess." She knew she sounded less than enthusiastic, but the whole thing with Alan was really bringing her down. The last thing she needed to witness was Will scoring with some beautiful brunette with big breasts.

Thad raised his eyebrows. "We did win, Meg."

"Okay. A Dark and Stormy, then. Better fits my mood."

Just then a pair of strong arms wrapped around her and picked her up, squeezing the air out of her lungs so she couldn't have protested even if she'd wanted to.

Will put her down and kissed her neck loudly. "Here's my girl," he said.

Meghan smiled and turned around, still in his arms. "I'm not your girl."

"Just for tonight, you are."

"What about the girl you were just talking to?"

Will grinned, his teeth white against his tanned skin. "You're jealous. How sweet."

"I just thought she looked a little young for you. It was sort of creepy."

Will let out a loud laugh and looked over to Thad. "Jealous," he said, and Thad nodded in agreement.

Meghan gently elbowed herself out of his embrace and grabbed her drink. "How many of these have you had?" she asked, eying him suspiciously.

"I don't know. Thad? You're keeping count, aren't you."

"One."

Will raised an eyebrow. "You sure?"

"Just the one, skipper."

"Then I must be high on victory," he said, picking Meghan up again and twirling her around once. Meghan couldn't help but laugh. No one, ever, was as full of life as Will. She'd forgotten how fun he was because he'd been so uncharacteristically intense during the past few weeks.

"Did you twirl Thad around, too?" she asked.

"Actually, he did," Thad deadpanned.

Behind them, the noise level rose ten decibels when the two college kids started arm wrestling. "Hey, I don't want anything broken," Will called over, and laughed when they booed him.

"It's not fair that they get to experience all this the first time out," Meghan said, looking at them with a small amount of envy. She'd been their age the first time she'd sailed an ocean race. It felt like so long ago when she'd been full of life and energy. Her only worry had been whether or not she'd get a hangover. And that hadn't really mattered because she wouldn't have had anything more pressing to do the next day than lie on a beach somewhere.

"Why not? Hell, it's always better to win than to lose. Doesn't matter how old you are."

"But they can't appreciate it like we can," Meghan argued.

"They'll appreciate it for the next twenty years when they crew on boats that don't win. They'll always look back on this night, on this boat, and say, 'we won the Newport-Bermuda when I was only twenty-one.'"

Meghan gave Will a small nudge. "You're not planning to win this again?"

"I doubt it. Not too many people have brought home the trophy more than once."

"You mean this is it? The end? Hang up the sail-cloth and go home? How can you say that?"

Will stared at her for a long moment. "Are you saying you're not saying it? I thought this was your last race."

It shouldn't have startled Meghan to be reminded of that pertinent fact, but for some reason it did. She'd become so enmeshed in the life again, so full of sailing and racing she actually forgot for a millisecond that this wasn't her life anymore. She was just borrowing it for a little while until she got back to her real life.

Her real life that, at this moment, was looking pretty crappy and unreal. She hadn't given a single thought to any of her clients in days. Honestly, she didn't care whether Alan had closed any deals—and she should.

"Let's take a walk," Will said.

Feeling a bit dazed, Meghan nodded and followed him outside into the warm, muggy Bermuda night. Bermuda muggy was different from New England muggy for some reason. The air here was invigorating, sensual even, while humidity back home seemed far more oppressive. A couple of guys were swimming in the pool, taking lazy strokes to where they'd left their drinks.

"I think I'll retire here," Meghan said. "I've always loved Bermuda."

"Do you think Alan would go for that?"

For the second time within minutes, Meghan was reminded that her life had changed. She knew who she was, she knew she would never retire to Bermuda. Then why the hell did something like that cross her lips? She shrugged. "People say stuff like that all the time and it never happens," she said.

Behind them, the pool was now empty. "Want to go for a swim?" Will asked. "For old time's sake?"

Meghan laughed and shook her head. "Nice try." She couldn't count the number of times she and Will had gone skinny-dipping, only to end up making love.

Will looked out over the dark waters of the Atlantic, the light from the house putting him in silhouette so Meghan couldn't see his expression. "I still remember you. Touching you," he said, his voice deep and rough, and Meghan closed her eyes in a desperate attempt to fend off the intense rush of desire that slammed into her.

"Will."

"God, you're so beautiful. I never told you how beautiful you are. I never told you anything."

"Well, it's too late now," Meghan said, her voice weirdly chipper in her attempt to sound casual because he'd sounded so raw, like a man about to say something irrevocable.

"Don't tell me that. He's not here, Meg. He's not and I am."

Meghan shook her head again and again as he walked toward her.

"I'm here, Meg."

All she could do was shake her head. She couldn't make her mouth move, couldn't make her tongue say what she knew she should. And she couldn't move her head away when he bent his toward her for a kiss. She couldn't move, she couldn't talk. All she could do is feel his warm breath against her lips as he waited for her to push him away or tell him no or say anything that would make him stop. But she stood there and let it happen, let him kiss her, let him put his arms around her, let him, let him.

She heard him groan, a deep, almost painful sound, as she finally responded. God, he could kiss. She'd missed that about him. His mouth was firm and soft and moving against her cheek, her neck, leaving her lips free to form the words she needed to say but for some insane reason wasn't saying.

And then it happened, sort of a spontaneous combustion of lust. He pushed up her shirt, she pulled down his pants, and they were on the ground, silent but for their harsh breathing, but for the roaring in Meghan's head. So good, so good. He kissed her breast, his beard rough against her skin, and then he took a nipple in his hot mouth and sucked until she arched her back and spread her legs to let him touch her. And he did, rough like she loved it, soft like she needed to come against his hand. But he stopped just before she climaxed, whispering something she didn't understand. He moved lower and she sighed, knowing what was coming—literally—next. She felt his mouth against her, his tongue, pressing against her, moving just right. He was so good at this. So damn good. His large hands cupped her bottom and he brought her closer, loving her until she arched her back and came, fighting hard not to scream because she'd hadn't come quite so hard in a very long time.

"Will," she whispered when her breathing was almost normal. "Thank you."

He chuckled softly, his smile showing even in the darkness. "You are very welcome," he said. "God, I missed you."

"Meghan."

That voice was almost like a sharp shard of ice piercing her heart. "Alan. Oh, my God, it's Alan," Meghan said, pulling up her panties and shoving down her skirt in a frenzy of movement.

"Shit." Will's head dropped to his hands, which lay on the sand. He was still between her legs; that is, until she pulled herself up and peeked between the bushes to see where Alan was. He was standing on the terrace, his eyes scanning the beach. A man came up next to him—Thad.

"I think she said something about taking a walk on the beach," Thad said over-loudly, sounding like he was reading from a bad script.

"Where's Will?" Alan asked, and Meghan's heart nearly stopped. Why would he ask that unless he was suspicious? Or was it only her guilty conscience causing her heart failure?

"I think he's in the head. The bathroom. After all those MREs, I don't think the mahi mahi sat very well with his stomach."

Meghan scuttled silently toward the side where a small wall divided the swimming pool from the lawn that eventually dropped sharply to the beach. Hunkering down, she checked her clothing to make certain everything was where it was supposed to be, her heart still thumping painfully in her chest.

"What are you doing?" Will asked. He'd made his way on his stomach like a soldier hiding from the enemy. It was too dark to see his expression, but Meghan was surprised to hear anger in his voice.

"It's Alan. I can't let him see us together," she whispered.

"Why not?" Will asked, as if challenging her.

"Will, please. I can't do this to him. He came here to surprise me and I was . . . Oh, God." She could feel her eyes fill with tears, as a deep sense of shame filled her. How could she have succumbed to Will's charms so easily when Alan was on a plane all this time trying to make her happy, trying to show her how much he loved her? It didn't matter that she'd been thinking about breaking up. Alan didn't deserve this.

"You can't do this to me," Will said, grabbing her shoulders and giving her a small shake.

"What?" She was so distracted by her own thoughts, by the horror of seeing Alan standing a few yards away from where she'd been writhing in ecstasy moments before, she didn't hear the agony in Will's voice, didn't see the desperation in his eyes that could only have meant one thing. All Meghan knew was that Alan was here and she was still tingling from the orgasm that Will had given her, that she was the shittiest girlfriend a man could have.

"You have to tell him," Will said, and his words, if not their meaning, finally reached her brain.

"Tell him what? About what just happened? Are you *crazy*?" she whispered.

She didn't look at him; she was trying to tell where Alan was, whether he was walking toward the beach, which would reveal their position. It was dark, but she was wearing a white T-shirt that would be easily seen even in the night. God, she couldn't believe Alan had shown up. She couldn't believe she'd allowed herself to be with Will. What was *wrong* with her? Will should have left her alone. No, she couldn't blame him. He was just being Will, trying to get a little, trying to celebrate their victory in the only way he knew how.

"Meghan." He touched her shoulder lightly until she turned her head. "You're going to him." It wasn't a question, but a statement.

"He's trying to surprise me. I cannot believe this is happening. Do you see him?"

Will moved his head so he was peeking over the wall. "He's talking with Thad," he said, his voice sounding oddly emotionless.

"Thad wouldn't say anything, would he?"

Will wanted to scream, wanted to yell at the top of his lungs that he loved her, wanted Alan to spontaneously combust so he would disappear. But she was there, hunkered down behind the wall, asking for him to help her sneak back to her fiancé. He could still taste her. His erection had just been throbbing, his hands still could feel her beneath him. And all she could think about was that Alan was here to surprise her.

"Thad's cool."

"How do I look?" she asked, and he could see the panic in her face, even in the darkness.

He knew what she looked like. Her eyes were still dilated from the passion, her lips were red and slightly swollen from their kisses, her cheeks were flushed from her orgasm. He didn't even have to look at her to know that. He knew exactly what she looked like, all he'd had to do was close his eyes for the past two years and he'd see her. "You look fine," he said.

"No grass in my hair?"

"Not that I can see."

Something in his voice perhaps tipped her off that her words were slowly killing him, like tiny pricks that, given enough of them, would bleed him dry. "Are you okay?" she asked.

"Sure."

"I'm going to sneak around that way," she said, jerking her head to the side of the house. "And walk up the path as if I'm coming from the beach. You stay here until we go inside and then go in the front door. Sound like a plan?"

"And what then? You go home with Alan?"

Meg looked away, as if suddenly realizing that he was more than bothered by Alan's appearance. She hugged herself and he felt the humiliating urge to comfort her. He clenched his fists to stop himself from pulling her into his arms and begging her to stay with him. Because he knew she wouldn't. She'd go to Alan the Tool, her fiancé.

"I don't know what to do," she whispered, and he could tell her eyes were filled with tears. "I screwed up, Will. I was mad and you were here and . . ."

He shook his head to stop her from pummeling his heart even more. He'd been convenient. A revenge. That's all he'd been. Well, isn't it what he deserved for letting her go? Didn't he deserve to suffer for being such a fool?

"Go ahead. I'll come in the front," he said, and gave her a gentle push toward the path.

He watched, torturing himself, as she came up the path and then pretended to be surprised to see

Alan there. He watched as she launched herself into his arms, but he couldn't bear it when Alan kissed her, so he closed his eyes, squeezing tight against the pain.

He didn't know if he could endure it, seeing her act as if nothing had happened, treating him like an old buddy. But he loved her and was finally figuring out what the hell that meant. He never should have kissed her. He shouldn't have put her in the position of cheating on Alan. Aw, fuck it. He should have done exactly what he'd done because he loved her and wanted her and he was pretty sure she felt the same way.

Will waited until the small group went back into the house, Thad giving a lingering look in his general direction. Then he snuck to the front of the house and let himself in. His body was bathed in sweat, so he supposed he did look a little sick when Alan spotted him and rushed over, his hand outstretched. If Will hadn't loved Meg, the look on her panicked face would have been priceless. As it was, it just cut into his already battered heart even more.

"Hey, Will, congratulations on your win. Saw it on the news this morning and got the first flight out."

Will grabbed the other man's hand, feeling slightly sick inside.

"Hear you're a little under the weather," Alan said, that bright smile on his face that Will found so damned irritating. Only now, he felt so guilty, so low, he couldn't bring himself to be irritated. He'd just shaken hands with the fiancé of the woman he'd just made come. Even if Alan was a tool, he didn't deserve that.

"Feel like shit, actually," Will said honestly, and let his gaze dart quickly over to Meg. She was looking at Alan, refusing to meet his eyes, as if she did Alan would suddenly know his mouth had just been between her legs.

"We're not going to be here all that long," Meg said. "I'm beat and so is Alan."

"Sure you don't want to stay a bit longer?" Alan said, looking down at Meghan like he wanted to devour her. "Looks like fun." He motioned with one hand around the room at the raucous crowd and Will figured the party was the last place Alan would want to be. The man hadn't seen his girlfriend in nearly a week, a girlfriend who could have died. Likely the last place on earth Alan wanted to be at this moment was at a crowded party. He'd want her naked in bed, that's what he'd want.

Will turned away before he killed him. He walked to the bar where Thad had taken over again, his entire body shaking.

"A rum," he said.

Thad didn't say a word, just poured the drink. He didn't even say a word when he obviously noted how badly Will's hand was shaking when he brought the glass up to his mouth. When Will turned back to the room, Alan and Meg were gone. So, that was it. They left, were probably holding hands, kissing. So happy to see one another after the long separation. Meg was probably mortified, scared to death Alan would somehow guess what she'd been up to. Maybe she was even contemplating telling him that she'd cheated on him.

None of that mattered.

What mattered was that she was sitting in a car next to another man who was thinking one thing: he couldn't wait to get her naked. He couldn't wait to be inside her. He couldn't wait to come. He was a guy like any other guy, so of course that's what he was thinking.

What would Meg do? Let him? Stop him?

And that, more than anything, was driving him insane. He couldn't let Alan do it. He could not touch her. Not tonight.

"What are you thinking, dude?" Thad asked.

Will could only shake his head.

"You can't. You have to . . ."

Will stood so suddenly his bar stool tipped over. "Don't tell me what I can't do," he said, low and savage.

Thad put his hands up. "Dude. Calm down. Have another drink. On second thought, maybe that's a bad idea."

"Where's Rachel?" Will asked suddenly.

"Why?"

"Because she knows where they're staying."

Thad looked like he wanted to say something, but instead he waved Rachel over. "Where are Alan and Meghan staying?"

Rachel looked between the two men as if trying to assess whether she could give them the information. "What's going on?"

"Nothing," Will said, trying to sound normal. "I've just got to tell Meg something important."

"Oh. Over in Newstead Belmont Hills."

"The country club time-share thing?"

Rachel shot another look over to Thad. "I don't know which unit, though."

Will gave her a tight smile. "I'll find it."

Chapter Eighteen

Meghan sat next to Alan in the taxi feeling as if she might be sick, not knowing what to do or say or even feel—other than the horrible grinding guilt that was consuming her. Everyone always said it was better not to tell, didn't they? Or did they say you should? Hell, she didn't know what to do or say. She only wished Alan hadn't come to Bermuda.

"You're quiet," he said, and to her ears it sounded like an accusation. *So, you've been screwing around on me.* "I expected you to be gushing about your big win."

Meghan tried to smile, but failed miserably. "I'm just really tired. It feels like jet lag. We hardly slept at all in the past twenty-four hours." She could feel him staring at her and she tried with all her power to hide what she was feeling. She knew how well Alan could read her, so she doubled her effort.

"What's wrong, baby?"

Shit.

Meghan tried to take a deep breath without Alan noting it. "Nothing. It's just what I said, I'm tired and . . ." *And I've just been with Will and it was wonder-*

ful and I'm scared as hell that you're going to want to make love and I'm not going to be able to and I won't have a good excuse so I'll fold and tell you and you'll hate me forever and I'm not even sure that's so bad.

"Just tired," she repeated, right before she started sobbing, just like that, so loudly the Bermudan taxi driver slowed down and spared a quick look to the back seat to make sure nothing awful was happening in his cab. Meghan quickly stifled her sobs, but the tears still flowed freely, a river of guilt down her face. She gave the driver an embarrassed wave and a shaky laugh to let him know she was okay, but she couldn't look at Alan, knowing she'd see alarmed concern in his face. She didn't deserve concern, she didn't deserve to have him there with her—even if deep down inside she was angry that he'd shown up when he'd said he wouldn't. *Don't blame him, it's not his fault you were lying almost naked with Will. It's not his fault you haven't felt that kind of desire and lust and passion since. . . . It's not his fault you're a horrible, horrible woman who doesn't deserve his love or concern.*

"I'm just so happy to see you," she said, hoping desperately he'd just let things go. But, of course, he couldn't. He had to probe, get down to her *feelings*, her true reason for crying. He couldn't let her be, couldn't pretend nothing was wrong even though she was desperate for him to believe she was simply tired and overjoyed to see him.

"No. What happened?" He had an edge to his voice that only made her panic increase. "You know you can tell me anything."

She shook her head, sharp, jerky movements. "No, I can't."

He sat back in the taxi and stared at her until she

had to look at him. "You're right. I don't want to talk about this right now," he said, and something in his voice made her shiver.

"There's nothing to talk about," Meghan insisted as the taxi pulled through the gates of the resort they were staying in.

For the next few minutes, they acted as if nothing were wrong, as if they were any couple on vacation in Bermuda. But Meghan felt a tingle of fear that Alan had somehow figured out what she and Will had done. It was the long looks he gave her, the way he opened her door, the way he smiled at her. Alan was angry. Far, far angrier than she'd ever seen him. In fact, Meghan had never seen Alan angry. They'd never fought, never disagreed about anything, she realized, feeling the heat of his eyes on her.

Their room overlooked Hamilton Harbor, and though it was just one step nicer than a hotel room, it was airy and pretty and way too far away from *Water Baby*'s crew. At that moment, Meghan wished hard that she was back in the house Frank had rented, tipping back Dark and Stormies, back joking around with Rachel and Thad. She wasn't afraid of Alan, but how could any woman be certain of a man's reaction when he suspected the worst of his fiancée?

"Wow, this is nice," she said, just to say something and fill the horrible silence in the room.

"I want the truth," he said, his voice steel.

Oh, God. "I don't know what you're . . ." she started, then closed her eyes. She *did* know what he was talking about.

"I didn't sleep with him, if that's what you're asking," she said quietly. She finally met his eyes, praying he would stop asking her questions, and stopped cold. She did not recognize the man standing in front of her.

"Did you kiss him?" he asked casually. Too casually.

"Alan."

"Did. You. Kiss. Him." He voice was low and vicious and very, very scary.

Meghan swallowed, and nodded.

"Did you like it?"

Tears filled her eyes and she shook her head, wanting him to stop.

"Liar."

"I was angry with you. You acted crazy when I got sick and then you said you weren't coming and . . ." She closed her eyes. "Will and I have a history together. It was stupid of me, I know, but nothing happened." Better to lie, better to lie. "Oh, Alan, I'm so sorry."

"Sorry. You're sorry," he said, shouting the last word so loudly she flinched. "If you didn't do anything then you don't have to be sorry, do you? I can't touch you now. I can't kiss you. I can't even look at you."

Meghan sat down on the pristine couch, feeling miserable. "I don't blame you," she muttered.

"Oh, you don't blame me. You don't *blame* me. Well, why the hell would you? What the fuck is that supposed to mean?"

"I didn't mean it like that and you know it. Can we please stop talking about this? Will and I kissed. I feel terrible about it. I'm here with you."

Alan walked over to her and planted his fists on his hips. "I want details."

Meghan shook her head. "That won't help matters."

"You did more than kiss."

Meghan kept her expression completely blank, because, frankly, he was frightening her now. She didn't like the odd light in his eyes. "We kissed," she repeated forcefully, knowing it was sort of an honest answer.

"You fucked," he shouted.

Meghan stood. "I'm leaving. I can't talk to you right now. I don't blame you for being angry, but you're scaring me, Alan."

"Good. And you're not going anywhere. I flew here to be with you. I wanted to surprise you. Well, I guess I did, didn't I?"

A knock at the door startled them both.

"Who is it," Alan called.

"Will."

The smile Alan gave Meghan chilled her to the bone. "I'm going to politely ask him to leave," he said. He held up a finger to his lips, keeping that awful smile.

Meghan watched as Alan took off his polo, ran his fingers viciously through his hair, then unbuttoned the top of his khakis before opening the door.

"Hey, Will. We're a little busy, if you know what I mean. Is this important?"

From Meghan's spot on the couch, she couldn't see Will, could only hear the hesitation. She wanted to call out, but was afraid that would only send Alan over whatever edge he was dangling near. He thought she'd slept with Will and he was probably more angry than he'd ever been in his life. She'd never seen him like this.

"No. It's not important. Sorry to disturb you."

"No problem, buddy," Alan said, his tone

friendly. "Maybe Meghan and I can catch up with you tomorrow."

Alan shut the door slowly, the smile fading when he turned to Meghan. "You fucked him," he said calmly, then slid, his back to the door, down to the floor.

Meghan swallowed, unable to answer.

"Do you love him?"

He sounded almost like the old Alan, but Meghan still couldn't answer him.

"No answer. Hmmm. Maybe you can answer this question, then. Do you love me?" He was crying, barely holding it together, as he looked at her.

Meghan felt tears prick her eyes. "Of course I do," she said.

He shook his head. "You don't. If you did, you couldn't have . . ." And then he began sobbing, a sound that was so startling, Meghan's first—and immediately squashed—impulse was to laugh. He was really letting it go, she thought, slightly stunned by the copiousness of his tears. She should have gone to him, crawled next to him, held him, told him she was sorry and everything was going to be all right, but she couldn't make herself do it. Instead, she sat on the couch and watched him cry until he got it together enough to stand up and join her on the couch. She knew what he wanted, what he needed her to do, and she was feeling just guilty enough to pull his head against her. When she felt the first kiss, she snuggled closer, ignoring her twisting stomach. And when he moved from her neck to kissing her jawline, heading for her mouth, she pulled away just slightly.

"I need you," he muttered against her mouth,

letting out a queer little noise that sounded oddly feminine.

Meghan pulled away. "We shouldn't, Alan. Not with our emotions so raw. I don't think it's a good idea. Tonight was crazy. We have a lifetime to figure this out, okay?" The mention of their lifetime together seemed to mollify him. Meghan could not make love to Alan tonight, not after all that had happened with Will, and she knew in her heart they would never make love again.

Alan sagged against her, sighing deeply. "Okay, baby. I understand." He lay his head on her lap, his face still slightly wet from his tears, and the only thought Meghan could dredge up was that she had to go pee and how long was she going to have to let him stay on her lap?

She caressed his hair, and lay her head back, closing her eyes. What an insane night, she thought, and that's when it hit her: Will had shown up at their door. Why would he do such a thing? And how had he in a million years found their apartment? She didn't want to think what it could mean, she didn't want to think at all.

"Why don't you want to make love, baby?"

Meghan almost groaned aloud. Alan never had been a person who could let go of a conflict until it was completely hashed out. "I don't think it would be fair to you. Or me. We just had a huge fight and I'm so tired I can barely think."

"I've never in all my life felt more angry than I did tonight," he said, keeping his eyes closed and his voice calm. "I wanted to kill you. Or him. Or myself." He let out another laugh.

"I'm sorry I brought you to that. I swear it."

Alan shook his head. "It doesn't matter now."

"Why not?"

Alan shrugged and his sudden secretiveness bothered her. Meghan wasn't sure what she should do now. She had a feeling Alan's mental state was fragile at best and she didn't want to get him upset again by suggesting she wanted to leave. For a long while they sat like that, Meghan sitting on the couch with Alan's head resting on her lap, pressing against her bladder.

"Alan, I have to go pee. My bladder's about to burst."

"I don't like it when you talk like that, baby," he said blandly, sitting up to allow her to escape.

"Well, I don't like it when you call me baby and I've told you that a hundred times."

He let out a chuckle. "Put it in our wedding vows alongside that part about not fucking other people."

Meghan stopped midstride and turned back toward Alan. "I don't think I can stay here tonight," she said, and walked as calmly as she could toward the door. Thankfully, she hadn't unpacked and her duffle was still near the door.

"If you go to him, that's it for us. We're through. I'm not a complete idiot, Meghan."

Meghan picked up her duffle and opened the door. "I don't think you're an idiot, Alan. I think you're very angry and you're not thinking straight. I'm not going to him. I don't know where I'm going right now."

"Why would Will come here tonight, Meghan?"

"I wondered the same thing. I don't have an answer."

Alan pretended to think about it. "Let's see. If I thought the woman I loved, the woman I just slept with, was going to sleep with another man, what would I do?"

Meghan snorted. "Will doesn't love me."

"He just went for a walk and ended up here." Alan's tone was ugly.

"I'm leaving."

Behind her, Alan laughed. "You don't love either one of us, do you?" he called right before the door slammed shut.

Meghan walked to the resort's taxi stand. It was close to midnight and she felt like a walking zombie, never mind that she'd never made it to the bathroom and was in dire need of one.

She climbed into the small Toyota, waving off the driving who wanted to take her bag.

"Where would you like to go?"

The driver smiled at her and Meghan tried to smile back. She wanted to go home—and not her apartment. She wanted to go to home to North Carolina and her mother and father. She wanted someone to give her a hug and tell her she wasn't a terrible person. She didn't want anyone looking at her with anger or passion or anything but unconditional love. Her mother, as much as she liked Alan, would know better than to say a word if she could see her daughter at that moment.

Meghan gave him the name of the marina where *Water Baby* was docked, and she smiled at her stroke of genius. No one would be on the boat, she'd be blessedly alone. And then she'd call her mother and cry and ask her how she could have raised a daughter who could ruin her life and very possibly the lives of two men in a single night. Heartbreaker.

Yup, that was her, all right. She was pretty sure she hadn't broken Will's heart, but she had pissed him off pretty good by going off with Alan.

The taxi driver tried to be friendly, and even asked if she'd been a part of the Newport-Bermuda race, but Meghan couldn't even attempt a civil response. Her need to be alone had overtaken her need to pee and that was saying something.

After paying the driver, Meghan ran to the boat, dug through her duffle for the companionway key and let herself into the boat, going directly to the head. Then she climbed onto one of the bunks, cell phone in hand, and called her mother.

"Meghan. Did you get your surprise?"

Meghan started crying, knowing it would freak her mother out, but she just couldn't stop herself.

"Meghan, what happened? What's wrong?"

She heard the panic in her mother's voice and tried to answer. "Alan . . ."

"Oh, God, no. He's dead."

She would have laughed if she wasn't feeling so completely awful. "No, Mom, he's not dead. We had a fight."

"You scared the hell out of me," she said, laughing. "A big fight or a little fight?"

"Big. Will and I . . ."

"Don't tell me. I don't want to know."

Meghan started crying again, feeling tired and so damned sad she wished she could reverse her entire life, like Superman had, and make the last six hours disappear.

"Okay, tell me. Meghan, calm down."

Meghan took a deep breath. "Will's been so nice to me. He was always nice. It wasn't his fault."

"You slept with him."

"No," Meghan said quickly. "Not quite." She winced at her own words. She would have made love to Will had they not been interrupted. They probably would have made love all night because that's the way they'd always been, especially if they hadn't seen each other in a while. "I didn't know Alan was coming," she said miserably.

"He caught you?" came her mother's flabbergasted question.

"Not quite. No. He interrupted and didn't know it and I pretended everything was okay, but of course it wasn't and he started asking questions and getting angry so I had to tell him something."

There was a long silence while her mother digested what she'd told her. "Where are you now?"

"I'm at the boat. Alone."

"That's good. Let Alan calm down, then the two of you can talk and if you can't work it out, that's it."

Meghan smiled. "That sounds like a good plan. Mom? I'm not sure I want to work it out."

"Okay, honey," she said after a long pause. "Call me tomorrow and let me know what's happening, okay?"

Meghan knew her mother would be like that, wonderful and nonjudgmental. "Mom, thanks. I love you."

"Yes, I know. But I do wish you'd marry someone nice like your sister did."

"Alan was a bit of a psycho tonight, so I don't know if he qualifies as nice anymore. Part of me doesn't blame him. The other part was a little scared."

"Scared?"

"He was extremely upset."

"I suppose," her mother said doubtfully. "Call me tomorrow or I'll call the Bermudan police."

Meghan laughed. "Bye, Mom."

Meghan snapped her phone closed and stared at the blue canvas bunk above her. She'd screwed up many, many times in her life, but this won the prize. She was dreading tomorrow, because not only was she going to have to face Alan, she was going to have to face Will and she didn't know which would be more difficult.

"He's back," Rachel whispered to Thad. They were sitting on the couch getting each other's opinions on everything from the Red Sox chances that year to who would win the next presidential election. They didn't agree on much—to Rachel's horror, one of Thad's favorite movies was The Big Lebowski—but she loved every minute of their discussion. The other crewmembers had long gone to bed or made their way into town to the clubs. But she was content to sit with her head in the nook of his arm, relishing the feeling of a strong, sexy man sitting next to her. When Will arrived back, Thad straightened up.

"You okay?" he asked. Rachel could feel the tension in Thad's body as he looked at his friend.

"No."

That single syllable nearly made Rachel shiver—or maybe it was the empty look in Will's eyes. She'd known Will for years and she'd never seen anything close to that look.

"You want to talk?"

Will made a poor attempt at a smile. "No. I'm going to bed."

After he was gone, Thad and Rachel resumed their previous positions. "He's messed up," he said, low so Will wouldn't hear him. "I didn't think she could do it again, but she did."

Rachel pushed slightly away. "Are you telling me that you somehow blame Meghan? She loved him. She wanted to marry him and he wouldn't."

"That doesn't mean he didn't love her."

Rachel rolled her eyes. "It means he didn't love her enough."

"What happened two years ago is ancient history. I knew he was asking for trouble when he went to get Meghan for this race. He never got over her."

"Well, she got over him," Rachel said with a certainty she didn't really feel.

"She's got a funny way of showing it. They were out there together when her boyfriend arrived."

Rachel's mouth hung open in shock. "Are you sure?"

"Sure I'm sure. When the guy showed up I knew there was going to be trouble. They were on the other side of the pool and I don't think they were just talking."

Despite the seriousness of the conversation, Rachel laughed. "You mean they were making out?"

He grunted. "Something like that." He was obviously implying that more was happening than mere kissing.

"Oh, my God. And then Alan showed up and Meghan went with him?"

"And Will went after her. Guess it didn't go well," Thad said, looking toward the darkened hallway where Will had disappeared.

"Poor Meg," she said, knowing it would rankle him.

Thad shook his head in disbelief. "Poor Meg? Are you kidding me?"

Rachel gave him a look. "How do you think she felt, knowing she'd been cheating on her fiancé with her ex-boyfriend and she had to go off with him and pretend nothing happened? Maybe some women wouldn't care, but I know Meghan did."

"She didn't have to go with him."

"Of course she did. It was either go with the man who loved her or stay with someone who was just using her because it was convenient."

Before Thad could spit fire, she laughed. "I'm only kidding. Will would never do that. And from the look on his face, I think he might actually love Meghan as much as you said."

"Might? He's so far gone, it's pathetic."

"Will loves Meghan? Did he tell you that?"

"Guys don't tell each other shit like that. But basically, yeah, he told me."

They settled back down, Rachel taking her position again. "I think Meghan might love Will, too. She just won't admit it because she's so afraid he'll hurt her again."

Thad let out another grunt.

"Getting bored with all this talk?" she asked, smiling up at him.

"I can think of better things to do."

Thad bent his head and Rachel met his mouth halfway. She might not have a lot of practice kissing men, but it sure was fun learning. There was something about the way he moved his mouth, slow and incredibly erotic, that made Rachel want to throw herself on top of him and rip his clothes off. She'd thought about it, oh, maybe a hundred times or so in the past few years. But now that the object of her fantasies was actually kissing her, moving his hands on her thigh, moving his hand to her breast, moving his thumb across her nipple, it was almost more than she could take.

"That feels so good," she said, every nerve of her body seemingly centered on that thumb moving slowly back and forth against her hardening nipple.

"I want to suck you," he said, and pushed her cotton wrap blouse aside along with her bra so he could do just that. "God, I love your nipples." He licked her, then took her rather embarrassingly large nipple into his mouth and . . . she let out a scream.

"Sorry," she said, laughing. It was obvious that Thad wanted to get back to business, but Rachel couldn't stop laughing.

"What's so funny?" he finally asked, his eyes moving from her enticing breast to her eyes.

Rachel swallowed and let out another giggle, right before she felt her eyes prick with tears. "I have to tell you something," she said, and looked down at her hands.

"Go on."

"I . . . You . . ." She looked up at his beautiful face, strong and masculine and a little scary unless you didn't know what a teddy bear he was. "I'm a virgin."

His eyebrows went straight up. "Like a *virgin* virgin?"

"Yes. Whatever that means."

"Wow." A slow smile spread on his face. "I think I'm up for the challenge. If that's okay with you," he added quickly.

Rachel nodded, all shy again. "You do like me a little, don't you?"

"I'm pretty sure I like you more than a little," he said. "You're the most beautiful, sexy, funny woman I've ever been with."

She gave him a look of obvious skepticism. "Don't forget I've seen a few of your girlfriends."

"I mean the total package." He kissed her, long and hot and almost made her scream again.

"If you're going to be noisy, maybe we should wait until we can get a hotel."

Rachel's cheeks blushed, but she nodded. "I think you're going to make me scream, Thad."

He closed his eyes as if in ecstasy and Rachel got such a rush of love and lust she almost dragged him outside and down to the beach. A hotel, she thought, would be much better.

"I'm finding a room tomorrow," he said with conviction. "And if I can't find one, I'll borrow one."

Chapter Nineteen

Meghan woke up feeling groggy and depressed. Nothing was going the way it was supposed to. Her well-planned, perfect life was dissolving beneath her feet and she didn't have a clue how to stop it. Or even if she wanted to. She knew, with a huge effort, Alan would forgive her. The problem was she wasn't sure that's what she wanted. What the hell had happened to the woman who knew exactly what she wanted and had that goal at her fingertips not three weeks ago? She knew what happened. She climbed aboard a sailboat with Will Scott, the love of her life, the man who could make her forgot who she was.

Or make her remember.

"Damn," she shouted, then put the pillow over her head and screamed. No need to alarm other boaters nearby.

Somewhere along the way, she'd lost who she was—or at least who she thought she was. Right now, she was the woman who'd broken one man's heart and possibly ripped another man's heart from his chest. She'd never been so wishy-washy.

She hated wishy-washy women. When had this happened? When had the girl she'd known and loved become this rotten, deceitful, indecisive woman?

Meghan heaved herself out of the bunk, scrubbing at the blond curls that had tightened overnight in the humid air. She stumbled to the head and caught her reflection in the mirror over the tiny sink. She saw a woman with dark circles beneath her red-rimmed eyes, skin bronzed from the sun, with tiny salty tear tracks lining her cheeks. "Who the hell are you and what did you do with me?" she asked her reflection.

Meghan washed her face with a bottle of water before making her way out of the boat to face the day and the consequences of her actions. Within ten minutes she was walking into the house Frank had rented for the crew, faintly shocked to see it was only seven in the morning and everyone still in their rooms, apparently asleep. Including Will.

Suddenly, she knew. She wanted to see Will, wanted to hold him, to tell him she was sorry, to tell him that she and Alan had done nothing but argue—about him. She wanted Will to know, maybe not that she loved him, but that she wanted to be back in his life.

Meghan walked toward Will's room, stopping when she got to the door, afraid he'd be as angry as Alan, afraid he'd tell her to go to hell.

"He's gone."

Meghan turned to see Thad, standing in his doorway wearing nothing but a pair of boxers decorated with New England Patriots helmets. "What do you mean?"

"Frank died last night and he's taking the first flight out this morning." He looked at his wrist, and seeing nothing but skin, backed into the room to check the time. "He's already gone. Took the seven A.M. out of Hamilton."

"Frank *died*?" She couldn't believe it. She'd known he was ill, but no one had ever indicated he was that sick.

"He was really sick. Why do you think Will wanted this so much? It was all for Frank," Thad said, and his eyes got suspiciously misty even as his tone was tinged with anger, as if she should have known, as if she would have done something differently.

Tears filled Meghan's eyes. "But I didn't get to see him. I didn't know. I can't believe he's gone. And Will." Her heart suddenly felt filled with something heavy and awful. "He must be devastated. Oh, my God."

"It wasn't a good night for him," Thad said, and the look he gave Meghan made her feel one step above a piece of dirt. And Thad was a nice guy.

Meghan wiped her tears away with the tips of her fingers. "I've got to go. He shouldn't be alone."

"I really don't think you're the person he needs right now," Thad said, and Meghan knew then that Thad was aware of at least some of the drama that had unfolded the night before.

"Thad, I never meant to hurt him. I didn't even know I *could* hurt him."

Thad's expression softened infinitesimally. "I guess you could say the timing sucked. But Will wants us to stay here to collect the trophy. He won't be back in time, with the funeral and all. He wanted you to accept the trophy."

Meghan shook her head, her throat aching so much she didn't think she could talk. "No," she finally choked out.

"It's what he wanted, Meg. At least give him that."

Thad shut the door, leaving Meghan standing in the hall with tears flowing down her face. Will had known Frank was dying. He'd known the whole time and she'd just thought all that intensity had been about the race. It had never been about the race; it had been about Frank and that promise the old man made to his son. All during the race Will hadn't said a thing, he'd just kept his eyes on the horizon and his mind on the race. When he wasn't at the helm, he'd been below, checking instrumentation and navigating the boat to victory, a man completely focused on victory.

And yet . . .

Meghan ran blindly for her door, closed it, and threw herself on her bed as a horrible, wonderful, devastating realization came to her. Will had been willing to end the race. For her. He'd been willing to board that Coast Guard boat with her and throw in the towel without even a thought about what it would mean to that promise he'd made. All for her. He hadn't questioned it, hadn't let her have an inkling what was at stake.

Only one thing could explain that. Will loved her. He loved her enough to give up a dream, give up a promise to a man he loved more than life itself.

Wave after wave of torturing awareness hit her. Will loved her, she was sure of that, and she understood why he'd shown up at Alan's door, how he must have felt when Alan opened the door and seen him standing there half naked. Alan had known and she hadn't. Meghan had entered a new level of self-loathing, one she wasn't quite sure how to climb out of.

She grabbed blindly for her cell phone and pressed Will's number, then hung up, realizing he was still on the plane. She didn't want to leave a message. What would she say?

She heard a soft knock on the door and quickly wiped her face when Rachel peeked in. "Are you okay?"

"No," she said, sounding stuffed and about as sad as a person can get. "One of my favorite people in the world just died, and apparently I've managed to rip out the hearts of two men in one night."

"Wow," Rachel said with a sympathetic grimace. "What happened, anyway? I've been guessing, but . . ."

"I'm sure what happened is far worse than your imagination." Meghan flopped back on the bed. "Will and I were getting sort of hot and heavy when Alan showed up." She squeezed her eyes shut. "Alan wanted to surprise me. Surprise." She waved her hands, a sad imitation of happiness. "Of course I felt sick. About Alan and what I'd been doing."

"And Will?"

"We were just messing around. I never in a million years thought it was anything but that. I felt guilty but Will and I, well, we sort of spontaneously combusted." She let out an embarrassed laugh, which quickly turned to a sob. "I didn't mean to hurt him."

"Of course not."

"But I really think I did. Will showed up at Alan's and I was like, what the heck is he doing here? Alan and I were in the middle of a huge fight because he guessed what I'd been doing with Will. Or at least part of it." Meghan let out a groan. "What a mess." She sat up and looked at her friend. "The thing is, I'm a nice person. I would never hurt anyone on purpose. I'm not vindictive or small or petty or anything. I'm nice," she shouted.

"You are almost a saint," Rachel said.

Meghan shook her head. "No, I'm not. I'm such a jerk."

"Well, it wasn't your most shining moment," Rachel agreed.

"I thought you said I was a saint."

Rachel laughed. "I'm really just trying to make you feel better."

Meghan walked to the bureau to get a tissue and blew her nose. "Tell me the truth."

"I think Will is madly in love with you. But you can't be blamed for not knowing it. I'm pretty sure he didn't tell you."

"He didn't."

"And from what I've heard about Alan . . ." Rachel shrugged.

"What have you heard?"

"You have to consider the source. Thad is Will's best friend and he's extremely loyal. I'm sure Alan's a nice guy," Rachel said hesitantly. "But no one could figure out what you saw in him."

"Why?" Then Meghan shook her head. "Don't bother. I already know. Alan is the opposite of Will. I thought that's what I loved about him."

"And now?"

"Now I'm so confused, I don't know what to think," Meghan said honestly.

Two hours later, Alan showed up at the door looking haggard, asking for Meghan. He refused to step into the house, as if it were something evil.

"I want the ring," he said, holding out his right hand. "I paid ten thousand dollars for it, and frankly, you were a bad investment."

Meghan stared at him, wondering why she didn't feel anything more than relief. And a tiny bit of irritation. "I don't have it with me. It's at the apartment. I'll give it to you when I get back."

"If I don't have it within two weeks, I'm contacting my attorney."

Meghan would be the first person to admit Alan had every right to be mad, but this imperious, arrogant attitude was beginning to grate. "I'm going to give it back to you, Alan, because I don't want it."

He started to turn away, then stopped, and Meghan wished he'd kept going. She could take his anger; she figured she deserved it and it made it easy for her to say good riddance. But when he turned back, it was old Alan, the one she'd fallen in love with, except now he had tears in his eyes. "I loved you so much," he said, and his face crumpled. "I would have done anything for you."

Meghan took a step toward him, but stopped when he jerked slightly away from her, as if he couldn't stand the thought of her touching him. "I'm sorry, Alan. I wasn't fair to you or to myself. I thought I could change myself, reinvent who I was. But I can't and I'm just so sorry that you got hurt by this."

He shook his head as if denying what she was saying, then turned and walked away. This time he didn't look back.

Will stood on the rocky beach in front of Frank's house, feeling battered and so worn down he could barely stand against the stiff breeze blowing in off the bay. Frank had loved days like this, when the usually calm bay turned choppy and gray and alive.

The funeral had been one of the saddest things he'd ever experienced, mostly because Nancy, who'd been a rock throughout Frank's illness, had finally let the stress and heartache of the past months out in a torrent of public grief that was torture to watch. Will, who'd wanted to rail against God and join Nancy in her grief, had held her as she sobbed a lifetime of tears against his best suit while horrified friends and relatives looked on.

Later, when she was calm and the tears long dried, she tried to explain to him and perhaps to herself why she'd lost it so badly at the funeral. "I think, even though he's been dying for years, I never let myself really believe he was going. And then, I was sitting there in the church and I knew in here," she said, tapping her head, "that Frank was in that coffin, but I turned to say something to him, to Frank. And he wasn't there. And it hit me, he's never going to be there again."

"I think we'll both be doing that for a long time. I actually picked up my cell to tell him something about the race. I was on my way to the wake." Will shook his head.

When his father had died, Will had gone to the funeral only because it was the right thing to do. The only other people to attend were a handful of drinking buddies. The entire event had left Will feeling depressed and wondering how anyone could waste a life the way his father had. He'd been blessed with a good brain and a son who would have loved him if he'd given him half a chance. But Jared Scott at some point had decided the world was against him and to hell with everyone—including himself.

If it hadn't been for Frank, Will might have

ended up like the old man and maybe that's why Jared hated his son so much. Will had gotten a shot that he hadn't; he had someone to love him, to teach him right from wrong when the only thing his own father could teach him was how to cure a hangover.

Will's cell phone rang and he dug it out of his pocket and glanced at the number. Meg. Yeah. He really wanted to talk to the woman who'd shattered his heart right before Frank's death had ripped what was left clean out. It was the fourth time she'd called and she never left a message. Might as well get it over with.

"Yeah."

"Will? It's Meghan."

"Okay."

He waited, gut churning, for her to say something.

"Are you all right?"

Considering that his eyes were burning and his throat felt like he had a golf ball lodged in it, there wasn't a hell of a lot he could say at the moment. The thing of it was, he didn't know if he was reacting to Frank's death or Meg's phone call. "No."

"Will. I want to see you. I . . ." He could tell she was losing it, so he figured he'd help her out.

"I'm real busy right now."

"Oh."

"Bye, Meg." And yet, he didn't close his phone, he waited for some reason, hoping she'd say something to make some of this godawful pain go away.

"I . . . I'm sorry."

Wrong answer. He hung up.

He walked back up to the house where Nancy was sitting with some friends talking about when their children were young, how things had changed. When Nancy saw Will, she stood up.

"Are you leaving now?"

"Unless you need me to stay."

Nancy smiled. "No, no. You go. I'll call you if I need anything."

"I'll be back next week and fix the lock on your slider," Will said, bending down to kiss her cheek, and then giving in and hugging her close.

"I know. It's so hard," Nancy said, giving him a squeeze.

"Call if you need anything."

Forty minutes later, Will was putting his key into his house in Newport, when one of his tenants peeked out of her door.

"How was the funeral, Will?" Louise had been living in his building for more than thirty years. When Will bought the place last year, she never even asked if he was kicking her out, which, of course, made it impossible to make her leave. She had the nicest apartment in the place at the time, but Will was slowly turning the old Victorian into a single family home. As depressing as it was, the only way he ever got to take over an apartment was when the tenant died or went into a nursing home. He'd already gained a one- and two-bed apartment that way. And Louise would be next; it wasn't a pleasant thought.

"It was very nice," he said, knowing it was what she expected to hear. "Very well attended."

"That's good. Mr. Walcott was such a good friend to you. Do you want to come in for some chicken soup?" It was eighty-five degrees out and humid. The last thing he wanted to put into his mouth was steaming hot soup.

"Sure, Lou. Sounds good."

He went into her morbidly hot apartment and sat in her kitchen at one of those old-fashioned metal kitchen tables with the plastic-cushioned metal chairs. "You can put the air conditioning on, you know, Lou. It's why I installed it last summer."

"Are you warm?" she asked, looking slightly alarmed.

"No," he said with an inward smile. "Just wanted to remind you that it's there."

"It's always better the second day, so I'll give you some to take home with you," she said, ladling some of the thick soup into a bowl and another portion into a plastic container. Will didn't protest. Louise made some of the best chicken soup he'd tasted, even on a hot summer's day.

He ate the soup with her looking on. He must have eaten in her kitchen a hundred times and she'd never eaten with him, just looked on with a happy light in her eyes that someone was eating and liking her cooking.

"How was that race of yours?"

"We won a trophy," Will said between bites.

"Good for you." She moved her hands across the faux marble top of the table. "You had Meg on the boat?"

"She was there. And so was her fiancé."

"Oh," Louise said, with a slight look of distaste. "That's too bad. I always said you'd end up together. Carla and I would talk about it all time." A bit of sadness entered her tone; Carla died six months ago, leaving Louise alone with Will in the building and Will with another piece of his house.

"Not this time. We're just old friends now," Will said, trying to keep his voice light even as his chest felt like it was filled with lead.

"She'll come around," Louise said, as if that were even an option. "I have a feeling. And you know about me and my feelings. I knew something was wrong with Carla months before she passed."

"She was ninety-eight," Will said, unable to suppress a grin.

"Still. I knew."

"You knew. You knew you'd have me all to yourself so you could fatten me up."

Louise laughed, and lightly slapped the table. "You're right. I'm making beef stew later in the week, if you're interested."

Beef stew was not a typical summer meal. "Just let me know when it's done." Will stood and carried his empty bowl to the sink, rinsed it and placed it in the dishwasher for her.

"Chicken soup makes everything better. Did you know that?"

Will wasn't sure if Louise was a bit batty or just being kind in her own eccentric way.

"Well, I do feel better, Lou." He picked up the container, not feeling even a little better as he walked toward the door.

Meg looked at the "call ended" message through blurry eyes. What had she expected? That he'd tell her he needed her, that he'd forgiven her? Not that she needed forgiveness. How was she supposed to know that he loved her? Heck, she still wasn't convinced because, guess what? He hadn't told her he did. Sure, all the signs were there, but maybe Will was just a nice guy. Maybe he did love her, the way someone loves an old friend. And old friend with benefits.

Who was she kidding?

If he just hadn't been so cold on the phone. If he'd just given her some sign that he'd left a tiny crack open to let her in.

She was leaving Bermuda today. In Will's absence, it had been left up to her to make sure the house was cleaned—or at least didn't look as though it had been the site of a half-dozen parties in the last several days. Most of the crew had flown out in the morning, except for Thad and the college kids who were sailing *Water Baby* and the trophy home. The house seemed strangely quiet. She could hear the surf, the frequent sound of scooters buzzing down the street, and the splash of the pool next door, and she felt incredibly alone.

Without much thought, she opened her phone and hit the speed dial for her parents' house. "Dad? I thought I'd come home for a few days, just to regroup."

Chapter Twenty

Meghan waited until she was certain everyone was out of the office before going in and clearing out her desk. She knew she was a coward for sneaking in late at night, but she wasn't up for a confrontation with Alan or anyone else in the office. She'd been in the office after hours many times, but felt like a thief this night, as if she didn't belong. And she really didn't. She'd been out of the office now nearly a month, and even though she hadn't officially quit, no one expected her to come back.

Her desk was neat, only because she'd done that right before she started practicing for the race. The cleaning crew had dusted, so even the pictures she had on her desk were spiffy. Finally her eyes came to rest on a picture of her and Alan on a skiing trip last winter. She braced herself for some emotion and was surprised when only a small bit of sadness hit her. She'd hated skiing, but she'd gone anyway. She'd tried her best and Alan had been incredibly patient with her, considering he was an amazing down-hiller. They'd ended up going cross-country skiing and she tried to convince herself she enjoyed getting sweaty in subzero temperatures and he tried to convince himself he liked cross-country when he really wanted to be flying down the hill. Meghan supposed they'd been trying to do that for their entire relationship, trying to convince themselves and each other that they were perfect for one another.

She was halfway done cleaning out her desk before she realized she really didn't want anything except the photo of her and her parents at their silver anniversary party.

Two years of her life ended up in the trash can. She walked over and placed her listings and the picture of them on Alan's desk. A parting gift. She'd contacted the sellers who were depressingly willing to let Alan take over the job of selling their homes. After all, he'd been handling them while she was gone anyway.

She hid the ring—the bad investment—in the back corner of his desk, then e-mailed him to let him know it was there.

> Alan. The ring is in your top drawer in the back. I'm sorry I couldn't be what you wanted—or even what I wanted.
>
> —Meghan

Considering she'd worked so hard to forge this new life, it was remarkably easy to walk away from it. The tough thing was figuring out what she was going to do next. Her father initially had her convinced to come home, find a job, save her money and buy a house near them. What did she have in Rhode Island to hold her? What had she ever had?

The problem was she really didn't have any skills. She could be a waitress or work in McDonald's. She could get her real estate license in North Carolina, but the thought of that made her slightly ill. The truth was, she wasn't very good at selling houses. She'd made enough to feel slightly less poor than she had been, but she'd never loved it the way Alan had. The only thing she'd ever loved, felt passionate about, was sailing, and God knew it wasn't easy to make a living doing that. She'd thought, ridiculously briefly, about going back to school, but she still didn't know what she wanted to be when she grew up. She was only good at one thing—other than screwing up her life and everyone she touched—sailing. Her father, strangely enough given the boat she'd ended up on, used to call her his little water baby. Growing up on the Outer Banks, she'd been in or on the water as long as she could remember.

Meg closed up the office and drove home, smiling when she saw her brightly colored walls. She didn't want to go into the bedroom, it held too many memories, it was too beige, too . . . Alan. So she went into her hall closet and pulled down her old purple-and-yellow-checked comforter and lay down on the couch, TV remote in hand. Turning on NESN, she watched the Red Sox beat the Yankees and took that as a sign she should stay in New England.

Marcy Matthews, one of Will's college student instructors, walked into his office smelling like sunblock and salt air, and placed a piece of paper on his desk. "You see this?"

"This" was the announcement of a new sailing school targeting tourists. The name of the business was Day Sailor and it promised to teach anyone to sail in a single, intensive one-day course. Students were "guaranteed" to pass any sailboat rental business's test. Conveniently, the new "school" rented boats. Fast-food sailing.

"I give it two months," Will said, wondering why anyone would start a seasonal business when it was nearly August. He wasn't worried that the new business would compete with him; it was targeting a completely different audience. But he did worry about some hack coming in and diluting the purity of the sport. Sailing was a religion to Will and he didn't much care for the thought of someone cheapening it like that.

"I had one of the parents ask me if you could really learn how to sail in one day and if so, why we were charging for six weeks of lessons."

Okay, maybe he was a tiny bit worried. "What did you tell them?"

She flashed him a smile, making Will think that she really was a very pretty girl. And she was brunette; she had that going for her. "Easy. I told them it was impossible to learn how to sail in a day. It's like learning to drive. Sure you can start a car and steer, but are you really ready go out on a super highway after one day? Would they want their kid behind the wheel of car with only one driving lesson?"

Will grinned. "You are a genius."

Marcy blushed and immediately looked away. "I think they put them on every car in town," she said, picking up the flyer.

Will had a feeling Marcy had a crush on him, and it wouldn't have been too long ago when he might have pursued it. But she was too young and too brunette, and too tall, and too not everything he really wanted, even though he figured she was exactly what he needed. He knew he was in for a long, long road back to the place where he'd actually want to be with anyone who wasn't Meghan. When she'd walked away the last time, it had taken him many agonizing weeks before he could think of actually dating someone. He'd screwed his fair share, but that was different, that was sex. He didn't even want sex at the moment.

He just wanted Meghan. Which meant he was a pathetic loser.

"Hey, see this?" Thad asked, slapping the flyer on his desk. Thad worked as manager for Bowen's Wharf, so he basically just hung around the sailing school bugging Will most of the day. At least that's the way it seemed since they'd gotten back from Bermuda. Thad would give him these weird long looks as if he was afraid Will was contemplating something crazy—like climbing to the nearest clock tower and snipering every blonde with curling hair he saw.

"He's seen it," Marcy said from the hall where she was pressing thumbtacks into the revised July schedule of available classes.

"You do know who's behind this, don't you?" Thad asked.

"Sanderson?" Will asked, baffled as to why Sanderson would bother doing something so pedestrian as to start a sailing school that was doomed to fail. The guy was a multimillionaire.

"Good thing you're sittin', dude. It's Meghan."

Chapter Twenty-One

Meghan's venture consisted of three sailboats, one of which probably shouldn't be in the water, but it looked nice and romantic and so far had been enough to draw a number of customers her way. She hadn't put the schooner out on the bay, but that was okay; it was the perfect place to string the sign for her school. Besides, it was easy to explain to the novice that the schooner was set aside for more experienced sailors. Over the winter she planned to have it refurbished so she'd feel good about renting it. She would have liked to have started her business in May at thc bcginning of the tourist season. She'd only have six to eight weeks to tap into the market before the weather turned cool and the tourists fled for warmer places. It meant that for at least this year, she'd have to use her realtor's license, but at least she'd have the summer to look forward to. And someday she'd have enough business to sustain her for the entire year. Of course, her decision to start a sailing school in Newport had nothing to do with the fact that Will lived there, worked there, and also ran a sailing school.

She told herself that, not believing a word she said. She also told her father that and he hadn't believed her either. He'd just grinned in a maddening way that made her feel like she was ten and was trying to convince him she could go to the mall by herself. She'd been back in town nearly a month—it had taken that long to get city licensing and harbor master approval—and she hadn't seen Will once. Not that she'd been looking at every sailboat that motored by her slips. Not that her heart would jump into double-time if she thought she saw someone who might be him. No, sir. It was only natural that eventually she'd run into him and she was prepared. "Hello, Will, how are you? I'm fine. Okay, I'm not fine. I miss you and I'm so afraid you hate me that I can't seemed to gather the courage to go see you because what if I do and you're all cold and distant? You've never been that way to me before and I think if you were I'd just die. So that's why I haven't been to see you. I'm a coward. But I knew we'd run into each other eventually and here we are." Yep. She'd be real smooth.

Meghan, who didn't have a lot of confidence in the relationship department, knew one thing. She was good at sailing. Real good. And she also found out she was pretty darn good at teaching it, too. When she'd first come up with the concept, she'd had doubts. But now that she'd gotten a few lessons under her belt and watched the new sailors handle boats with confidence, she was convinced she'd made the right move. None of her students could crew in the America's Cup, but they could go for a day sail and be safe.

Meghan's Day Sailor charged two-hundred-fifty dollars per student for the one-day lessons and five hundred to rent a boat for a day, and had more tourists than she could handle. Her course was an intensive, eight-hour class in which she immersed the students—usually a couple—into sailing by making them raise and lower the sails, pull into a slip, reef the main and jibs, drop anchor and hook onto a mooring. They tacked, they headed into wind, they learned basic navigation. Nearly everyone who had hired her had complained she was a female Captain Bligh, but she refused to put her students at risk or her reputation on the line by letting someone out on the bay alone who shouldn't be there. For the last two hours of the course, she sat back and gave orders. By that point she rarely had to correct her students. She hadn't failed a student yet, but then again, she'd only been in business for a week. She'd put a flyer in every hotel and bed and breakfast in Newport, as well as an ad in a tourist-targeted weekly paper. It was a one-woman business and she loved every minute she'd been in operation.

Day Sailor was a seven-days-a-week operation, but Meghan couldn't foresee a time when it would become boring. The only days she'd have free were when the weather didn't cooperate. Her office was really an old ticket shack for a now-defunct tour boat that used to bring people beneath the Newport Bridge and back. She'd painted the outside a bright yellow trimmed in marine blue and hung a ship's wheel above the bright red door. When people entered, a bell tinkled above them, a cheery sound that made Meghan smile every time she heard it.

Her bell sounded and Meghan looked up to see a young couple standing uncertainly in the door.

"Welcome to Day Sailor," Meghan said.

The woman was clutching one of her pamphlets. "We'd like sailing lessons. Actually, he'd like sailing lessons," the woman said with a nervous laugh.

"I can teach you both or just one of you, but I'd recommend you both take lessons if you plan to sail together," Meghan said, watching the woman carefully. She looked as though she'd been dragged to her execution.

"I think we should both take lessons," the man said, then turned to the woman. "If you take lessons, you won't be so afraid."

The woman began shaking her head.

"I'll tell you what," Meghan said. "I'll sign up the two of you. If she fails the course, you get your money back. Extreme fear would definitely mean you fail the course. I'm betting that once you get out there and see how easy it is and how much fun, you'll get right into it."

The woman looked uncertainly from one to the other. "That sounds fair, I guess. When do you have an opening? We're leaving next week," she ended on a hopeful note.

Meghan smiled. "You're in luck. I have a class available Wednesday."

"We'll take it," the man said quickly.

Meghan began taking their information, including their hotel and cell phones, when her bell tinkled and her heart stopped. Will stood in her doorway, looking more handsome than she remembered, and her memory was pretty vivid. He was even more tanned than he'd been in Bermuda, making his brown hair more sun-kissed than usual. He seemed leaner, his face harder, which for some reason only made her heart beat faster—even when she realized that hard expression meant Will was angry. His expression cleared immediately when the couple turned to look at him.

"I'll be right with you, sir," Meghan said, looking blindly at the paperwork in front of her. Think, think. She couldn't breathe with Will standing in her tiny office, yet alone act professionally in front of new clients. God, she could even smell him, that wonderful combination of sea and sun and Will. "Yes. Um. Sign here to reserve your lessons. And here. It's a basic liability statement saying that if you're captured by pirates or eaten by sharks, it's not my fault." The couple laughed and she could have sworn she heard a snort coming from the doorway. "If you plan to rent a boat for Thursday, you should book it now, either with me or another agency. They go fast. I'm booked for the weekend already. By the way, they all give a ten-minute test and you'll have to pass mine the same way you'd have to pass theirs." Another snort, this one rather obvious.

"Do you need a tissue, sir?" she asked Will.

Will gave quick negative shake of his head, his eyes betraying nothing of what he was thinking, which worried her even more. Will had never had to hide what he was thinking—at least not to her.

"If you reserve the boat, there's a one-hundred-dollar nonrefundable fee. Of course, if the weather prevents you from going out, I will return that fee."

The couple reserved the boat and Meghan mentally ticked off a quick thousand dollars—five hundred for the lessons and another five for the rental. If things worked out, she could make a thousand dollars a day during the summer, more when she expanded her fleet of rental boats.

Apparently, Will was thinking the same thing, because when the couple left, he said, "I think you're the pirate the people should be warned about."

Even though he was belligerent, Meghan couldn't help but feel glad to see him. She just wasn't ready to show him yet. "What are you saying?"

"I'm saying you should be banned from ever stepping foot on a legitimate sailboat for what you're doing here."

Of all the things she thought would come out of Will's mouth when they finally did see each other again, that was not even close to one of them. She'd actually fantasized about him congratulating her on her brilliant business plan, then taking her into his arms, proclaiming his undying love, and begging her to love him in return. She suddenly wasn't so glad to see him after all.

"I'm teaching willing students how to sail."

"That's like saying the guy flipping burgers at McDonald's could work as a chef in Paris. It's bullshit."

Meghan felt a rush of anger. "You don't know what you're talking about," she said, trying to remain calm and losing the battle. "You don't know anything about my course, which means you're basing your opinion on what I can only think is regret that you didn't come up with such a brilliant idea first. Or is it that I'm a threat to you? Is that it?"

He stared at her a long time, as if trying to figure out which language she was speaking. Finally, he shook his head. "I don't know what I was thinking," he said softly, before turning and walking out the door.

Now what the hell did *that* mean?

Meghan leaped from her chair and followed him

out the door. "Will." He stopped, but she could see he was mad enough to rip a piling from its berth.

"Do you really think I'd put people's lives in jeopardy for a buck? Is that what you really think of me?" she said to his back.

She could tell when his anger deflated, because his entire body sort of softened. Will had never been one to stay angry longer than a few minutes. He just didn't have it in him. Will turned to her, and she could hardly look at him because it hurt so much.

"Why did you set up shop here?" he asked.

Meghan shrugged, because the answer to that question was so simple and so difficult to say. *Because of you. Because I couldn't bring myself to say goodbye forever.*

"This is home to me. Plus, there's all these rich tourists. And I really teach them, Will. You'd be amazed how much a person can learn in a day. I give them an eight-hour lesson and I'm telling you, by the time we're done, they're pretty competent sailors. They couldn't sail to Long Island and back, but they can tool around the bay and tell their friends back in Ohio that they went sailing in Newport."

Will shook his head. "You can't teach a person to safely sail in a day. It's reckless and it demeans the sport. I can't believe you would do this."

"And I can't believe you think this is a negative thing. It's introducing sailing to people who might never have the chance. I'll bet one of my students could sail as well as one of your students," she said rashly.

"Fine. It's a bet," he said, pointing a finger at her. He was far too happy with the bet.

Meghan went cold. "I didn't mean that literally."

"How did you mean it, then? You said very clearly that one of your students could sail as well as one of my students. I'm taking you up on that claim."

"I wasn't really . . ."

"Are you saying you can't teach a person to sail in a day?"

Meghan was getting angry again. "I'm saying that I can teach a person to sail competently and safely in a day."

"As safely and competently as I can?" he asked, all smug and superior, and Meghan wanted to smack him.

"Yes." *Oh, shit.*

"It's a bet."

"Fine." *I'm so dead.*

"And the wager?" he asked.

"Dinner. At the Black Pearl."

He pretended to think it over. "Not quite what I had in mind," he said, and for a moment Meghan could have sworn she'd seen that old wicked gleam in his eyes. "I want a sentence in your pamphlet stating that people wanting a more thorough knowledge of sailing should take a more intensive course, such as the one I offer."

"As long as you include a sentence in *your* brochure that states people wanting to learn only basic sailing can obtain that in a single-day lesson, such as the one I offer."

Will shook his head. "But you can't."

"We'll see, won't we?" she said, lifting her chin.

For the first time since she'd seen him in Bermuda, Will gave her a genuine smile. He shook a finger at her, still grinning, "You are in so much trouble, kiddo." And then he turned and left her standing on the pier, once again wondering what the heck he meant, but knowing whatever it was, made her feel good about herself.

Meghan felt a little silly going to his apartment with the flimsy excuse of presenting him the bet in writing. She filled a paper with ridiculous legalese that had her laughing aloud as she read it. "Said party shall, as the condition of the wager agreed to in the above paragraph 1, section 1a, blah blah blah." She'd actually typed in "blah blah blah."

She entered his building and tried to open the door that led to the second floor, only to find it locked. So she knocked and waited. "Weird," she said to herself.

"Can I help you?"

Meghan turned to see Louise standing in her doorway peering at her over her reading glasses. "Louise," she said, happy to see the old woman. "It's Meghan."

"I knew it," Louise said, clapping her hands together.

"Knew what?"

"That you two would get back together," she said, her grin exposing her startlingly white false teeth.

"Oh, no," Meghan said, feeling her face flush. "I'm just dropping this off for Will. It has to do with sailing."

"Oh." That single syllable expressed a great deal of disappointment. "Well, I suppose I can let you in. I have a key." Louise disappeared into her apartment and came back with a key.

"How is everyone?" Meghan asked as the woman struggled with the lock.

"Dead." It seemed Louise's enthusiasm for seeing Meghan had lived as long as her hope of Will and her getting back together.

"I'm so sorry," Meghan said.

Louise opened the door and gave it a little shove. "He's probably on the roof if he didn't hear your knock," she said, then went into her apartment.

Meghan walked into the hall and stopped short. This was not the same place Will had lived in two years ago. Will had a small apartment on the second floor that was reached by going down a small hall and up a set of stairs. Instead of a hall, Meghan found herself walking into a large airy living room. Painted bright yellow. With green trim. She closed the door quietly behind her, taking in the room with wide eyes. The living room stretched in front of her, encompassing half the house. The other section of the floor held a large eat-in kitchen with bright white cabinets, blue trim, and stainless steel appliances. It was as if she'd come to this place unknowingly and painted the entire house. A staircase curved to the second floor, where Will's small apartment used to be. Instead, she found three large bedrooms, all with their own baths—the largest a soothing green with cream trim. This was getting scary, because that was the color of her bedroom before Alan suggested she paint it. This green was slightly less vibrant than what she'd had, but the color scheme was nearly identical.

She couldn't catch her breath, suddenly confronted with such tangible evidence that Will loved her—and loved her in way she never could have comprehended. She slowly went down to the main floor, noticing small marks on the wall, little flaws that told her this hadn't been done recently. She couldn't wrap her mind around the fact he'd done this, created a home that she would adore. Even the furniture, eclectic and cottage-y, were items she could have picked out.

Meghan moved blindly down the hall and through the door, only to run into Louise. "Oh. The key," she said, handing the older woman the key.

"Wasn't Will there? I thought sure he was . . ." Louise said, her voice trailing off.

"I got a call," she said, digging into her pocket for her cell phone. "Emergency at work."

Louise looked behind Meghan as if she might see him barreling after her.

"Louise, do you know when Will painted his house?"

Louise wrinkled her nose. "Don't know what he was thinking of with all those bright colors. He did it right after he bought the place. But he's gotten sick of them, finally. Saw a painter come in the other day to give him an estimate."

"Oh."

"Maybe you could help him pick colors. I believe he's lacking that talent," Louise said with a wink. "Hey. Would you like some beef stew? Got some left over. I always make too much now that everyone's dead and gone and Will can only eat so much." She moved into her apartment, fully expecting Meghan to follow. Apparently, she'd been forgiven for not getting back together with Will.

Meghan held up her phone to remind the woman of her fictitious emergency.

"Won't take more than a minute," she said, waving Meghan in. Meghan followed, looking fondly around the apartment that hadn't changed a bit since the last time she and Will had been invited in to eat some of her pot roast and brown potatoes. The old multicolored crocheted throw still lay on the back of a hideous brown couch and Louise's rocking chair, the one with the chewed-up runner from a long-dead dog, sat in the corner.

"Will's big friend was by here yesterday and I gave him a good amount to take home. Ted?"

"Thad," Meghan said.

"He's a nice boy. Scary-looking, but nice. He's got a girlfriend. Sounds pretty serious. How about you?"

Meghan grimaced a smile. "Right now I'm between boyfriends. I was engaged, but we broke up."

"Will told me."

Meghan's eyebrows shot up. Will had talked about her with Louise? "What did he say?"

"Only that you were engaged to a fellow and it didn't work out. What happened, anyway?"

Meghan shrugged, trying to remain indifferent when the fact was she was still a bit raw from the entire ordeal. Alan had called her on her cell a couple of times, leaving bitter messages thanking her for giving him her clients and another for giving back his ring. And he'd shown up at her door once, leaving a note that he'd dropped by. Meghan knew that eventually she'd have to sit down with Alan in some calm and distant future to talk to him. Meghan had a lot of regrets, including the way she'd hurt Alan, but she didn't regret breaking up with him. She just wished she had done it in a better way, and it scared the hell out of her that she hadn't seen how wrong they were for each other. If she hadn't gone on the race, she probably would have married Alan and ended up trying to convince herself she was happy for the rest of her life. The entire thing made her doubt herself—at least when it came to love.

Meghan thought of Will's apartment, the bright colors, the care and time that had gone into every choice. He'd loved her when she'd walked away from him two years ago, but she still didn't know why he let her go.

"He cheat on you?" Louise prodded.

"No. We weren't a good match. Alan is a nice man and he'll make someone a good husband. Just not me."

"*You* cheated on *him*," Louise nodded smugly.

"Louise," Meghan said, laughing. "It's none of your business."

Louise fairly cackled, the old witch, and Meghan wouldn't have been surprised if she started stirring her beef stew and chanting some incantation. Instead, she opened her fridge, took out a large soup pot and proceeded to scoop the thickened beef stew into a container.

"I don't need it back," Louise said, implying with her tone that she definitely wanted the container back.

"Next time I stop by I'll bring it. I have a bunch of these at home."

"This'll put some meat on your bones," Louise said, handing over the surprisingly heavy container. Meghan would bet anything that she'd told Thad the stew would put hair on his chest—or maybe on his head.

Louise followed her to the door. "He hasn't been the same, you know. You can see it in his eyes," she said, tapping the wrinkled skin near her own faded blue ones.

"He loved Frank like a father," Meghan said, praying that's what Louise meant.

Of course, she didn't. "I'm talking about whatever else happened in Bermuda. He never said what happened."

"Nothing happened," Meghan said, wishing she believed her own lie.

"Well, then, I supposed I can stop worrying about him."

"Oh, don't do that, Louise. He needs someone to worry about him," Meghan joked.

"I'll leave that up to you. I have a feeling about you two, you know."

"I know, Louise, I know."

So, she'd seen it. Walked into his house, knew that he'd painted it all those ridiculous, eye-hurting colors because he'd known she would like them. At first, it hadn't been a conscious thing. It started out with him standing in front of a paint display not having a clue what to put on his walls. He'd thought about just painting them white. With white trim. And then a voice that sounded an awful lot like Meg's whispered that white walls were boring. Before he'd bought the house, the walls were eggshell, the trim white and he'd had to admit it was a little boring.

But putting color on walls was such a dangerous thing. Wouldn't he get sick of them? And what if he picked something that looked really bad? So, he stood there staring, picking up those little cards, trying to picture each color on his walls and failing so completely he almost hired someone to do it for him.

Then he'd seen it, a picture of a room with bright yellows and greens and reds and he thought: that's what she'd pick. And before he'd let himself think about what he was doing, he'd picked the brightest, gaudiest colors in the place and, with his gut twisting weirdly, he lugged the gallons to his car along with all the other stuff he needed, the rollers, the blue tape. He painted and painted, a frenzy of painting until he was standing in his apartment surrounded by color.

And damn if he didn't smile, then feel his heart break all over again. Then hate himself for being such a coward and letting the best thing that had ever happened to him walk away.

Now, more than a year later, he hated his house, his life, and especially the fact he'd been pathetic enough to paint his rooms—*his* rooms—colors that Meghan no doubt loved. He only had to look at her apartment to know that. The worst thing was, now she knew. She had to know that he'd been pining away for her for nearly two years, all the while telling himself that if he screwed enough tall brunettes he'd get one petite blonde out of his mind forever. The proof was in the paint. He'd never thought she'd see it; had, in fact, plans to change it. Two weeks after he'd gotten back from Bermuda, he'd gone back to that paint store, picked wonderfully neutral guy colors, and grabbed a business card off the store's bulletin board.

The painters were coming tomorrow, an exorcism of sorts, to wipe away all signs of the man who'd found himself shaking with rage and desperation standing at the door of his ex-girlfriend and her fiancé. What a jerk he was. A bigger tool even than Alan. Made Alan seem like a normal man's man.

Why the hell had Meg taken it in her head to come to his house after all this time? And why the hell was she back in Newport, walking around as if she owned the pier?

"Goddamn it," he shouted at his bright yellow wall, trying to eradicate the abject terror he'd felt when he'd discovered Meg had seen his house. How the hell was he supposed to get over her if she was working that ridiculous business two piers away? He was bound to run into her, bound to see her ads, bound to lose at least some of his business to hers.

Okay, calm down. You didn't let a little fiancé get in your way. Sure, you stayed away two years. But you knew, didn't you, that all you needed was a good excuse to see her and you'd be there. He'd known, somewhere deep in his mind, that he was going to try to win her back. But he'd failed, and here he was still alone and painting his walls beige.

Chapter Twenty-Two

Charlotte and Richard Lawrence stepped aboard the twenty-five foot Catalina with the awkwardness of people who'd never boarded a boat in their lives. Meghan nearly grimaced, thinking there was no way in hell these two people would be able to beat two of Will's students. She was as pale as a ghost and he smiled grimly, as if telepathically trying to tell her how hard it was for him to get his wife on the boat that morning.

Of course, Will had sent over a note yesterday morning saying he wanted his students to go up against the couple he'd seen signing up for lessons. Meghan had read the note in disbelief. She'd had an idea of who she'd wanted to go up against Will's students and it sure wasn't the Lawrences. A pair of brothers who had sailed sunfishes on a New Hampshire lake when they were kids were the perfect pair to match against Will. She couldn't back down now; she had said *any* of her students could match up to Will's students. She could picture him rubbing his hands together in anticipation of her humiliation.

"I think I'm seasick already," Charlotte said with a nervous laugh.

"Well, I'm about to make you two very happy," Meghan said, forcing a smile and an enthusiasm she wasn't even close to feeling. "I've entered into a friendly bet with a colleague. He doesn't believe I can make you two competent sailors in an afternoon. I disagree."

"I don't want to be part of any bet," Charlotte said quickly.

Meghan nearly groaned. Some people had no sense of adventure. They were the ones content to watch from the sidelines, the cheerleaders. Charlotte was one of those. Her nails were manicured to perfection, her red polish unchipped and decorating nails long enough to interfere with typing. Meghan had nothing against pretty women dressing pretty. But this particular woman was supposed to win a bet for her.

"Oh, come on," Richard said. "It'll be fun. What do we have to do?"

Meghan smiled her gratitude. "Just sail from the harbor to the Newport Bridge. There's a red buoy right before you go under the bridge, and that will be the finish line. It should be a pretty straightforward sail, and if the wind is right, you won't even have to tack."

"Tack?" Richard asked.

"Turn." And then Meghan gave the pair a lesson in wind direction and sail position on a wipe board she always used.

"That doesn't seem too difficult," Charlotte said warily.

"Easy as pie. If you win, the lessons are free. For

your participation, I'll cut the price in half. How does that sound?"

"Terrific," Richard said, with a huge smile.

"Okay, we've got a lot to learn today. Let's turn the two of you into sailors, right?"

Richard put his arm around his wife and jerked her close. He was clearly excited and Meghan could tell their enthusiasm was beginning to rub off on Charlotte. Maybe she'd surprise her, after all.

Meghan spent the first hour getting the couple familiar with the boat. She had the pair walk up and down the boat several times, pointing out the various things they would have to know in order to sail safely. They learned how to use a winch and how to tie off a line. Charlotte was a quick learner and Meghan decided to change her assessment of her. Then she told them it was time to head out to the harbor and Charlotte turned green.

"Charlotte, can you swim?"

"It's not that. Really. I'll get over it."

"Tell her, Charlotte."

Meghan looked from one to the other. "Tell me what?"

"I grew up on Lake Michigan and when I was a kid we had a sailboat."

"My God, you're a ringer," Meghan said happily, clapping her hands together.

"No, no," Charlotte said, shaking her head. "I'm scared to death. When I was little, we capsized and for about thirty seconds I thought my father was dead. He was just on the other side of the boat and he was calling for me, but I was so panicked I didn't hear him. I never went out again. It was a long time ago, so I hardly remember anything."

"No wonder you were so good tying the line on

the cleat," Meghan said. "What about you, Richard, have you sailed, too?"

"No. My first time. I grew up in Indiana in the middle of a cornfield."

"That's all they have. Cornfields," Charlotte said dryly.

Meghan smiled, and almost laughed aloud. Will had insisted the Lawrences be part of the bet. Ha. Now she wanted to rub her hands together with glee.

"Charlotte, I promise you we will not capsize. It must have been a small boat."

"It was. It was a little dinghy. We'd tipped over in the past and I just laughed. But that time, it was really choppy out there and windy and I was already a little scared. And then I thought my father was, you know, dead."

"Completely understandable. A Catalina is one of the steadiest little boats around. I promise you I won't let you out on the bay with winds over fifteen knots."

Charlotte smiled. "Okay. Let's go sailing."

At the end of the day, Meghan felt like doing a little happy dance as she said good-bye to the couple. They not only would qualify for any test a boat rental would give them, she was pretty sure they'd give any of Will's students a run for their money. Meghan did a final check of her boats to make certain they were secure, then went to her office to do some last-minute paperwork before heading home to Cumberland. It was a fifty-minute drive and she knew she'd have to find a new place when her lease was up. She loved her little place, but it held too many bad memories for her to stay after her lease ended in November.

Her bell tinkled and she knew without looking up who would be standing there.

"Hello, Will."

"Your couple looked pretty good out there," he said without preamble.

"Want to get out of the bet? Sorry."

Will looked around her small office, noting a picture of her and Thad standing next to the St. Davis Lighthouse Trophy. Neither looked particularly happy, and he wondered why she even bothered putting the picture up.

"I'm trying to impress my clients. Though I doubt anyone who walks through that door has even heard of the Newport-Bermuda race."

She was sitting behind her desk wearing a navy polo, her hair bleached from the sun and curling around her tanned face. She didn't have a bit of makeup on, unlike when he'd met her at her real estate office, when she'd been all corporate and put together. Now she was windblown, her cheeks a light pink from the sun. This was the Meg he knew, the one he'd loved with all his heart. He probably still loved her, but at the moment he could only think what a fool he'd been. He had to say it, had to let her know that he knew she'd been in his house, had to tell her he'd had the place painted to more sane colors. Beige and white and, in one room he'd gone a little crazy and picked out a nice eggshell. Burnt eggshell was the name of the color on the little piece of paper he'd given to the paint store clerk. He'd painted her out of his life, out of his heart. Out of his dreams. Stupid, romantic dreams of the two of them sailing around the world together, then settling down and raising a couple of kids. God, those were the worst memories of all, the memories of things that never happened and now never would.

"I painted my house," he said abruptly, and her head shot up and he would swear her cheeks turned a brighter pink.

"Louise said you were planning to."

"It didn't mean anything," he said, and he couldn't bring himself to look at her as he lied. "You know, the way it was."

"I know."

Ah, fuck it. "Okay. It did mean something. I guess I missed you. At first," he moved his knuckle back and forth across the top of her desk. Man, he was such a jerk. "I wasn't ready. For marriage. I didn't have a house or a real job and you were pressuring me." He looked up and couldn't read the expression in her blue eyes; she just stared at him as if she didn't quite understand what he was talking about. "I couldn't marry you."

"I kind of figured that when I gave you that brilliant ultimatum and you let me go."

"No. You don't get it. It wasn't that I didn't want to. I *couldn't*."

"Why didn't you just tell me that?" she asked softly.

"I did." She starting shaking her head. "I told you I wasn't ready. I wasn't."

A little crease appeared between her eyes as she tried to recall that part of their bitter breakup. Looking back, all they'd done was argue. "I thought you meant . . . Oh, Will, I thought you were just making an excuse. Letting me off easy. Putting me off until I just went away. And then when I did go away, you didn't come get me."

Something twisted painfully inside him. "I got over you," he said, knowing his voice soundly oddly flat.

She smiled brightly. "Me, too. Obviously. I mean, I got engaged to someone else."

"You sure did."

"Well. I'm glad we talked about this. Finally."

"I just didn't want you to think the way I painted the house meant anything now. I did that a long time ago," he said, driving home a point he didn't even really want her to believe.

She smiled and shook her head. "Honestly, Will, I just figured we liked the same colors. You must have been shocked when you saw my apartment."

"A little."

Her phone rang and he let out a silent sigh of relief. This had to have been the most excruciating exchange he'd had with Meghan. His old eloquent self. He wanted to tell her he'd painted it for her, he'd bought the house for her, he'd expanded the sailing school so he'd make enough money so they wouldn't be poor. So she'd be happy.

So she wouldn't leave him. God help him, but even he knew how obvious a reason that was, given his wonderful childhood. Looks like the old man messed him up after all Frank had done to deprogram him. Of course, Will couldn't tell her any of that. The words, as they always did, stuck in his throat. He didn't want to grovel, wasn't that kind of guy. He'd always let his actions speak louder than his words. Sure, he knew women liked to hear "I love you's" and he'd given that to Meg. At least he was pretty sure he did. He'd said a lot of "me too's" and wasn't that the same?

She sat there looking like she wanted him to leave and all he could think was how much he wanted to pull her into his arms and show her how much he loved her. And all he could see was her walking away from him and into Alan's arms. It didn't matter how many times he told himself she didn't have a choice, because she did have a choice, and then she'd gone back to their apartment and they'd . . . God, it killed him to think about it.

She hung up and he was still standing there beating himself up over things he couldn't change. "I'll see you at the starting line tomorrow," he said. "Weather's supposed to be nice. Light wind." There, a safe topic. He could almost feel the tension in the room fade away.

"You know, Will, I was thinking that it would only be fair that I pick your team because you picked mine."

He shrugged. "I have sixteen beginner sailors, most are under twelve. I had to pick the fourteen-year-olds for safety reasons."

"We're going against kids?"

Will smiled. "Ninety percent of my students are kids, Meg. Who did you think you were going against?" Kids were great, they were fearless and ferocious, and these two kids were the best he'd seen come through his program, but they'd only completed four weeks of the six-week session.

"Okay. Fine. My couple did great on the bay today."

Will gave her a level look. "I saw them out there."

"Oh?"

"And my kids are going to kick your sweet, pretty ass."

She smiled and batted her eyes comically. "Do you really think it's sweet *and* pretty?"

"You know I do," he said, grinning as he turned toward the door. "See you tomorrow at the pier. I've got a little egg beater so we can monitor the race."

"I'll be there bright and early."

"What the hell are you doing?" Thad asked as they sat together at the Black Pearl's tiny inside bar.

Will gave Thad an exaggerated bewildered look. "Listen, I know it's not imported, but I'm on a budget," Will said, nodding toward his Bud.

"You just can't stay away from her, can you? Dude, she's a cancer eating away at your soul."

Will just laughed.

"You got to find someone stable. Someone who gets you." He beat his chest. "Right here."

"Like Rachel."

Thad smiled. "Right. She gets me. She'd never give me a freakin' ultimatum, then marry some other dude."

"Listen to you, an expert. You've only been dating a month."

"Five weeks."

"I stand corrected," Will said dryly. "Date her for four years, refuse to even discuss the future with her and then see if she's," Will banged Thad's chest a little rougher than he had to, "right there."

Thad rubbed his chest and took a deep drink of his Bass Ale. "What she did in Bermuda. That was harsh."

Will had to agree with Thad. Getting his heart ripped out of his chest wasn't the most pleasant experience he'd ever had. "And I suppose Rachel's an angel."

"Yeah, she is," Thad said, unabashedly. Will never figured Thad would be the type to wear his heart on his sleeve. Girls were hot, according to Thad, or not. They sure as hell weren't "angels."

"Go slow," Will warned. He liked Rachel, but what did they really know about her other than she was a hell of a sailor?

"Why the hell should I? I'm thirty-six. I've screwed enough women to know what I want." He turned toward the bar and pressed his fingers lightly against his glass. "I'll tell you how much I love her," he said into his ale. He darted a quick look to Will. "We haven't even, you know . . . done the deed."

"You're kidding." Will was truly flabbergasted.

"No. I'm not," Thad said, sounding slightly defensive. "She's special. She's not like the other women I've gone out with."

"Jesus, Thad, you sound serious."

"I'm scared to death," he said after taking another deep swallow. "She's perfect. She thinks I'm funny. And smart. And the way she looks at me." He shook his head. "She's got to be crazy, you know?"

"If I was a chick, I'd like you," Will said.

"You're so full of shit. You think I lost it."

"Five minutes ago you were telling me I was nuts."

Thad straightened. "Yeah. We were talking about you and how Meg's got you wrapped around her little pinky." He made a whipping motion with his hand, complete with sound effects.

"I just got pissed off about her opening that Mc-

Sailing School and paid her a visit and the next thing I know she's betting me her students could beat my students. A simple wager between friends."

"Nothing is simple between the two of you and you know it."

Meghan tried really hard not to be too smug at the Black Pearl the night of the challenge. Charlotte and Richard had won the race, albeit by only a half a boat length. Still they won, which meant she won the bet. Will had been surprisingly gracious about the whole thing, which was slightly disappointing. It sort of took away from the joy of beating him when he was so darned nice about it.

She scanned the menu, looking for the priciest items in a transparent attempt to bother Will. "I'm in the mood for lobster," she said, pretending to peruse the menu. "Do you think they have any Dom Perignon?"

Will gave her a grim smile. "You can get whatever you want."

Meghan frowned at his ability to suck the wind out of her sails at every turn. Winning would have been way more fun if Meghan didn't suspect Will was secretly proud that her students had won and she was a bit suspicious that Will had given her team an advantage by positioning them in a way that gave them better wind.

After ordering the house white wine, Will raised a glass for a toast. "To your new boating school," he said, pretending to choke on the word "school."

Meghan held her glass firmly on the table. "Before I accept your toast, I have a question for you. Did you purposely give my team the wind advantage?"

Will pulled a look of shock, which made Meghan even more skeptical. "Someone had to have it. I flipped a coin."

"Oh. I didn't see you do that."

Will let out a laugh. "You don't believe me? Why would I let you win? Anyway, the boys made a race of it."

Meghan had been impressed that the kids knew enough to tack away from the other boat to find some better wind. But that tactic didn't work well enough to push them over the finish line first. Meghan couldn't help but smile at the pride Will felt for his students and her heart gave a little tug. Will and the salt air were like an aphrodisiac to her. He always looked so sexy with his hair blowing back from his strong forehead and his cheeks ruddy from the wind and sun.

Meghan had to admit that as sexy as he was out on the water, he was just as sexy wearing a jacket and tie, his hair finger-combed back and just messy enough to make a woman want to brush it into place. She couldn't quite believe she was sitting in restaurant with Will. A little less than two months ago, they'd been on the Atlantic heading toward Bermuda. After that week and what had happened, she'd never imagined herself having any kind of relationship with Will. She didn't know if he was angry or hurt or embarrassed by what had happened. Will had never been a guy to talk about his feelings and he probably never would be. For now, he was friendly, but Meghan wished that when he looked at her she saw the old intensity, the old . . . Will.

He didn't say much about how he felt, especially about that night in Bermuda when everything had fallen apart. Even weeks after that night, she could still feel her body burn with mortification for how she'd treated Will. She missed him, she realized. She missed the man who'd kissed her softly when she'd been so sick during the race. She missed the way he flirted with her, the way he looked at her as if he were a hairsbreadth away from stripping her naked and screwing her silly.

She missed the man who'd painted his house all those bright colors because *he'd* missed *her* so damned much.

Meghan had killed that guy, she realized, that awful night in Bermuda when he'd made love to her and she'd gone off with Alan.

"We didn't do it," she blurted.

"Who's we and what didn't you do?" he asked as he took a spoonful of seafood chowder.

"That night in Bermuda. Alan and I." His spoon stopped for the briefest of moments before he shoved it into his mouth, the only clue that Will had even heard what she said. She waited for him to say something, but he just kept spooning in the chowder. "Did you hear me?"

"I heard you," he said, but he wasn't looking at her. A muscle along his jaw bunched and she knew he was angry.

"He wanted you to think that we . . ."

"I really don't care, Meghan." He looked at her then, directly into her eyes, and Meghan almost flinched from the cold anger she saw. "Ancient history."

"Oh." Will was pretending Bermuda had never happened, when it had been the only thing she could think of for weeks.

He nodded toward the last roll. "You going to eat that?"

Meghan shook her head and he grabbed the roll, taking a bite and chewing angrily. She hadn't known a person could chew with anger until she witnessed it. As he sat there and ate everything edible at the table, Meghan watched feeling sick. Why had she brought up one of the worst nights of their life just when they were starting to get along?

"You're mad at me," she said, stating the obvious. Of course, he denied it.

"No." Other than salt and pepper, Will had run out of things to munch on. Until the waitress arrived with the main course, Will was out of luck.

"I don't blame you for being mad."

He gave her a sharp smile with about as much sincerity as a politician. "Meghan. I don't care."

He did. She knew he did. Otherwise why was his jaw muscle bulging, why was he looking for the waitress to come with the food and save him?

"What should I have done, Will?"

He closed his eyes. "You are so damned stubborn," he muttered.

"I'd already decided that Alan and I probably shouldn't get married before that night. And then he showed up to surprise me, all happy. And we'd just been . . ." she waved a hand. "You know what we'd been doing. Which was very nice, by the way." She ignored his low growl. "I didn't want to go with him, but he was still officially my fiancé."

Will let out a long sigh. "I know you didn't have a choice. I know this. But it doesn't change the fact that you'd been with me. Making love with me," he said, jabbing a thumb against his chest with an audible thump that made Meghan blink. "And you went with him."

"But nothing happened," Meghan protested.

"Hell, Meghan, it just doesn't matter anymore." He looked around for the waitress. "Where the hell's our meal?"

Meghan sat in her favorite restaurant with the man she was pretty sure she loved and felt miserable. Why hadn't she just let things lie?

The waitress finally arrived, smiling brightly as she put blackened tuna in front of Meghan and broiled mahi mahi in front of Will. Without a word they exchanged plates and began eating.

"Have you been to see Nancy?" he asked, abruptly.

Meghan felt her face heat with guilt. "No, and I know should. I feel so guilty about not going to the funeral and then I went home for a while. The more time passed, the harder it was to see her. I haven't even called."

"You should go to see her. She likes you."

Meghan gave him a sharp look. "I thought she was mad at me."

He looked genuinely puzzled.

"For breaking up with you," Meghan said, slightly exasperated.

"No. She was mad at me. For months she kept telling me to go get you back and what was I thinking letting you go. Then she read about your engagement in the *Journal* and she never really mentioned it again."

Meghan cringed inwardly. "For the record, I didn't want an announcement, but Alan insisted. I think he thought it would help him with his clients."

"Go see her," he repeated.

"I will."

Will took a drink of the beer he'd been nursing for about an hour. "I'm sorry I was such an ass before."

"When? You mean before when you dumped me or just now?"

"Just now," he said with forced patience. "And you dumped me."

Meghan raised her eyebrows. "Will, I don't think you've ever apologized for anything before."

"I'm not usually wrong."

Meghan let out a laugh.

He looked at her straight in the eye. "And I think we're better off friends."

If she thought she might love Will, she realized at that moment, when her heart gave a painful jab that was stunning in its intensity, that she did love him. Had never stopped loving him, despite everything else that happened. "Friends with benefits?" she asked, joking because she was so very close to crying.

"I don't think so."

Meghan pressed her lips together in a grim smile and nodded. "I think you're probably right," she said, even though her throat was closing painfully. She coughed and took a deep drink of her chardonnay, and thought of that Alanis Morissette song about irony. A black fly in your chardonnay. Realizing you love a man who doesn't love you anymore. Ha.

Even though Will knew he was doing the only thing that could save his sanity, he still couldn't believe she'd accepted the friends bit so easily and so blithely. Friends with benefits. Right. Maybe she could do that—she obviously was doing just that in Bermuda—but he knew if he made love to her again, he'd fall in love all over again. And he just wasn't up for that kind of self-destruction.

Thad had been right. He had to stay away from Meghan, because sitting this close to her, not touching her, was eating him alive. Meghan was a pretty woman, but tonight, in the soft light of the restaurant with her blond hair curling around her face, she was damn beautiful. Better that he set the ground rules that seemed all too easy for her to follow. He'd get over it. Hell, he'd even started to like the browns and whites he'd painted his house. He was man enough to admit he couldn't bear getting his heart broken yet again by the same woman.

"Where are you going during the off season?" he asked, one friend asking another an uncomplicated question.

"I was going to hang around here, maybe work part-time in real estate until next summer." She shrugged. "But the market's way off and I wasn't even very good when the market was hot. What do you do?"

"I'm up and running through October, but I usually don't hang around. Last year I was in the Volvo race as a professional. And I'm looking at the Transat race. I'm not really sure." Will finished his last bite and waved the waitress over. "I'll take the check now," he said, ignoring Meghan's look of surprise.

"You in a rush?" she asked.

He glanced at his watch, knowing he didn't have a thing to do except go home and suffer Louise's third degree about his "date." He was going to have to set her straight once and for all about about Meg and his relationship. "I'm meeting up with someone later," he said.

"Hot date?" Meg asked, smiling.

It really got to him that she could sit there smiling about his "hot date." Didn't she have an ounce of jealousy in her body? "Yes I do, as a matter of fact," he said, feeling mean, because there was no way anyone could classify Louise as a hot date, nice as she was. Meg was still smiling, still killing him with her absolute indifference, when he noticed her eyes were glittering suspiciously in the candlelight.

"I'm sorry, Will," she said, sounding angry as she dashed the tears away with her fingertips. "I can't be happy about your so-called hot date. I don't want to be your friend. I don't want anything to do with you." She stood up and left, only to turn around awkwardly to grab the purse she left behind. He sat there dumbfounded as she left him with a parting shot. "I can't believe I was actually looking forward to tonight."

With that, she left the restaurant. He let her go only because he knew where to find her and he really couldn't trust himself at that moment not to fling himself at her knees and beg her to take him back. Will let out a curse that caused a few of the other diners to turn to him with disapproving looks.

Chapter Twenty-Three

When Meghan arrived home after her dinner with Will, she felt raw and empty. She pulled into her parking space and opened the door to the sound of crickets and tree frogs. It was humid, the air heavy with moisture from a tropical storm off the coast, making the night seem darker. Looking up, she couldn't see any stars and only the barest shimmer of light where the moon was—not enough to brighten the bleakness. Or maybe it was just her poor broken heart making everything seem so dark and dreary.

Pulling out her keys, she walked to her front door, feeling foolish in her pretty dress and heels that she'd put on just for Will. Her *friend* Will. Ugh. The dress was a wrinkled mess now from the long drive and humidity and it hung on her like a wet rag.

"Where were you?"

Meghan spun around, her heart pounding fiercely in her chest, even when she recognized the man standing behind her. "Jesus. Alan? You scared me half to death."

He didn't move, a man-shaped shadow standing near her car. "Where were you?" he repeated.

"You could have called me, you know," Meghan said lightly, trying to quell the irrational fear she felt. It was Alan, after all, but she couldn't help thinking of all those movies where the victim thought she was talking to a man she knew only to be brutally murdered by a serial killer wearing a hideous mask. "What are you doing here, anyway?"

He just stood there and Meghan was beginning to think he might be drunk. Or might not be Alan. She suppressed a tingling of fear. He walked toward her and she had to stop herself from turning around and jabbing her key in the lock. Common sense stopped her. Even if Alan were drunk—something she'd never witnessed in more than a year of them being together—he'd never hurt her.

"I stopped by and you weren't here, so I thought I'd wait," he said, sounding blessedly normal and not like a serial killer at all.

"I was out to dinner with a friend. Why didn't you just call me?"

"I was worried when you weren't home. It's late."

"It's only ten," she countered, not liking the way he sounded . . . almost too calm, robotic and emotionless. She turned to open her door, feeling another bit of fear sliding down her back. After flicking on the outside light, Meghan turned back to him, feeling safer now that she was nearly in the house and a light was on. He looked normal, like Alan, like he always looked—calm, self-assured, handsome. She let out a sigh. "Why are you here?"

"I . . ." His face crumpled as he tried to maintain control of his emotions.

"Come on in," Meghan said, watching him get

himself together. She didn't want to encourage him, but she wasn't heartless enough to slam the door in his face. After all, they had been planning to get married and she'd been the one to break his heart. Didn't he deserve a little kindness?

He walked by her stiffly as if he might snap in two if she touched him, and she shut the door behind them, flicking lights on as she moved into her apartment. She sat in the living room's only chair and he sat at the edge of her loveseat.

"Who were you with?" he asked with a tight smile. He must have seen something in her face because he frowned. "Will. You were with him."

Meghan almost lied, but she had the horrible thought that maybe Alan had followed her and knew she'd been with Will. The last thing she wanted to do was to set him off.

"We had a bet and I won. Will had to buy me dinner. That's all it was, Alan." She watched with some alarm as his entire body stiffened, almost as if shot with electricity.

"Is he your lover?"

Meghan's cheeks heated, with anger, with guilt; she wasn't certain. "Not that it's any of your business, but Will and I have decided to be just friends." Meghan took a deep breath. "Alan, have you been following me?"

"Don't flatter yourself," he said sharply. "I just wanted to talk to you and you weren't here."

"Because if you're going to turn into some crazed stalker, I'm not afraid to go to the police."

Alan stood abruptly. "I was *worried* about you," he shouted, his face contorting in odd mix of anger and pain.

"Don't be. I'm not yours to worry about."

Meghan tried to talk calmly, tried not to let him know how very crazy she thought he was acting. "I think you should leave. I don't want this to turn ugly. We were never ugly, Alan."

He stared at her with cold, emotionless eyes, before turning to leave. He stood at the door with his back to hers, his head turned just slightly so she could see his profile. "I came here tonight to see if there's hope for us. I brought the ring," he said, his voice cracking slightly at the last word.

"Alan, I don't want to be mean, but I don't think we're going to get back together. I'm sorry."

He slammed his head against the doorjamb so hard, Meghan let out a small scream and rushed toward him. "My God, Alan . . ."

Alan thrust the door open and slammed it shut, leaving Meghan staring with horror at a small spot of blood near her door. "Oh, God," she whispered, feeling sick. When he was out the door, Meghan hurried to her bedroom window to watch him go. Alan half-ran across the street to an apartment complex parking lot where he'd parked his car and she couldn't help thinking it hadn't been the first time. When he was finally gone, Meghan sat, stunned, on her bed. Alan had gone psycho on her and she didn't know what to do. She was pretty sure the police couldn't do anything because she didn't have any proof that he'd been "stalking" her.

She picked up her bedside telephone and dialed.

"Will?" She started crying the minute she heard his voice.

"What's wrong? Meghan?"

Meghan gulped. "It's me. Will, Alan was here and . . ."

"What happened?" he asked, his voice like steel.

"Nothing. But . . ." Meghan took a deep breath. "I'm sorry. He just scared me. He was waiting for me to come home and . . . He just scared me because he was acting so weird."

"Had he been drinking?"

"I don't think so. No. Alan doesn't really drink."

"I'll be right there."

Meghan shook her head. "No. You don't have to." She let out a watery laugh. "I'm okay now. I needed to talk to someone, that's all."

"I'm hanging up the phone and driving there."

Meghan heard a click as Will did as promised, then stared at the phone and smiled through the tears in her eyes.

While she waited for Will, she had a rousing internal debate whether to call the police about Alan and her pragmatic side was winning. Ten minutes into her debate, she had herself half convinced that she'd been overreacting to the entire thing. After all, what horrible thing had Alan done? Okay, slamming his head against the doorjamb had been pretty, well, crazy, but what would she have told the police had they come to take a statement? That her former fiancé had shown up at her door because he'd been worried about her, then hurt himself when he got angry?

Clearly, Alan was having trouble with the breakup, but she didn't think it was time to get a restraining order. Other than a few polite messages left on her answer machine, Alan hadn't made any attempt to contact her. *That you know of*, a voice whispered in her head. What if Alan had been following her for weeks without her knowing it? What if finding out she was seeing Will had finally cut the fine thread of sanity that had been holding him together?

By the time Will knocked on the door, Meghan had gotten herself so worked up again (so much for her pragmatic side), she gave a small scream at the sudden noise—and a louder one when Will barreled through the door with murder in his eyes and a small wooden baseball bat in his hands.

Will drove like a madman, keeping his ear tuned to his radar detector and his mind on what could be happening to Mcghan at that moment. In his rush to leave his house, he hadn't brought his cell phone, and cursed himself a hundred times for forgetting it. Newport to Cumberland was nearly an hour drive on mostly highway—a long time for his mind to picture Alan coming back to Meg's apartment and hurting her. He drove himself mad with images of Meg trying to defend herself against a much larger, stronger man, valiantly fighting as the life was slowly ebbing out of her body.

Alan hadn't seemed like a crazy person, but you never knew what was really going on inside someone's head. He'd seemed like an average Joe, perhaps more slick than most, but that could mean he had an inferiority complex. Or it could mean he was a sociopath who didn't care about anything but himself and appearances. The kind of guy who wore Armani suits and talked about buying a waterfront house, not because he loved the water but because of the prestige of it. The kind of guy who would fall for a beautiful woman like Meg and not know a single thing about her because he didn't really care what made her tick, only that she did what he said and looked good while she was doing it. The kind of guy who would go a little psycho when that perfect woman turned out to be not so perfect, not so malleable, not so loyal as he thought. It might make a guy like that turn into a murderer who would stalk his girlfriend, then kill her.

"God damn it," Will shouted as he pulled off the highway and had to stop at a red light at the end of the ramp. A cop pulled up behind him, lights off, but Will, in his frenzied panic, wondered whether he was on his way to a crime scene involving a beautiful blonde. No need to hurry since the victim was dead. He let out a frustrated sob as the light seemed to take a lifetime to turn green.

Meg lived another mile down the road, and as soon as the cruiser turned off down another street, he pressed his foot on the gas and flew to her apartment complex. Spotting her car, he pulled in directly behind her, not bothering to search for an empty space, grabbed a Pawtucket Red Sox souvenir bat he kept in his car, and was out his door and running to her apartment while his old Jeep was still knocking.

He was about to rush into her apartment when a bit of sanity returned. He didn't want to scare Meg to death if all was well, so he knocked . . . and heard her scream . . . and died just a little before rushing in and finding her . . . sitting on her couch reading.

She sat cross-legged, her eyes wide, the book forgotten on her lap, staring at Will as if wondering what the hell he was doing there. And there he was, bathed in sweat, heaving his breath in and out, hands on knees, trying not to get mad at Meg because she was still alive and he'd almost been scared to death.

"You thought I was in trouble, didn't you. When I screamed."

"Maybe," he said, finally straightening up to glare at her. "You did call because that boyfriend of yours had gone a little nuts."

She held up her thumb and forefinger. "Just a little nuts," she said, sheepishly. "Just enough to scare me and call you." She walked up to him and he opened his arms and pulled her against him.

"Jesus, Meg, you keep scaring me like that and I'm going to die young."

"Sorry," she muttered against his chest.

He held her, fending off a small amount of panic to find Meg in his arms when he'd finally come to the conclusion he was better off protecting his heart by staying away from her. But that was before the phone call.

"Did he come back?"

She shook her head against his chest, then pulled back. He expected to see a tear-stained face, but he should have known better. She was smiling up at him. "My hero," she said.

Will pulled away and was about to walk into her living room when he saw her eyes dart to the door. Following her gaze, he was startled to see a small smear of blood, and felt his entire body tense. "Whose blood is that?" he said, trying to remain calm.

"Alan's. He did it do himself."

He let out a hiss of breath.

"He knocked his head against the doorjamb right before he left. Freaked me out a little. That's when I called you."

Will walked over to the mark. "He's a fucking idiot," he said softly, turning back to Meg. "He must have really slammed his forehead pretty good."

"He did."

"You should call the police," Will said. "This guy is not right. I can understand him punching a wall. Hell, I've even put a hole in the wall. But slamming his head? It's almost as if he was trying to punish himself."

"And putting hole in a wall isn't?"

Will grinned. "Maybe it is, but the idea of it is much more civilized. I hit the wall instead of someone's face."

"Anyone I know?"

My father. "No. It was a long time ago. Anyway, that's a different kind of crazy. That," he said, nodding toward the blood, "is *crazy* crazy."

"Maybe I should call the police. That might be enough to embarrass him back into being the man I know. He's never even raised his voice to me before."

Will gave her a disbelieving look.

"It's true. He was always very gentle, very nice."

"Sounds like me," Will said, smiling.

"It was a different sort of nice."

"Like creepy nice? All that hand-holding and gazing into your eyes." He made a grimace. "It was enough to make a person physically ill."

Meg ignored him and flopped down onto her couch, pulling up her knees and hugging them. At that moment she looked so young. She looked like the girl he fell in love with six years ago, the girl he knew even then would be under his skin for the rest of his life. Except he'd blown it, taken too long to grow up.

"You're obviously all right. I guess I can go now."

Meg leaped up and ran to the door, spreading out her arms comically, as if to stop him. "You aren't going anywhere. I'm still freaked out and you're staying here."

"On one condition," he said suggestively, just to mess with her head, just because he was still a little angry with her. Might as well prove to her he was exactly what she said he was: a guy who didn't really care about much of anything but getting laid.

To his surprise, she smiled. "Okay."

And she walked into her bedroom, pulling off her T-shirt as she went.

Chapter Twenty-Four

Will stood there, and being a man, as well as a man who loved the woman who'd walked away stripping, he was instantly and painfully aroused. But he'd be damned if he was going to be made a fool of by Meg one more time. So he took a deep breath and sort of sauntered to the entrance of her beige bedroom and stopped, leaning one shoulder against the door. Meg faced him and dropped her sweat shorts, revealing a lacy pair of bright pink panties hugging the wonderful curves of her body. He swallowed and tried damned hard not to let her know he was about to fall to his knees and beg her to let him take off those panties with his teeth. While he was distracted by the panties, her bra dropped down.

"You just going to stand there?" she asked, hands on hips.

"I'm not sure," he said slowly, wondering when he'd gone insane. He couldn't remember the last time he'd taken more than a second or two to decide whether he wanted to have sex with a gorgeous woman. "We're supposed to be friends."

She smiled. "Friends with benefits. Come on, Will, or I'm going to start getting self-conscious standing here naked."

Beautiful woman. Asking for sex. Aroused, heterosexual man. Broken heart. Beautiful woman asking for sex.

It seemed the cards were stacked against him.

When he saw the real need in her eyes, he couldn't resist. He'd think about all that emotion crap later. For now, they both needed to make love and Will wasn't idiot enough to say no. Even thinking about touching her again the way he'd wanted to for years made him break out into a cold sweat.

"We're more than friends," he said, walking to her and stripping off his polo. "I don't want you to ever call me a friend again."

"Okay."

He pulled her into his arms and nearly cried out from the feel of her naked flesh against his. God, it felt good. More than good. It felt right, like they'd never been apart, like none of the past two-and-a-half years had happened.

"Jesus, Meg, I don't know how I lasted this long without you."

She didn't answer him; he'd think about that later. At the moment, he just wanted to touch every inch of her, lick every soft, moist inch of her incredible body. "You have condoms? Please tell me you have condoms."

She wriggled out of his arms and dove across her bed to fish around in her bedside table, producing in triumph a pink-foiled condom.

"Giddy up," he said, and she laughed aloud.

God, she'd missed him. Sex with Will had always been so much fun with no hang-ups, little talking except to make the other person laugh. He'd never told her he loved her while they were making love, never told her she was beautiful, never said any of the things other men said and probably didn't mean. Will loved making love and she loved making love with him. It's the way it had always been with the two of them and that's the way she wanted it now. When they'd been dating she'd wanted more of him. More and more and more. Now she didn't.

Really.

Honest.

The minute Will took her in his arms, her heart took a nosedive back two years in time to when she'd wanted all of him, when she wanted him to love her.

Will growled and fell onto the bed, pulling her into his arms. "You are so beautiful," he said, and she felt something squeeze her chest. He wrapped his arms around her, letting her feel his erection, his strength, his entire body enveloping her. He suckled her nipples for long, drugging minutes, and was blessedly silent. Meghan wasn't certain she could take another endearment, another kind word. She caressed his penis and it felt so familiar, she almost laughed. He sensed she was smiling, so he lifted his head.

"You're exactly the same," she said, sounding almost relieved.

"You," he said, putting his hands between her legs. "Are definitely better. And wetter."

She laughed softly, then inhaled sharply as he began caressing her. Will knew what he was doing; he always had. She arched her back, closed her eyes, and let out a soft moan as she lost herself to the exquisite feeling of his finger dipping inside her.

"I could watch you all night," he said, softly, and it was such an un-Will-like thing to say, her eyes snapped open. He was putting on the condom so she couldn't see his eyes, but when he looked up he had the same devilish expression he always did right before they made love.

He moved down her body, kissing her along the way, and then brought her so close to orgasm, she groaned with frustration. Then he came inside her, and she came in such an unexpectedly violent rush, she screamed.

"Wow. Wow. Oh, wow," she said, as she slowly became aware of herself. She opened her eyes and saw Will smiling down at her and she nearly blurted out that she loved him then and there.

Will started moving, sliding in and out, and it felt so delicious after her incredible orgasm that she hung on for the ride. When he came, it was like hearing a favorite song you haven't heard in years, and it made her sad and happy at the same time.

They lay together listening to one another breathe for a long time before Will broke the silence. "I still don't understand how you ended up with someone like Alan."

Meghan smiled. "So that's what you were thinking about. Boy, was I way off. Here I was thinking you were about to whisk me away to some tropical island where we could live out our lives. Naked."

"There was that, too."

She trailed a finger along his jaw, liking the way his beard stubble felt against her fingertip. "Alan was like a life raft. He was what I needed at the time, until I figured out I could rescue myself. I think I lost myself for a while," she said quietly. "I just wanted to be . . ." She shrugged. "Normal. Have a car, an apartment, a real job. I wish I could be more like you. You don't care, do you? You could be a bum your whole life and it wouldn't bother you."

Will felt that old anger creeping up on him, like when he was a kid and people assumed he was going to be a loser just because his old man was. Even though he got good grades, even though his worn, slightly too small clothes were clean, they thought he was trash because of where he lived. More than once, cops pulled over to "talk" to him when he was on his way home from school. His hair was longer than it should have been, and sometimes it stuck out all over the place because they ran out of shampoo and he had to use Dial. He couldn't believe that Meg, the woman who knew him best, could think he'd be happy being a sail bum.

"I run a school and own a home. I don't know too many bums who have that," he said, knowing he sounded angry and not caring.

Meg raised her eyebrows in surprise and shoved herself onto one elbow. "I didn't mean it like that. I meant that you could bum around. Not that you arc now. Likc onc of thosc aging surfcr dudcs." Shc gave him a sick smile. "I'm just digging myself a deeper hole, aren't I?"

"You could say that."

"Don't be mad. I meant it as a compliment. You don't get all bent out of shape about stuff other people do. You could take it or leave it."

She was so wrong. How could she be so wrong about him? It was *all* he cared about. For as long as he could remember he lived in fear of being nothing, having nothing. He figured that was why it had taken him so long to try to own a house or a business—the fear that he'd fail, that he'd prove to the world he was just like the old man. He was so angry with her, he couldn't trust himself to speak. All Meg needed was another insanely mad man in her house tonight. So he got out of bed and slid on his boxers, mumbling that he had to go to the head. He went into the bathroom and flicked on the light so he could stare at the man in the mirror. All he saw at that moment was his father's face, which had been so much like his own before alcohol and neglect had turned him into an old man. He'd always hated when people commented on how much they looked alike, even though he knew he was different. Frank had been the only one to see it then, that he was more than the son of the neighborhood drunk.

He couldn't stay with Meg right now, couldn't trust himself not to say something he might regret. He heard a small knock on the door and quickly turned on the faucet to splash water on his face. "Yeah."

"Can I come in?"

"Sure," he said, grabbing a towel and scrubbing himself dry. When he looked up, Meg was there, her big blue eyes looking all sad and worried, and all the anger he'd been feeling sort of washed away.

"I hurt your feelings, didn't I?" she asked.

Will gave a quick nod. "Maybe." He shrugged. "I know I'm not a millionaire, but . . ."

"No, Will. You should be proud of yourself. You did all this on your own. My father had to help me with my business. I'm the bum, not you. I'm the one who'd love to be an aging surfer dude."

He smiled. "Somehow I can't picture that. Listen,

I'm going to head out. You're okay now, aren't you?"

He ignored her look of disappointment she couldn't hide before she flashed him a smile. "Sure. I'm okay. Maybe I'll stop by the school tomorrow. Weather's supposed to be pretty rotten tomorrow so I'm probably going to have to cancel my lessons. You want to get lunch?"

"I'm going to be in Providence most of the day," he said. It was the truth, but somehow it came out sounding like a lie.

"Oh. Sure. I'll call you later in the week then."

By the time Will was dressed and in his car, it was almost three o'clock in the morning. What kind of guy left a woman at three in the morning? He already knew the answer: A guy who was running scared. Of what, he just didn't know.

Chapter Twenty-Five

Rachel took in Meghan's little brightly colored shack and smiled, happy that her friend had found her way back to sailing. She hadn't been down to Newport in weeks and so hadn't gotten a chance to check out Meghan's new business. Thad had been less than enthusiastic, of course. His loyalty to Will would have been annoying if Will hadn't been such a great guy.

Thad was worried that Meghan was trying to get Will back by setting up business so close to him. And if she was, Rachel couldn't see why that was a problem. Thad did. "The guy has it bad for her. He's just going to end up a basket case again," Thad had said.

"I think they belong together. Just like us," Rachel said, giving him a hug.

She just couldn't get enough of her big, muscular bald man. The drive from Maine and seeing each other on weekends was getting old, so Rachel decided to look for a job in Rhode Island, something she'd thought would have freaked Thad out. Funny thing was, Thad not only was enthusiastic about the idea, he'd pulled out a ring and proposed. You could have knocked her down with a feather. But Thad had been so confident, so sure that they were going to be happy, he drove away any doubts that they hadn't been seeing each other long enough to make such a commitment. It was so strange to have a man love her so completely.

The ring felt wonderfully foreign on her hand, and it was as if she was carrying around a big neon sign that announced to the world she was in love and going to marry the sexiest, most wonderful man in the world.

Who would have thought that Thad, the man she would have voted to remain single the longest, was talking about babies and houses and weddings. There was only one problem. Thad had gotten it into his head that they were going to wait for sex, like her being a virgin was the most wonderful thing in the world when she'd just as soon get rid of her hymen and get on with life. Plus she was finally discovering what it truly meant to be hornier than hell.

At that moment, the wind changed directions and slashed her face with raindrops that fell so fiercely, they stung her skin. She ran to Meghan's shack and heaved open the door. Meghan was sitting at her desk doing paperwork, but stopped immediately.

"Hey. What are you doing here? Want to finally learn to sail?" Meghan joked, then her eyes grew wide. "Omigod, is that an engagement ring?"

Rachel felt her cheeks flush red. "It is. Can you believe it? He asked me last night."

"Let me see," Meghan said, standing up and moving around her desk to pull the beringed hand for closer inspection. "Holy shit, it's huge. I had no idea Thad did that well."

Rachel shrugged, but couldn't help holding her hand out so she could admire the way it looked on her hand. "It's freakin' crazy, isn't it? It's all happening so fast."

"You're not worried, are you?"

"No, but Thad wants to get married in October."

Meghan's mouth opened in shock. "*This* October? What's the rush?" Then Meghan clutched her arm. "You're pregnant."

"Hardly. We haven't even . . ." Rachel let her voice trail off and her face turned red again.

"You haven't had sex yet?" Rachel suspected Meghan's eyes could not have physically gotten any wider.

"Not officially."

Meghan laughed. "Honey, you have got to get that man in a bedroom. And fast."

"Tell me about it. It's become this *thing*. You know, he's making so much of it that by the time we actually do it, on *our honeymoon*, it won't be any fun."

"He's put your virginity on a pedestal," Meghan pronounced. "I suppose there could be worse things. Like if he wanted to wait so you wouldn't find out he can't get it up."

Rachel felt the blood drain from her face. "Do you think he'd do that?"

"God, no," Meghan rushed to say. "I'm just saying that would be worse than his being so old-fashioned about it."

"That's just it. Thad's not old-fashioned. He's just got it in his head that this is what I should do."

Meghan pressed her lips together in thought.

She'd never come across this problem. "That's a tough one. You say he's picked October? That's not all that long to wait."

"Yes, it is," Rachel said through gritted teeth. "Especially since we'll be seeing way more of each other in about a month. I've given my notice at work and I'm moving here mid-September. Will's letting me stay in one of his guest rooms until the wedding. Thad and I are supposed to go house-hunting this weekend. That means *hours* in a car together. I just don't think I can take it."

"You do know there are alternatives," Meghan said cautiously.

"I have a vibrator, if that's what you mean."

Meghan burst out laughing, half shocked that Rachel would admit such a thing. "Actually, that's not what I meant. I meant oral sex and stuff."

Rachel gave Meghan a withering look. "I'm a virgin. Not twelve. Of course we've done all that."

Meghan waved her hand and shook her head. "I'm getting more information about your sex life than I need."

"Speaking of sex," Rachel said. "What's wrong with Will?"

Meghan turned away on the pretense she wanted to sit back behind her desk. "What do you mean?"

"Thad said he's been a bear around the school the past week. He said it had something to do with you and Will going out a date."

"That was four days ago and I haven't any idea why Will would be in a bad mood." Meghan made herself busy straightening her desk, since she was going to close up shop early today anyway, thanks to the weather. It had been raining nonstop for four days, something that was really putting a strain on her bottom line.

"Thad said he was actually in a good mood until then."

Meghan shrugged. "We sort of had a fight. I guess." And then, out of the blue, Meghan's eyes filled with tears. She hadn't even known she was upset about it, but there she was crying.

"What happened?" Rachel said.

"I don't know," Meghan said, shaking her head. "Everything was going great." She put her head down onto her desk. "We slept together," she said softly.

"And that's a bad thing?" Rachel asked.

"No. It was good. At least it was good until I said something that got Will mad."

"What did you say?"

"I said I wished I could be more like him. Be a sailing bum my whole life."

"I don't know why that would make him angry. Up until two years ago, he was a sailing bum," Rachel said.

"See? That's what I was thinking. But somehow I insulted him and he left. And . . ."

"And?"

"I want him back," Meghan said, her voice agonized. "I really want him back but I think it's too late. He said . . . he said . . ."

"He said . . ."

"He said he wanted to be *friends*," Meghan wailed.

Rachel fished in her bag for a tissue and handed it to Meghan and waited until her friend blew her nose before asking, "Was that before or after you made love?"

"Before. What's the difference?"

Rachel looked at her as if she were crazy. "If he meant it, he couldn't have gone to bed with you."

"I stripped naked. I really didn't give him an option. Oh, God. I was a pity fuck."

Rachel looked stunned for a moment, then burst out laughing. "That's ridiculous," she said when she could talk. "Will loves you."

"Will *loved* me," Meghan said, feeling the pain in her heart give a sharp twinge. "I think I hurt him one too many times." Meghan wiped her face, feeling slightly embarrassed by the whole thing, and just a little jealous that Rachel was the one who was engaged now and doling out advice. "Did he say anything to Thad?"

"Nothing specific. Nothing even about you at all. But Thad really knows Will and apparently he was right. Will's bad mood did have something to do with you. Hey, you want to go get lunch? We can both get a big margarita."

"Sounds good," Meghan said. She'd need a little fortification for what she had planned later that afternoon: a visit with Nancy. All she needed was to spend an hour with the woman who knew Will best.

Chapter Twenty-Six

Meghan pulled up to the Frank's house, her car tires crunching on the broken quahog shells. Nancy was sitting on the porch of the hip-roofed colonial in one of two rockers set up facing the bay, and she stood when she heard her car. Other than the time Nancy sent Meghan away when she'd wanted to see Frank, Meghan hadn't seen her in more than two years, and she was suddenly filled with an overwhelming sadness looking at Nancy sitting alone, when for so many years she'd had Frank to sit by her.

Meghan got out of her car and walked up to the porch and went into Nancy's open arms. "It's so nice to see you," Nancy said, giving her a squeeze.

"I'm sorry I waited so long to come."

Nancy waved at her dismissively and sat down, indicating that Meghan should take the other rocker. The porch protected the women from the rain, letting only the finest mist from the sea hit them, something neither woman seemed to mind. "Will's been filling me in about you. I hear you started your own business."

Meghan felt herself tense at the mention of Will. "I did. But on days like this, I have to close up shop. Thankfully, I still have my real estate license. As much as I dislike that business, I have to keep it up until I'm in the black with Day Sailor."

The two women chit-chatted for a while, mostly small talk that thankfully had nothing to do with Will, until Nancy stood. "I want to show you something. You wait here."

When Nancy returned, she handed Meg one of those cheap black plastic certificate frames. In it was a letter written on lined notebook paper and for a second Meghan thought it might be a bit of Will's homework kept for sentimental reasons.

Then she read:

Dear Jared:

I'm leaving you because you're nothing but a bum and that's all you'll ever be. I just can't stand being poor a minute longer. Marrying you was the biggest mistake of my life. And so was William. I'm just not cut out to be a mother right now. I'm too young for this crap."

Diana

Meghan read the framed letter twice before she realized what she held in her hand and looked up to Nancy for an explanation.

"Frank went over to the house Will grew up in when his father got evicted. He found it hanging in their kitchen. He brought me over there to look at where our boy had grown up and it tore at my heart." After their wonderfully innocuous small talk, Nancy had deftly turned the conversation to the last place Meghan wanted to go.

"It was little more than one room. A shack, really. Frank bought the land and had it knocked down while Will was still in college. I've never seen Frank so angry in his life as the day he walked in that house and saw that letter hanging on that wall.

"Do you realize that Will saw that poisonous letter every day of his life? His father hung that letter as a reminder that Diana might be coming back. He waited for years until he got word that she died. And every day Will saw the reminder that he was the reason she'd left."

Meghan hardly heard her. All she knew was that she'd called Will a bum. Certainly not in the same context his mother had called his father a bum, but now she understood why he'd been so angry, why he'd left that night. "I don't know anything about Will's childhood," she said, feeling sick inside. "He never talked about it," Meghan said.

"He never got anything handed to him. He went to college on scholarship and student loans, even though Frank was more than willing to pay for him. He wouldn't accept a dime. Even after Frank died, he left him *Water Baby*, did you know that?"

Meghan shook her head numbly. "No." But she assumed Frank would. She also assumed that Frank had helped Will go to college, get that sailing school, buy his house. She'd assumed a lot of things that now made her feel slightly ashamed.

"He's donated it to the Providence Boys and Girls Club so underprivileged kids can learn how to sail. And he's volunteering to teach them."

So he really was going to Providence, she thought. "He never told me that, either." He never told her anything, not that he loved her, not that he wanted to marry her, not that he wanted their children romping around him. Will never told her anything—in words. And God, sometimes a girl needed to hear the words. Sometimes.

"It took years of Frank's prodding to find out what happened to his mother. Will's not a big talker," Nancy said.

"A vast understatement," Meghan said dryly. "He never told me any of this. If he had, I would have understood him more. We dated for four years, and he never told me he loved me, at least not in any meaningful way. And when I told him I was leaving unless he married me, he let me go. Why?"

Nancy shook her head sadly. "I wondered about that too, especially when I saw how torn up he was about your breakup. Believe me, it took a lot of prodding to get the truth out of him and then I gave him my two cents about what I thought about him letting you go.

"Sometimes when all a person has known is hurt and abandonment, they can't let themselves show how much someone means to them." She turned to Meghan then, her gray eyes red-rimmed. "I have a feeling that boy loves you, more than you'll ever know. And I'm not issuing platitudes. I mean it. I don't think he can express himself. Now Frank, he told me he loved me so many times, it almost lost meaning. There wasn't a thought that came into that man's head that he wouldn't tell me about. Got damn tiring." Nancy laughed. "Still, I guess that's better than trying to be a mind reader."

"What was Will like as a boy?" Meghan asked, her heart hurting for the boy as much as the man.

"He was a fierce little thing. Very serious. Frank and I worried about him, but there wasn't much we could do. His father never beat him, kept him fed and clothed. His biggest sin was drinking too much and being too poor. I supposed nowadays child services could have stepped in. But back then, people didn't get as involved. And he never complained. Never said a bad word about his father."

"He sounds like a saint," Meghan said dismally, her guilt growing.

"Oh, Lord, no. By the time he was sixteen, he was a hellion. He was the only one in his school with long hair. By then it was out of style to be so long, you know. He drank and smoked and, well, everything he could do, I suppose. And then one day, Frank pulled him aside and Will showed him some bad attitude and Frank slapped him. Hard."

Meghan gasped. "Frank hit Will?"

Nancy laughed. "You should have seen Will's face. He was nearly seventeen and looked like a tough guy. But he burst into tears and threw himself into Frank's arms and had himself a good cry. That was the end of it. He turned himself around. I think he was just seeing how far he could push himself toward the dark side before anyone cared. Well, Frank cared, and that was enough. Sometimes, a man like Will just needs a good slap in the face." Nancy laughed again as she looked at Meghan's thoughtful face. "If I were you, I wouldn't walk up to Will and slap him."

"I just might," Meghan said darkly.

Meghan didn't bother heading back to Newport after her visit with Nancy. She was feeling gloomy after her conversations with Rachel and Nancy and wanted nothing more than to fill the bathtub with warm water, light some candles, and sip a cool glass of chardonnay.

Instead, she got another visit from Alan.

When she saw him standing at her doorstep, she nearly ran away, but something in his face stopped her.

"I'm sorry I was such an ass the other night," he said, sounding and looking completely normal except for the vivid bruise on his forehead. "I'd been drinking."

"You?"

He shrugged. "You broke my heart so I figured I was good for one bout of drinking. Big mistake, huh? Now you know why I don't drink."

"How much did you have?"

He gave her a sheepish grin. "Two whole beers."

He was so much like himself, so like the Alan she'd come to care for, she forgave herself for thinking she could have been happy with him. "If I invite you in, are you going to go psycho on me?"

He held a hand up like a Boy Scout. "I will not. Promise."

Meghan had a little mental war with herself before turning and unlocking her apartment door and letting Alan enter in front of her.

"I just came here to apologize. And to thank you for not calling the police," Alan said, letting out a nervous laugh.

"I almost did, you know."

"I guess I would have deserved it. I went a little crazy and I'm sorry. That's why I'm here. I want you to know you don't ever have to be afraid of me. To be honest, I really hated myself for doing that to you."

Meghan hugged her arms around herself. "You really scared me."

Alan looked slightly ill. "I know. I didn't want to end our relationship like that. It was ugly, like you said. That's why I stopped by. I really didn't expect you to be home." He pulled a letter out of his suit. "I really came to slide this under your door. Then I thought that might scare you that I'd been here and I was going to leave without giving it to you. Here. You might as well have it now. No crazy stuff. I promise."

Meghan reached out for the envelope and held onto it as she re-crossed her arms.

"Are you with Will?" he asked, then shook his head. "Sorry. None of my business." He turned to leave, then looked back. This time there was nothing in his eyes but regret. "I really just want you to be happy."

"Me, too," Meghan said with a small smile. He closed the door softly behind him and Meghan let out a deep breath, feeling as if a bubble of stress had just popped inside her, leaving her feeling slightly giddy. It was finally over.

Chapter Twenty-Seven

Meghan coiled the lines to her teaching boat in preparation for the next day as the sun dipped closer to the horizon. It was only seven at night, but already the sky was turning milky pink as another summer day slipped away. August was almost over and Meghan dreaded the next few months of trying to eke out a living in real estate until next summer. Maybe Will was right—setting up a seasonal business in a part of the country that only had two months of summer might not have been the best decision. She was feeling tired and drained and incredibly lonely.

She'd gone over and over what Nancy had told her about Will. In the end, it all just made her feel even more uncertain of their future. She'd slept with him, loved him, spent nearly every minute of the day with him for four years, and she hadn't known a single meaningful thing about his childhood—or about anything other than sailing and having fun. He'd close up just the way he'd close up when she'd talk about the future. She didn't want a touchy-feely guy like Alan; she knew now that wasn't a good match for her. But she sure as heck didn't want to play twenty questions just to find out basic facts about the man she loved.

The more she thought about it, the angrier she got. How dare he get mad at her for calling him a sail bum. That's what he'd been the entire time she'd known him. She didn't know he'd been saving up for a house and business. How could she? She didn't read his bank statements, she didn't have a secret copy of his life plan.

She threw down the last line, and started walking, down the docks, past her car, skirting by a group of tourists milling around for the launch to their cruise ship, getting more and more angry with every step. By the time she got to Will's house a half mile away, she was winded, sweaty and really mad.

She yanked open the front door, walked into the building's foyer, rang his doorbell and waited. Then she made a fist and knocked. And waited. Of course, Will didn't hear her, but Louise did. She poked her head out through the door, her white dandelion-fuzzy hair making Meghan smile.

"He's home. He goes up to that deck of his every night. How'd you like that stew?"

"The stew was wonderful. And I had so much I froze a bunch for when the weather gets cooler."

"That's a girl. As soon as the apples come in I'm making an apple pie."

Meghan wasn't certain she'd ever be back to collect, but she said, "That'd be wonderful."

"You go on up," she said, handing Meghan the key. "Will won't mind. You tell him I gave you the green light." Louise winked. "I knew you'd be back, Meghan." She closed the door and Meghan found herself blinking back tears. This was bad. She wanted to be good and mad at Will before she saw him with his gorgeous smile and fabulous body and my-life's-a-closed-book attitude. There. She wasn't raging mad, but she was majorly annoyed and that was good enough for what she had to do.

Meghan opened the door and stopped cold. The bright colors in Will's house were gone, the life of the place sucked dry by beige and cream. Blech. What had been a cheerful haven was now a man's dull, masculine space. Even the furniture, which he hadn't changed, looked lifeless under the new neutrals. She walked to the end of the hall, peeking into the kitchen, which he'd left stark white and bright nautical blue, and up to the second floor. At the end of the hall connecting the bedrooms, all blandly neutral except the master bedroom, was finally a familiar sight—the old staircase that led up to the rooftop deck.

Meghan walked up the stairs, noting that Will had been working hard sanding it down. Her hand trailed along the smooth banister that had once been marred with several coats of paint. The screen door at the top was the same, which she found oddly comforting. When she opened it, her eyes immediately found Will squatting by a row of tomato plants, a basket half full of ripe tomatoes next to him.

The rest of the deck had been converted to a box garden, with one small section reserved for a set of teak deck furniture.

"Hey."

He turned around and looked downright unhappy to see her. "Louise said it was okay to come on up."

"She would," he said dryly.

Meghan bit her lip. It was damned difficult to stay mad at him when he was standing there in the last glow of the setting sun, his hair tousled, his cheeks ruddy from being out on the bay. But she was going to try.

"I have something for you," she said, swallowing heavily as she walked toward him.

He straightened and she couldn't tell what he was thinking at that moment. Certainly he couldn't have guessed what she had come here for. Meghan stopped about two feet away and gave him a small smile. This was so, so hard, she thought, as he smiled back at her.

Whack. She slapped him as hard as she could, and was shocked to see the vivid red handprint that immediately formed on his cheek.

"What the *hell,*" he said, his face losing any sign of that smile.

"Oh, God. I guess was angrier than I thought. Hold on." In a panic, Meghan ran down two flights of stairs and hurled herself into his kitchen and to his freezer. Grabbing the first frozen thing she could find—a package of Oscar Mayer Light Beef Hot Dogs—she ran back to the deck where Will stood still staring at the door where she'd disappeared one minute ago.

"Here," she said, thrusting the hot dogs at him.

"I'm not hungry," he said darkly.

"It's for your cheek. The one I hit. I'm sorry, but I thought I could knock some sense into you." The last came out more like an uncertain question than a statement of fact.

Will took the hot dogs and pressed them against his still-pink cheek. "How's that again?"

"I had a talk with Nancy."

He sagged a little, then turned away to look at the setting sun. "I take it it was an enlightening conversation."

"You might say that."

"Go on."

"I know you love me," Meghan blurted out and waited for him to deny it. He was still turned away from her so she couldn't see his expression. "I know you had a really tough childhood. I know you've worked hard your whole life to prove to yourself that you weren't like your father." His head jerked slightly, but he kept staring at the bay. Meghan took a deep breath. "I know you've always done everything yourself. You're a self-made man. The complete opposite of a bum. And I know you're going to drive me crazy for the rest of my life because for some reason you couldn't tell me any of this. The woman you love. You couldn't say it so I always have to guess or come to the wrong conclusions, which you could say I'm pretty good at."

"Are you finished?"

Meghan shook her head. "No. I'm not. Because I need to know. I need to hear the words out of your mouth, Will. I'm going to need a hug sometimes, I'm going to have to hear how much you love me and that you think I'm funny and smart and beautiful. I need to know when you're sad." She stopped because her throat was closing up and she was about to cry and she knew how much Will hated tears.

"Are you done now?" he said, finally turning to her. All she could do was nod.

"You know." He stopped and cleared his throat. "You've got to know how much I . . ." he closed his eyes briefly, ". . . love you. I love you." He took a deep breath as if he'd just done the most momentous thing.

And he had.

Meghan threw herself into his arms. "I knew you did. I knew it."

"I thought I was being pretty damned obvious about it," he said, laughing.

Meghan looked up at him as if he were a bit crazy. "I love you too, Will. Can I hear it, say, once a year?"

"I think I could handle that." He smiled and his eyes shone a bit brighter than normal. "I'm not happy without you. I tried it out and it just doesn't fit." He smiled. "How's that for expressing my feelings?"

"Wonderful," Meghan said, holding him tight, breathing in his sea and warm-sun smell that she knew she could never do without.

And would never need to.

Epilogue

"Are you okay?" Meghan whispered to Rachel as she hugged her friend good-bye.

Rachel had changed from her wedding gown and was wearing a scarlet wrap dress that hugged her curves so nicely, Thad had hardly been able to take his eyes off her.

"I'm so nervous I feel like I'm going to throw up. I can't believe I let Thad do this to me. Do you know how long the flight is to Paris? Do you? And could he have booked it so we could leave tomorrow *after* our wedding night? He's a sadist. And a masochist."

Meghan smiled at her friend's agony. "But I have to say it makes the whole honeymoon thing memorable. There aren't too many women in your position on their wedding night. I think it's sweet. I almost wish Will and I were as fresh and new as you two."

Rachel rolled her eyes. "You're plenty fresh, the two of you. I think the dance floor is still smoldering from that dance."

Meghan blushed. "I've been visiting my parents and we haven't seen each other in three days."

"Wow. Three whole days."

"Once you break the dam, it's hard to stop the water, if you know what I mean," Meghan said, giving her friend a little jab with her elbow.

"I wouldn't know."

"But you will. Believe me." Meghan's cell phone vibrated in her small purse and this time she chose not to ignore her mother's call.

"Hey, Mom."

"How was the wedding?"

"Beautiful. The bride was gorgeous." She winked at Rachel. "Will and I had a wonderful time."

"About that . . ." her mother said, hesitation clear in her voice. And from the background she heard her father yell, "Tell her."

"Tell me what?" Meghan said, walking away from Rachel to find some privacy. Will, the best man, was at the bar toasting Thad with the other groomsmen as a send-off for the honeymoon.

"You have our blessing."

"Really, Mom?" Meghan said, feeling her eyes prick.

"Really. I've never seen you so happy as when you were here. I think I might have gotten the wrong impression of Will." Her mother let out a heavy sigh. "There was a boy, before I met your father. He was a baseball player. Almost good enough for the majors, but he never quite made it. He was always making promises to quit, to get a real job." She lowered her voice. "He cheated on me. All the time, though I didn't find out until later. Will reminded me so much of that boy. And then I met your father and he was so much nicer. More like Alan."

Meghan nearly choked. "Oh, Mom, Alan is *nothing* like Dad. Honest. I know I've made the right decision." She looked across the room at Will, saw him throw his head back and laugh at something Thad had said, and she smiled.

"I know you have. That's why I called. Anyway, I just wanted to tell you that."

"Thanks, Mom. And tell Dad thanks, too."

Meghan closed her phone and walked over to Will, who immediately slung his arm around her and pulled her close. He bent down so only she could hear him. "I love you," he said, his voice barely above a whisper. His hand found hers and he touched the ring on her left hand.

"You scared?" she asked.

"Yep. It's like heading into the Gulf Stream in a pea-soup fog."

"I love sailing in the fog," she said.

"I do, too. But only if you're on my boat, kiddo. Only then."